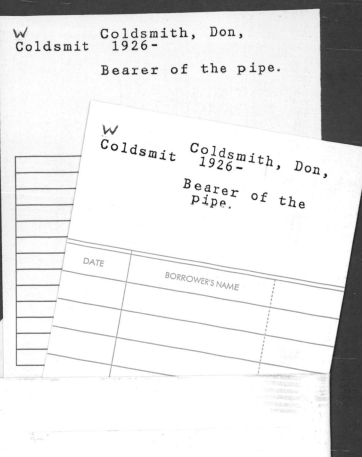

W
Coldsmit   Coldsmith, Don,
              1926-

              Bearer of the pipe.

W
Coldsmit   Coldsmith, Don,
              1926-

              Bearer of the
              pipe.

DATE	BORROWER'S NAME	

Bearer of the Pipe

Also by Don Coldsmith

Bearer
of the Pipe

»»»»»»»»»»»»»»

DON COLDSMITH

Doubleday
NEW YORK   LONDON   TORONTO   SYDNEY   AUCKLAND

PUBLISHED BY DOUBLEDAY
a division of Bantam Doubleday Dell Publishing Group, Inc.
1540 Broadway, New York, New York 10036

DOUBLEDAY and the portrayal of an anchor with a dolphin
are trademarks of Doubleday, a division of
Bantam Doubleday Dell Publishing Group, Inc.

Library of Congress Cataloging-in-Publication Data

Coldsmith, Don, 1926–
    Bearer of the pipe / Don Coldsmith. — 1st ed.
        p.   cm.
    1. Indians of North America—Great Plains—Fiction.   I. Title.
    PS3553.O445B4   1995
    813'.54—dc20   94-37178
    CIP

ISBN 0-385-47030-4
Copyright © 1995 by Don Coldsmith
All Rights Reserved
Printed in the United States of America
September 1995
First Edition

10 9 8 7 6 5 4 3 2 1

vᴧↃ

To my assistant
ANN BOWMAN
who has suggested for years
that I write about a tornado

Bearer of the Pipe

1
>> >> >>

On the day of his birth all who saw this, the child of Dark Antelope and Gray Mouse, smiled. It was a smile of amusement at the baby's droll appearance. Some infants have this quality. It brings out the best of feelings, a warming of the heart and a sense that the spirit in this new being is a good one.

Partly, it may have been the appearance of his hair. It was not unusual for babies of the People to possess a quantity of hair at birth. Some had more than others, of course. There seemed to be no particular connection. Facial hair, which appeared on males as manhood approached, was sometimes heavier than usual, especially in the Southern band. This was assumed to be because of the influence of Heads Off, the Spanish outsider who had brought the First Horse to the People. That story was told in pictographs on the Story Skins.

Many young men boasted when a fringe of dark hair began to sprout along the upper lip. This was a sign of noble ancestry, an evidence of a link with the fabled Heads Off. Though his status as an outsider had prevented his rise beyond the office of a minor band chieftain, Heads Off had held great prestige. His heroic deeds against the Head Splitters were legend. Head Splitters were now allies of the People, but at that time, long ago, had been a dreaded enemy.

The possession of heavy facial hair might be a thing of pride for a young man, but it was a mixed blessing. The extra time and discomfort required for plucking a heavy growth with the clamshell tweezers was certainly a thing to test one's manhood.

All of this, though, seemed to have no connection to the amount or texture of the hair on the heads of newborn babes of the People. And this child, son of Antelope and Mouse, had a considerable amount. It did not lie flat, as it might have, but stood on end in a furry round globe, some two finger breadths long. This, with his deep-set eyes, wide with wonder at this new world, gave a serious yet comic appearance. And smiles . . . The sort of smiles that one might see on the faces of people watching a litter of fox pups at play.

Yes, that was it! The emotion evoked by the charming appearance of a young, furry creature.

"Where did this pup get the fur?" asked an old woman. "It is not that of an Antelope."

"Nor of a Gray Mouse, either," teased another.

"But," reminded another, "the grandfather of this one is Singing Wolf, the holy man. Maybe that is why it looks like a wolf pup."

It was all good-natured, happy bantering, a teasing of new parents to have a part in their joy. The result in this case, however, was that a name was created which this child would wear for many years.

Wolf Pup. There were other names. Little Bear was one which might have been more appropriate considering the color of the fur on the child's head. He was also somewhat plump and roly-poly, like a cub of the black bear.

But no name seemed quite as appropriate as Wolf Pup. The keen understanding in his gaze, even in his first days of life, told of far-seeing thoughts. And, with his grandfather being the respected Singing Wolf . . . *aiee*, how could it be otherwise? In a matter of days, the new child in the lodge of Antelope and Mouse was known to everyone as Wolf Pup.

The name fit well as the child grew. He was serious and thoughtful, yet fun-loving, and could move from one approach to the other in the space of a heartbeat.

"His is a spirit that is old and wise," proclaimed Running Deer.

No one remembered any longer how many winters the old woman had seen. She was the grandmother of Dark Antelope, but had also raised the orphaned Gray Mouse. Thus she was twice the "grandmother" of this, their child. There was no blood relation to Mouse, of course. That point had arisen when the two young people, raised within the extended family of the holy man, Singing Wolf, had decided to marry.

"Of course it may be done," Wolf had explained to the council. "The girl is not even of the People. You all remember how we found her as an infant in the Camp of the Dead? Her people had died of the spotted sickness, the *poch.*"

There were nods of agreement. The Year of the Spotted Death was recorded on the Story Skins.

"My mother, Running Deer, took the child who seemed to be dying. It was thought that she, too, would die. But both lived. That is how these children were raised in the same family, but in different lodges. So, I am made to think there is no problem here. These may marry."

The marriage had taken place, and it was good.

Now, with such strong ties of family, this child was blanketed with love and affection. His grandparents, Singing Wolf and Rain, showered him with adulation, and his twice-grandmother thought that there had never been such a child. Not even since the People came through the hollow log into the world.

This is not to say that the upbringing of Wolf Pup was overly permissive. With so many adults feeling such a closeness, the child could hardly move unobserved. And, according to the customs of the People, any adult might also discipline a wayward child. Thus there was plenty of direction and guidance for this special child.

Yet little guidance was needed. Wolf Pup cheerfully adapted without complaint to whatever occurred. His unquestioning acceptance of the day-to-day problems of the People was remarkable. Cold, heat, rain, or snow might cause most infants to complain at such discomfort. Yet this one seemed unimpressed. It was as if he understood the ways of this new environment. The placid look in his large dark eyes seemed to say so. It was a look of patient insight, as if his thoughts were expressed without words. *If this is the way of things, let it be so.* Insight, understanding, possibly even gratitude for those good things that did happen to go his way.

His baby name still seemed to fit. There were a few suggestions in the family as to other possibilities. In his more solemn moods, the expression on the child's face—especially the eyes—was positively owlish. And had there not been an ancestor long ago called Owl? Nothing, however, seemed as fitting as the name he already wore. Wolf Pup.

As everyone knew, it did not matter anyway. The baby name was quite a temporary thing. This, the eldest son of Dark Antelope and Gray Mouse, would receive his real name at the end of his second year. Already, before he could walk, the early preparations had begun. The child's hair must not be cut or trimmed. It was fortunate, though, that it was soon long enough to begin to twist it and plait the strands. Narrow strips of finest otter skin were interwoven with the natural hair to produce a heavier plait on each side. It would create a handsome effect at the child's First Dance, the ritual day when he would also receive his name.

That name, the People assumed, would be that of his grandfather, Singing Wolf. That part of the ceremony belonged to the older man, and the name would be his choice. Almost always, a man would bestow his own name on a young relative. There was good reason for this. Among the People, it brought ill fortune to speak the name of the dead. Therefore, some living person must wear it.

There had been an extreme case, many generations ago, when a popular young subchief was killed in battle before he had given his name. No one else in the entire nation happened to be wearing the name at the time, and two words were dropped from the language to be replaced by new ones. No one now even remembered what the old words for the young chief's name had been, because they must never be spoken again.

So it seemed logical that at the time of the Naming ceremony and First Dance, little Wolf Pup would become Singing Wolf, the younger. No one even spoke of it, so certain was that expectation.

Even that name might be changed later when the young man reached the age of maturity. He might earn a name of his own through some significant act or event in his life, and give it away in turn to his heir. But for now he was Wolf Pup, and the name seemed to fit, and he grew and played and learned with the other children in the Rabbit Society.

The day came for the ceremony of the First Dance and the Naming. There were several children who had become eligible, and it was a day of joy. A little bit of sadness, too, for Gray Mouse. *One does not have babies long,* she thought. *They grow up too quickly.*

Still, she was proud. The children circled the dance area, hopping to the rhythm of the big dance drum as they performed the Rabbit Dance. Then the other simple steps, and finally the most vital of ceremonies, the ritual of Naming.

One by one, each small boy was presented to his older relative and received the name he would bear for many seasons. For his entire life, maybe. Red Dog . . . Bloody Knife . . . Yellow Hawk . . . Each youngster stood with pride as he received his name.

Then came Wolf Pup, grandson of the holy man. His was a family of great prestige, and it was an honor for the spectators to even be present at this ceremony. The boy stood straight and tall, and there were quiet murmurs among the old women that this generation would continue the greatness of the family and of the Southern band.

". . . and your name will be," Singing Wolf announced, half speaking, half chanting, "Wolf Pup!"

There was a quiet gasp of surprise. Had the holy man made a mistake? He was expected to give the boy his *own* name, Singing Wolf. Instead, he had reassigned the same childhood name by which his grandson was already known. No one spoke aloud. To do so would be unseemly, but there was a quiet mutter of whispered questions. Why had Singing Wolf done this?

Probably no one noticed the twinkle in the eye of the holy man. No one except his wife, Rain, that is. She knew him well, and smiled to herself. *He must have a reason,* she thought. She would ask him later.

"A reason for what?" he asked innocently.

"You know quite well, my husband," she answered. "Why did you not give our grandson your name?"

Wolf shifted his shoulders against his willow backrest and settled in more comfortably. Rain handed him a glowing twig to light his pipe, and he took a puff or two to get it burning well before he answered.

"Oh, that," he said casually. "I am still using it." His eyes twinkled.

"Yes, but . . ."

He raised a hand to stop her protest. "Wait, Rain. I know. But look . . . the name he now bears fits him. It is partly mine anyway, the Wolf part. And he *is* a pup. He will earn a name, because I am made to think that this child is special."

He paused to draw on his pipe.

"But for now . . ." Rain protested.

"For now, what? I have drawn some notice to him, but it is good notice, no?"

"Well . . . maybe. But . . . *your* name."

The holy man nodded. "I know. I will give it to him later,

maybe. But I am made to think I will need it for a while. There is no danger of losing it from the language of the People."

Rain was exasperated. "I know that you understand many things, my husband, but how can you be sure of this?"

"Oh, *that,*" he said calmly. "I am sure, because there is a boy in the Red Rocks band who is called Singing Wolf, too."

"And you did not want our Wolf Pup to have the same . . . ?"

"It does not matter," he interrupted. "As I have said, *this* one will earn a name of his own."

2

>> >> >>

As Wolf Pup grew, his parents had more hints that this child would be different, somehow. Special, destined for greatness in some special way.

It is, of course, the privilege of parents everywhere to believe this. Especially mothers. There is a unique bond between a mother and her son, as there is between father and daughter. Possibly more so. But the mother's love carries more conviction, perhaps. There is in her heart a surety that no matter what others may think, hers is a unique situation. *My son is special, and will do great things.* Gray Mouse was no different. To her, Wolf Pup was the most perfect baby ever seen. She resented his name a little bit at first. It did not seem to carry the dignity that such a child deserved. Yet, by the time that his grandfather shocked the People by letting the name stand, she had become resigned to it. The name fit. *Anyway,* she told herself, *he will earn a name when it is time. One more appropriate to his status.* She said nothing aloud, of course.

Both of his parents were pleased at Wolf Pup's accomplishments. The child did well in his learning of the ways of the People. The lessons of the Rabbit Society were very informal. Play is, in essence, the work of children. It is the manner in which they learn, through pretending to be grownups. A child may, in play, become anything or anyone he chooses. He develops leadership by becoming the leader of a hunting party. A girl, looking ahead a few seasons, establishes her own lodge. Toys are merely replicas of the tools and implements that will be used soon in the world of adults.

The instruction among children of the People came about by means of adults who spent a little time to teach their own skills. Not as a chore or a duty, much less an assignment. This was only what one *did.* A little while playing with the children of the band.

Some things, of course, require more instruction than others. The dance steps require a rhythm. Someone must not only teach the steps but beat the cadence on the drum and teach the songs.

All children, both boys and girls, must learn the use of weapons for hunting and for self-defense. Contests in running and throwing develop athletic skills. Races help develop swimmers in the deep clear pools of the prairie streams on hot afternoons. Many of these skills require little instruction, but only a suggestion now and then. A better grip to hold the bowstring with the fingers . . . A stance to produce more leverage and more distance with the throwing stick . . .

The Rabbit Society may have started as a joke originally, as a contrast to the deadly serious activities of the warrior societies. The Bowstrings, the Elk-dog Society, the Bloods . . . These held great prestige, and sometimes political power. There had once been an almost fatal split in the Southern band as the young reactionaries of the Blood Society followed a banished leader for a season. That was depicted in the Story Skins, and reenacted in the Warriors' Dances each autumn.

So, though it possibly began generations ago as a joke, the Society was now, like all of its own activities, an evolving picture of things to come. It held a miniature reflection of that which would be, later.

So, each adult, in contributing suggestions, helped to give a glimpse of his own expertise. Stone Breaker had inherited both his name and his skills from his father, who had learned from *his* father. Stone Breaker had no son. But, as he demonstrated the techniques of creating a beautiful and useful flint knife or arrow point, some of the children would show more interest and more proficiency. To those, his own interest would demand that he bestow special consideration. One would someday bear his name.

Wolf Pup seemed to take an interest in everything that was presented. He danced well, with a sense of rhythm that was above average. He remembered the songs and stories quickly. His athletic skills were developing nicely.

"He would be even better," Dark Antelope observed, "if he tried a little harder."

Gray Mouse was furious at even this slight question of their son's ability.

"How can you say that? He won the race, no?"

"Yes, yes . . ." Antelope retreated before his wife's wrath. "I only meant, Mouse, that . . . *Aiee*, woman, how can I say . . . ? Look, he won by only a little. He tries only hard enough to barely win. If he misjudges his opponent . . ."

He did not continue, for he had made his point. This would bear watching, though. Antelope was pleased somewhat more as he saw that Wolf Pup was interested in his own skills. Antelope, as a boy, had been expected to follow in the footsteps of his father, the holy man. Yet it had not happened.

He was not certain why. Maybe it was partly that he saw the dedication and sacrifice that were required of Singing Wolf. There was honor, to be sure, but to a young boy, the responsibility required of the holy man seemed overwhelming.

Antelope's interests lay along other lines. He enjoyed the hunt and the physical activity required. It was easy for him to become impatient with the long-drawn ceremonies of Singing Wolf's medicine. He had never been certain that he wanted to immerse himself as deeply in the spiritual qualities of life as his father was required to do. In short, the skills of his father's brother, Beaver Track, had been of more interest to young Antelope.

Beaver Track had been a skilled tracker and scout. Here was something to see and observe and touch. It had seemed more interesting to the young Antelope. He had followed the way of his uncle, not that of his father.

He was grown when he realized that this must have been a great disappointment to Singing Wolf. There was no other son to become the apprentice to the holy man. Antelope's brother had been killed by a bear when they were small.

There had been times when he realized that he *could* have studied the ways of the holy man. Sometimes when he studied the tracks of some wild creature he could almost feel himself inside that creature's head. He could feel the fear in the heart of the tiny mouse that hid in the grass and watched the shadow of the hawk that circled above. He could have immersed himself in the mysticism, and let *it* become his life, he realized in later years. It was so in the life of his father.

There had been some guilt, that he had been a disappointment to Singing Wolf. Yet, his own feelings . . . Antelope doubted that he could have carried the responsibility.

One influencing factor, of which he was probably not even aware, was the bitterness of old Running Deer, his grandmother. During his formative years, he had dreaded being in her presence. This was an angry old woman, bitter over the loss of her husband to his profession. True, it had ultimately led to his death, because of a broken taboo. Her hatred of all the aspects of his life as a holy man had been felt plainly by the young boy, and he had followed the other path.

Now he, Dark Antelope, was the chief tracker and scout of the Southern band. Beaver Track had been killed in a hunting accident when a running bull had turned in the wrong direction, goring Beaver's horse and throwing him beneath the hooves of the herd.

Antelope had inherited his uncle's position and prestige. He was uncomfortable with it, but finally had a talk with his father which helped him to place his feelings in proper perspective.

"Some things are meant to be, my son," Singing Wolf said. "Could you have prevented Beaver's death? Stopped the bull?"

"No, Father. I am made to think no one could have done that."

"So be it. Some things are meant to be. Maybe this is why you studied his ways, to learn his skills."

"But I am not as good a tracker as my uncle, Father."

"Of course not. But how many winters have you, Antelope? Twenty? Oh, more than that . . . Look, are you not as good as Beaver Track was at your age?"

Antelope began to understand.

"Father, there is another thing . . . I . . . I am made to think of my brother, Little Owl, who was killed. Owl would have been your son who became a holy man. Now you have none. I . . ."

The old man smiled. "And you think that you should have followed my ways, Antelope? Is that it?"

"I am made to think so, Father."

"Yes, you could have. The spirit was there. You had the gift."

"Then I should . . ."

"No!" Singing Wolf held up a hand to stop him. "No, that is not the way, my son. You were offered the gift, and you refused it. I was made to wonder why, I admit." He paused and smiled. "But now, look! If you were a holy man, the Southern band would now have two holy men and no tracker!"

"That is true. But if I had taken a different path . . . You have said that I was offered the gift of spirit, Father . . ."

"I am made to think so. But Antelope, it is no disgrace to refuse the gift."

"No honor, either," said Antelope glumly.

"Exactly. But honor comes in many ways. So do the gifts of the spirit. It is ours to choose, and no disgrace."

Slowly, Antelope had felt the guilt of his choice lifting from his shoulders. Now, as he watched the interests of his own son, he recalled that conversation. It would be of help to him.

Even so, it was pleasing to him to see the interests that young

Wolf Pup displayed. It was nearing autumn of the child's fourth year when Antelope watched him squatting under a dogwood bush near the camp. Wolf Pup was studying the ground, then looking up into the leafy growth.

"What is it?" his father asked.

"I am tracking a caterpillar," the boy said seriously. "Look, here is its spoor. A big one."

Antelope looked at the droppings under the bush. "That is true," he agreed.

"But they are dry."

"A day or two, maybe?" asked his father.

"Yes. Why are there no fresh droppings?"

"Maybe it moved on, like the buffalo."

The boy laughed. "It does not move on, Father. How could it?"

"Maybe it was killed by a hunter . . . Who hunts it?"

"A bird?"

"Maybe."

"But I was looking to see how it eats. See, where the leaves are chewed on the bush, here? *Aiee!*"

"What is it?"

"Look! What is this?"

The boy was pointing to a curled leaf, which was wrapped around a new cocoon. It must be fresh, because the leaf was still green.

"Your caterpillar has built its lodge for winter," Antelope suggested. "It will come out in the spring as a moth."

"It is inside?"

"Yes."

"Is it a caterpillar now, or a moth?"

"Neither one. It is in between."

"Can I see it?"

"Yes. We can cut it open. It would kill it, of course."

The boy was quiet for a little while. "How did it build this lodge?" he asked.

"With tiny strings. Like a blanket."

"That was much work, Father."

"Yes, maybe so."

"Then it should not be undone."

"As you wish."

Wolf Pup rose from his squatting position. "It is good," he said. "Let him stay."

Antelope was pleased. It had not mattered to him whether they opened the cocoon or not. But it was pleasing to see that the boy was thoughtful. To realize that there must be a reason why there were no fresh droppings . . . To learn from it that there could be more than one reason . . .

Best of all, it had been a superb job of tracking. He must be sure to tell Gray Mouse.

3

>> >> >>

It was at about the tenth summer that Singing Wolf noticed
there was something unusual in the spirit of his grandson, Wolf
Pup. The holy man had known from the first that the child was
quick and intelligent, but was that not to be expected? It is the
right of grandparents, as it is of mothers, to believe this.

Wolf could not have explained why he did not choose to give
the boy his own name at the Naming. It only seemed right, and
who can argue with that? He remained proud of Pup, and expected great things. Maybe, even, he would bestow his own name
later. That was permissible.

The event that really caught the attention of the holy man was a
strange one. That which revealed the sensitivity of young Wolf
Pup was a fight. This would seem to be an impossible combination, a contradiction on the face of it.

Singing Wolf had been for a walk around the camp. It was late
spring, the Moon of Growing. The holy man had gone to empty
his bladder, and the day was so inviting that he decided to take a
walk. The green of the prairie grasses was the clear, clean color

that is seen only in springtime. Likewise, the blue of the sky was radiant and alive. The prairie was humming with life. The buzz of insects blended in harmony with bird songs and the distant whinny of a mare who had temporarily lost sight of her foal.

The hum of human activity came from the cluster of lodges behind him. *Life is good,* he thought. He watched a circling hawk a little longer, and murmured a short greeting to the bird as it swept past and over him.

"Good hunting, my brother!"

He turned back toward his lodge. He had brought no pipe or tobacco with him. The scents of the prairie called to mind the mixture of tastes that would make themselves apparent in his pipe, and the thought was good. Yes, his willow chair and a pipe in the sun . . .

He strolled on toward his lodge, not hurrying but enjoying every step of a fine day. He could remember no better. His wife often teased him about that.

"Every day," she joked, "is the best one yet, for you."

He nodded. "Is it not true?" he would ask. "The one we have today is better than any we do not have."

There had been bad days, of course, in the lives of both of them. But memory is kind. The remembrance of good times is sweet, so we treasure it in our hearts while we partially forget that which has brought us pain. And a day like this one with its warmth, its smells and sights and sounds, was a day to treasure. It brought back memories of a thousand such days through his lifetime.

The pungent odors of the plants of the grassland touched his nostrils. He had often wondered at this. The sense of smell is powerful. A mere whiff of a forgotten scent transports us instantly to some scene from long ago.

This was such a day. The smells were those of his childhood, when he was like those two boys near the camp. They knelt, talking over something on the ground between them . . . Singing Wolf paused, curious. Then he recognized one of the youngsters. His own grandson, Wolf Pup. *Aiee,* how the boy was growing! The holy man edged closer, trying not to interrupt whatever discussion was in progress.

It appeared that the object of concern was an ant hill. As nearly as he could tell, Wolf Pup had been watching the creatures and the other boy, a little older, had joined him. The distance was too great to tell what the ants were doing, but he was sure that the boys would find it interesting. He smiled to himself at the memory. He had spent such afternoons watching ants too. It still fascinated him, the manner in which the creatures could systematically cut up and carry off large insects. It had always reminded him of a butchering party after a buffalo hunt. The meat was carved up and carried to the ants' underground lodge in the same way.

One thing he had puzzled about . . . There was an invisible path, a trail of some sort, traveled by every individual ant. Not one varied from it as they traveled back and forth to the door of their lodge, carrying their burdens. He had seen them pause sometimes as they passed, to touch together the whiskery feelers on their heads. *Is that a way in which the ants talk?* he had wondered. *Do they tell each other of the trail? Or is it marked with scent, like that of the coyote?*

He smiled as he watched the two youngsters. Maybe they were wondering about such things, as he had long ago. Wolf Pup had shown much interest in the skills of his father, the tracker. This would be part of it.

There was a brief moment when Singing Wolf felt a twinge of regret that Dark Antelope had not sought the way of the holy man. But no matter. It is for each to choose, and Antelope had chosen well. Singing Wolf continued to watch the boys.

Now the larger boy had picked up a stick and was poking at the ant hill. Wolf Pup seemed to be trying to dissuade him . . . What . . . ? Suddenly the boy laughed derisively, and swung his stick in a destructive arc, sweeping back and forth across the ant hill. It was apparent that such an action was destroying or crippling scores of individual ants, as well as seriously damaging their abode. No matter. The creatures would soon start to rebuild . . .

He was totally unprepared for the next development. His

grandson attacked the other boy in a fury, grappling and rolling on the ground, fighting hard. Both boys were panting and grunting from the exertion.

Singing Wolf did not reveal his presence. There would be no serious injury, and such wrestling bouts were a part of the learning process. Among the People, blows were not struck with fists, only with weapons, and then only in serious combat. To use a weapon against another of the People would be a serious breach of conduct. A fight like this was nothing. Like the play of children, it was considered training for future adulthood. Skills of self-defense learned here might well be life-saving someday.

But in this case . . . *Aiee!* Singing Wolf could not understand what had precipitated the argument. The boys had been watching an ant hill, and then . . . Even though he had seen it himself, he could hardly believe it. Wolf Pup, the happy, well-liked, quiet, and easygoing child, had actually *attacked* his friend.

He was still reluctant to interfere, so he continued to watch as the combatants tugged and grunted and rolled. More slowly now. It was obvious that both were exhausted, but that neither would concede defeat. That, of course, was good. Unusual, but good.

They lay panting now, too tired to continue. There was a brief exchange of words and the two rolled apart to sit up, still glaring. *This is not over,* thought Singing Wolf.

Both boys rose unsteadily, and backed away. Wolf Pup cast one last glance at the ant hill and turned his back to stalk away.

It was nearly dark when Singing Wolf found occasion to seek out his grandson for a moment of talk. They sat down and Singing Wolf lighted his pipe as they watched the sunset. He did not mention an obvious abrasion on the boy's left cheekbone, where it had ground into the dirt.

"*Aiee*, today was a beautiful day!" Singing Wolf began conversationally.

The boy only nodded, saying nothing.

"What did you do?"

Wolf Pup glanced at his grandfather suspiciously, but then decided that it was a harmless question.

"Nothing much. I saw a hawk . . . a red-tailed hawk, Grandfather. It was circling. Hunting, I thought."

"Yes, I saw it. Did it find meat?"

"I do not know. It flew north to the trees along the river."

"It is good," Singing Wolf nodded.

It *was* good. The boy had seen something not really significant, but had observed its outcome anyway and remembered it. This showed good powers of observation. But how could he bring up the subject of the puzzling fight at the ant hill?

"You have something on your face," he said cautiously. "*Aiee*, it is scratched! A bush?"

There . . . Pup could minimize it and drop the subject if he chose. Singing Wolf waited, hoping that the query would not end their conversation. The boy studied his grandfather's face for a moment, and finally spoke.

"No. A fight."

"Ah! It is good. Did you win?"

"Nobody won, Grandfather. But . . . this was not like a race. We were angry."

Singing Wolf waited, hoping that the story would continue. But it did not. He drew a long puff on his pipe and blew a cloud of fragrant bluish smoke into the evening air.

"What angered you, Pup?" he asked finally.

Another long silence . . .

"Do you want to tell me of it?" Singing Wolf asked.

"No . . . yes, I . . . Grandfather, I was watching ants today." The boy was looking at his grandfather's face for any sign of reaction.

"Yes?"

"Well, I . . . they were butchering a grasshopper!"

"*Aiee!* How did they skin it?"

The boy laughed and began to relax.

"They could not do that, Grandfather, but it is much the same. They cut it up to take to their lodge."

He nodded. "I watched them when I was a boy too."

"They can carry great burdens, Grandfather. A load as big as themselves!"

"That is true."

"Some were bringing rocks from beneath the ground."

"Rocks?"

"Grains of sand," the boy chuckled. "For them, they were big rocks. That makes room for their lodge below?"

"Yes."

"It would be good to see their lodge, Grandfather."

"Yes. But to be small enough to do that . . . *aiee*, they would eat us!"

Pup laughed. "And to dig it up to see destroys it." He became sober again, and then continued. "Grandfather, that was the cause of the fight."

"What?"

"Otter Tail . . . my friend. He was poking a stick into their lodge."

Singing Wolf was astonished. *That* had caused the fight? He could think of nothing to say.

"The ants were nearly finished carrying their meat," Pup said. "They needed to get it stored." He was becoming excited now. "I said *let them finish, they are storing food.* And Otter laughed and destroyed their lodge."

"But they will rebuild it," said his grandfather.

"That is true. As the People would, if our lodges were destroyed while we were butchering and drying meat. But it would be hard."

"Yes." Singing Wolf's mind was racing. Here was a child of only nine or ten winters, showing wisdom beyond his years. "But now you can watch them rebuild," he offered.

"I will watch alone next time," Wolf Pup said. "Otter does not understand."

"Understand what?"

"I wanted to get inside their heads, to follow them down into their lodge and feel their spirit. It is a different spirit, Grandfather! A spirit made of many."

"Like a buffalo herd?" Singing Wolf suggested.

"Yes . . . No! The buffalo have a spirit that is a herd of many spirits. But I am made to think that the ant lodge has one spirit and that each ant is a piece of it."

There was a sensation at the back of his neck that made Singing Wolf's hair stand up. This child was talking like a person who had been on a vision quest. At least, one who was *ready* for such a quest. It was a little bit frightening.

"It is good," he managed to say, "and yes, it would be better to watch ants alone."

4

》》》

By the time he was twelve, Wolf Pup had become the best tracker in the Rabbit Society. His father was very proud.

"See," the boy pointed to the tracks in the soft mud along the stream, "it was the horse of Yellow Hawk. The left forefoot turns out a little. It stood there to drink. Then it jumped back. It was startled, maybe, by something across there. Shall we go and see?"

Dark Antelope nodded, and allowed the boy to lead the way across the stony riffle to the other side. They turned back along the shore, and Antelope was pleased to see that his son stepped only on stones or areas of grass to avoid stepping in the moist earth and sand. Just now, that might destroy the tracks for which they searched.

More important, it was a good habit. One should *leave* no more tracks than necessary. The People had been at peace for a generation, but there was no guarantee that it would continue. A traveling trader had told of conflict to the north. There was always some shifting among the tribes and nations of the prairie. A change in

the weather, with a bad season or two for growing crops . . .
Growers were only semi-permanent in their towns.

The People, their allies the Head Splitters, and others who were
primarily hunters moved constantly. That was their advantage. If
an area suffered too much or too little rain, they could strike the
big skin lodges and transport them to a better site. This was carried out several times each season anyway. The People came together annually for the Sun Dance at some previously selected
location. Each band was on its own for the rest of the year, but
each had favorite areas for summer and winter. They might move
to a site a few days' travel away at any time if grass for their horse
herds became scant. Or if the migration of the great buffalo herds
caused the animals to take a slightly different route that season. A
move might be considered simply because they had been in one
place too long. The scent of human habitation could become over-
powering to those accustomed to the fresh clean air of the prairie.

With all of this constant motion, it was almost inevitable that
someday the People would encounter other people whose habits
were more aggressive. It was necessary for the young to learn this.
A generation unprepared for self-defense would be like a newborn
calf before the approach of the great gray wolves that followed the
herds.

For all of these reasons, Dark Antelope was glad to see his son's
manner of tracking. There was an instinct here . . . Wolf Pup
seemed to avoid stepping on the muddy spot that would leave a
track almost without thinking about it. He seemed completely
unaware that he was doing it.

"Here, Father," he said eagerly. "It was a deer. Two deer, a big
doe and her yearling. She did not have a fawn this year."

Dark Antelope tried to maintain his composure and make it
seem that he had seen these things all along. Actually, the boy was
probably correct, Antelope thought. But Wolf Pup had realized so
quickly . . . *Aiee*, almost before he had seen it himself.

"How do you know these things, Pup?"

The boy was eager to share his reasoning. "Two sets of tracks, one big, one small . . . But not small enough for this year's fawn."

"Maybe the fawn is hidden and did not come to water."

Wolf Pup shook his head. "No. The doe would chase her yearling away if she had a fawn, would she not?"

"Maybe. But maybe this is an old buck with a younger one following him."

The boy considered, but only for a moment. "No. The track is big, but not big enough for an old buck. I am made to think it is that of an old doe, a big one, and her daughter from last year."

"Not last year's *son?*"

Wolf Pup laughed. "No, you are teasing me, Father. At this season, the bucks stay together and so do the does."

"That is true." *Aiee,* the boy was skilled for his age!

Now Wolf Pup chuckled. "Look! The horse startled them, at the same time! They frightened each other, just about sunrise."

"What?" his father asked in amazement.

"Look!"

Pup pointed to a set of tracks that were smeared and pushed to one side. A small clot of mud had been thrown up as the animal jumped, and lay isolated near the track. It had not had time to dry, so yes, about sunrise. Antelope realized that the boy had been correct at every point.

"Why did you say 'the same time,' Pup?"

The boy laughed. "Ah, Father, both the deer and the horse were frightened enough to jump. They were just across the stream from each other . . . A stone's throw. Why would they jump at *different* times?"

The logic was flawless, and Dark Antelope's heart was filled with pride.

"Our son will be a great tracker," Antelope told his wife that afternoon. "Just the right mix of looking and thinking."

"It is good," said Gray Mouse. "Will he be as good a tracker as his father?" She came and sat beside him and he put an arm around her. "His father tracked me all the way to the Horn People's town and beyond."

She expected some teasing in return, but there was none. Dark Antelope was serious.

"I am made to think he may be better, Mouse. He reminds me of Beaver Track, who taught me."

"Is this true, my husband? Our son is this skillful?"

"I am made to think he will be."

She clapped her hands like a child. "It is good then! But why are you surprised?"

Antelope laughed now. "*Aiee*, woman! You are right, of course. How could he be otherwise?" Then he became serious again. "I am made to think, though, that he does see things of the spirit. The way he seemed to know what the deer were *thinking* and *feeling* when they made the tracks . . . That will make him a great tracker. Mouse, I did not feel such thoughts until my vision quest."

Her curiosity was aroused.

"What was that like . . . your quest?" she asked.

He looked at her, surprised. A woman could undertake a vision quest, but most did not. It was strange that she would be interested now, at this stage of her life.

It would be impolite to ask about another's vision quest, but he understood. Their relationship was very close. His wife was not asking him the private details, but only how it *felt*.

"It is something that cannot be described," he mused. "Mine was before we married, you know."

"Yes," she teased, "while you waited for me to grow up." There was a difference of several years in their ages.

"And then, you had to follow *your* quest, to look for your people."

She nodded. "Yes, that was foolish. But Antelope, you do not know how it feels to be an orphan. Anyway, that was a search, not a vision quest. A vision quest is a thing of the spirit, no?"

He held her closer for a moment. "That is true."

"But my husband . . . Why do we speak of vision quests?"

"We spoke of the spirit of our son."

"Oh, yes . . . Antelope, you spoke as if he is ready *now* for a vision quest. Can that be?"

He was quiet, and when he finally did speak, it was very slowly and thoughtfully. "No . . . he must reach manhood first. I am made to think that his spirit is ready, but his body must wait. *Aiee*, that is strange."

"Your father would know of such things, no?"

"Yes. I wonder if he has noticed. He and our son are very close."

"That is true. There is more than the name between them. Singing Wolf and Wolf Pup . . . Maybe you could speak with your father about it."

Singing Wolf was very thoughtful about it, as Antelope tried clumsily to explain what he meant. His old eyes twinkled with amusement as the younger man stammered in confusion.

". . . and I . . . we, Gray Mouse and I . . . are made to think that there is a thing of the spirit . . . *Aiee*, Father, do you know what I am trying to say?"

The holy man nodded gently, took another pull on his pipe, and spoke.

"So . . . You have noticed it, too?"

"What?"

"*Aiee*, of course you have. But you thought that it was only your joy as parents that made it so."

"Well, we . . ."

But Singing Wolf held up a hand to stop him.

"No, my son, it is true. There *is* more here than meets the eye. You have noticed it too."

"But Father, what . . . ?"

The old man shrugged. "Who knows? There are many kinds of spirit-gifts. This boy knows things, has understanding beyond his years. It is a thing of pride for me, as for you."

"Then what is to be done?"

"Find ways to encourage him, to teach him."

"But Father, I am made to think that already he sees things as quickly as I."

Singing Wolf laughed. *"Aiee,* I know the feeling. I remember when you showed me things about tracks that I had not noticed."

"I did?"

"Of course. You were only a little older than Wolf Pup is now. You were about to choose your path, to follow my medicine or to become the tracker that you now are."

"Father, I . . . ."

The old man dismissed the protest with a wave of his hand.

"No, no, Antelope. Each must choose his own path. One cannot follow another's path. Your Wolf Pup is about to choose, and it is his to do so."

"But he is too young!"

"Ah, yes. A parent always thinks so. Yet, Pup has the same right to choose as you did . . . or I! And it will take him a little while yet."

"We are made to think that his spirit is wise but that his body lags behind."

"No . . . his spirit runs ahead."

"Yes, maybe. What shall we do?"

"Wait. That is hard, too, my son. But I have an idea! Let us show him the Story Skins."

The Story Skins, the history and legendry of the People! Antelope had been fascinated by the rolled skins, several of them, stored behind the lining in the lodge of his father. Pictographs, usually one for each year, depicting some momentous event in the history of the band or of the whole nation.

"It is good," agreed Dark Antelope. "He will learn more about the People, and can choose his path."

"Yes. But he must not know that it is for that purpose. Then he would feel pushed to choose, and maybe he is not really ready. Let us wait for the right moment, no?"

5
>> >> >>

Dark Antelope held up a hand to halt the column. The Southern band was in the process of moving to winter camp. They would settle in the shelter of the oaks to the south of their summer range. Where the Sacred Hills of the open grassland met the forested slopes, there was protection from Cold Maker's onslaught.

It is made that way for the use of the People, Singing Wolf said. It had been told to him by his father, and his father before. All the way back to Creation, maybe. In that region there are heavy thickets of oak, almost impenetrable to walk or to ride through. The grassy strips between provide a means for travel and the thickets a barrier to the wind.

Yet there is more. Most of the trees in the region drop their garments in autumn, the Moon of Falling Leaves. It is not so with the scrubby oaks of the thickets there. The leaves die, but cling tightly to the stems for most of the winter, providing more defense against the north winds. Not until the return of Sun Boy from his journey south does the leaf-fall occur to the oaks. The dead foliage is pushed free by the awakening buds of a new season's growth. It is part of the plan, and part of the year's routine for the Southern band.

The Red Rocks and the Mountain band usually moved westward to winter in the shelter of the geographic features that gave them their names. The Northern band had favorite wintering places among the hills along the rivers, and the Eastern band in the deeper forested areas east of the River of Swans. The New band, who had joined the People a generation or two earlier, had largely followed the pattern of the Southern band.

Just now, the People were moving into their selected areas to prepare for the winter. The weather was still warm, but it would take some time to erect and winterize the lodges. They would build snow fences and stuff the dead storage space behind the lodge linings with dried grass to hold the warmth of the lodge fires. Besides all this, they would need a Fall Hunt. There was much to do before Cold Maker's arrival.

Travel was a somewhat cumbersome thing. Thirty or forty families, sometimes more, each with two or three horse-drawn pole-drags . . . *travois,* the French traders were calling them . . . Then the other horses, those ridden by women and children, as well as the prized buffalo runners and war horses of the warriors. In addition, there might be hundreds of horses in the loose herd, driven by a few of the young men.

This was the task of Wolf Pup this season, and he was very proud. He had seen fifteen winters now. This was the first year that he had been permitted to ride with the herd instead of with the family, and he reveled in the responsibility. His younger sister, at three seasons of age, was tied to the back of a dependable old mare. Pup could dimly remember when he had been tied in place in that fashion. Children of the People felt a familiar safety on the back of a horse because of this custom. If a mother had other duties, which a mother always does, she would tie a child to the back of a "family" horse and turn it loose to graze. The rocking motion of the horse's gait became a comforting, familiar thing.

Children of the People could ride well almost before they could walk. It was for good reason that others called their nation the Elk-dog People, the People of the Horse.

During travel, of course, the family horse that carried the children would be kept with the family's baggage, drawn by other animals.

Wolf Pup looked across the dusty fog raised by the horse herd to see that his father had stopped the column. He signed to the nearest of the other herders, and they began to circle the herd to keep it intact.

"What is it?" the other youth called as they came within speaking distance.

"I do not know. Antelope stopped the column. The wolves must have seen something. Ah, yes! There he comes!"

One of the scouts who had been out of sight ahead of the straggling column was loping down the slope of the ridge ahead. He did not appear unduly excited, only returning to report on what lay ahead.

The young man pulled his horse to a stop before Dark Antelope, talking and pointing. Wolf Pup had another reason for pride during this move. His father had been selected as the leader. Election of the band chieftain was usually based on political prestige, and would remain in effect for the lifetime of the individual selected. But though the wisdom and experience of such a chief was valuable, the operation of a hunt or a move such as this often required the vigor of a younger man. Such a temporary leader would be elected by the band council for a specific project. The manner in which he handled the responsibility would mark him for consideration when the next election of a band chief must take place. Dark Antelope had proved himself before. He might well be a candidate, but the present band chief, Walking Crow, was still vigorous. It might be many seasons before an election was needed.

Antelope now turned and motioned to a couple of young men near him. One turned to ride down the column and spread whatever news there might be. The other kicked his horse into a gentle lope toward the herd, slowing as he came near to maintain a calm among the driven animals.

"Another party, beyond the ridge," he explained. "We wait here, a little while."

"A war party?" Pup's heart beat faster.

"The wolves think not. They appear to have *travois*. Women and children. Circle the horses, wait here a little while."

He turned and rode to inform the other herders.

Dark Antelope was not unduly concerned. He knew the young men who served as wolves, and they were the finest. Their task had been his many times, and would be again. He was proud of the honor to be asked to lead this move, but he enjoyed the scouting assignment too. His skills at that had resulted in his selection as leader now.

In a way, Antelope would have preferred the circling and exploring that went with the task of the scouts. Wolves, they were called, because of the similarity of their activities. As the great buffalo herds migrated through the season, there were always the gray ghosts circling the herd, looking for stray, sick, or defenseless animals. Someone in the past had noticed the similarity to the scouts who circled a traveling column of the People. Their purpose was the opposite, of course, that of protection rather than predation. Again, something that was once a joke had become part of the culture.

The wolves had reported today that another column, a band on the move, was straggling along in a generally similar direction. There was little cause for alarm because the strangers, too, had their families with them. Both groups were vulnerable, and only a madman would provoke an incident that would put wives and children at risk. Even enemies in such a situation would stop and visit. Cautiously, to be sure. There was always the remote possibility of a trick. Or the even more remote chance that the strangers *were* led by a madman.

The accepted protocol now was to meet and talk to the strangers. Walking Crow would do the negotiating, and he now joined Dark Antelope.

"Do we know who they are?" he asked, drawing his horse to a stop.

"No, Uncle. Head Splitters, maybe."

"They do drag lodge poles? There are families?"

"The wolves are made to think so."

"Could they be our own New band?"

"I am made to think not, Uncle. They spent the summer to the east of us, and this band seems to come from the west or southwest."

"That is true. Well, let us meet them."

"It is good," agreed Dark Antelope. "Now, we will close up the column and move it slowly into plain view. The wolves say there is a level place over the ridge, a good place to meet. Does this meet your wishes, Uncle?"

"Of course. This is your decision, Antelope."

"I know, but to be sure . . ."

"Yes, it is good. You have another rider to go with us?"

"Broken Wing. Maybe my father too?"

"Good. Singing Wolf lends dignity."

The entire band moved slowly forward, and the four emissaries drew ahead toward where one of the wolves waited on the ridge. The setting was a large grassy basin surrounded by low rolling hills like that on which they now stood. On another of the flat-topped ridges a group of horsemen was visible, and beyond, a straggling column. A horse herd was held in a little canyon.

"They look much like our band," observed Walking Crow.

"Yes, Uncle," the scout said. "They do. We are made to think that they are not Head Splitters. They may be the Trader People."

"This far south?"

"Maybe not."

All of this was speculation, without much alarm. Head Splitters were allies of the People for many generations back. The Trader People, by virtue of the very characteristic which had led to that name, were usually friends of everyone.

These might be strangers, but what sort of strangers? Newcomers might be aggressive and dangerous, or peaceful and neighborly. The purpose of this meeting for both groups would be to gain as much information as possible about each other.

Now five riders from the other band rode slowly down the slope on the opposite side of the basin. Walking Crow, flanked by the others and joined by the scout, rode down to meet them. On level prairie, Crow reined his horse to a stop.

"Let them come to us," he murmured.

Antelope smiled. The politics of diplomacy . . . By stopping first and making the other group approach, Walking Crow had already won the first point. The implication was clear: *This is our land and you have entered it.* Antelope was not certain that he would want the position of political leadership held by Crow. Possibly his father could have handled it, because he dealt well with people. But the gifts of the spirit had always been more important than politics to Singing Wolf.

The other party drew up in a line, facing that of the People about twenty paces away. A handsome, athletic-looking man in the middle of the line raised a palm in the greeting sign. In essence, *I carry no weapon.*

Walking Crow returned the greeting, and continued in hand signs.

"How are you called? Who are your people?"

The other nodded and signed in answer. "I am Blackbird. My nation, Snake. And you?"

"Elk-dog People. I am Walking Crow."

"The weather is good."

"That is true. But you did not come to talk of weather."

The other man nodded. "It has been a hard season for our people. Dry, a poor fall hunt. We look for buffalo."

That might be true, or not, Dark Antelope thought. In such a situation, it was always proper to make small talk about the weather and the hunting. This allowed the two groups to evaluate each other at their leisure. Both knew that there would be no trouble at this time, because the families of both groups were present.

He looked over the horses of the strangers. Good stock, though small. A bit thin for this time of year . . . Yes, the strangers may have had a very hard season. It would be logical for them to search for a better place to winter. It was unusual, though, for a tribe to the south to move northward as winter approached.

"You are traveling in the wrong direction," Walking Crow was signing. "Winter is coming."

"We know that," returned the other haughtily. "But we must find meat."

"You have seen no buffalo?"

"Only a few."

This, too, seemed odd. But there was no predicting the actions of the great herds. It was quite possible that this band from the south had merely failed to make contact with a major herd of migrating animals.

"I am made to think he speaks truth," said Crow aloud, in an aside to his companions.

"We had heard that your fall hunt was good," Blackbird was signing. "The herds have gone somewhere."

"We have not had our big hunt yet. But we summered well. We will find a winter camp and then hunt."

The fact that hung between them unsaid was that both bands would need a large number of buffalo kills before the winter season. This could lead to much friction between the two, if the buffalo continued to be scarce. Wars have been fought over lesser conflicts.

Walking Crow now demonstrated the diplomacy that had made him a leader.

"Let us camp together tonight," Crow suggested. "You are welcome in our country. We will talk of the hunt."

How clever, thought Antelope. In one move, Crow had managed to accomplish several goals. He had plainly established the claim of the People to this region. He had extended a hand of friendship which would enable the two groups to become acquainted. It is much harder to go to war with someone with whom you have shared a campfire. But possibly more important, this would enable the men of the Southern band to evaluate the strength of the newcomers.

6
>> >> >>

A few families erected their big lodges. Primarily that was to impress the strangers.

"That is much work just to boast a little," giggled Gray Mouse. "Do you want to set up our lodge?"

"I see no need," her husband smiled.

A few of the newcomers, too, set up lodges, a few bow shots away, apparently for the same reason. The majority of both bands, however, settled into camp sites marked only by a fire and some sort of temporary shelter . . . A brush arbor, perhaps, or a robe or two over a flimsy frame of poles.

Most important to each family was the lighting of the fire. This was a ritual. Wolf Pup watched his father use the fire-sticks. Many of the People now used steel strikers obtained from the French. Antelope possessed one, and frequently used it. But this, the first fire in a new place, had special meaning. It was always the first communication with local spirits, and Antelope, under the influence of his father, the holy man, felt somewhat differently about it than some of their neighbors. He could not have explained it, except in vague and general terms. There were good relationships that the People had always enjoyed with the spirits of the prairie. It only seemed to him that this good contact would be best maintained by means of the old and proven ways. The spark from a blow of steel on flint might be equally acceptable, but why take chances?

The fine powder that was spilling out of the notch in his yucca fire-stick quickly became darker, then black as the spindle twirled. Now the smoke rose in a tiny spire, now thickened . . . A glowing spark . . . Antelope dropped the fire-bow, removed the stick, and picked up the little wad of shredded cedar bark, carefully wrapping it around the precious spark. Even as he did so he was blowing gently on the tinder, breathing life into it. A few more breaths and the cedar bark burst into flame. He thrust it under a cone of small twigs and dry grass that he had prepared, and watched the orange tongues lick upward through it. A pinch of tobacco from his pouch . . . That, to attract and appease whatever spirits might inhabit this place.

"Here we will camp" the informal ritual stated in simplest terms. It was a notice, an announcement of intent, and in a way, a request for permission to camp here. Other families around them were carrying out similar rituals. Some were simpler, some more formal. Probably the Snake People across the stream were carrying out similar ceremonies.

Have not other cultures in other times often done much the same in the form of a "housewarming" custom? What is that but a ritual lighting of the first fire? *Here I intend to stay.*

As the routine chores of preparation for the night were completed, people began to bring wood for a fire. Not a council, but much the same. This would be a way for two groups of strangers to learn about each other.

It had been agreed that the newcomers would join the People. It was still light when they began to straggle across the gravel bar in the stream to gather at the site of the larger fire. Its lighting was delayed until just before darkness fell, to avoid waste of the scarce firewood.

At the appropriate time, someone brought a burning brand and thrust it beneath the pile. Flames crackled upward, and a column of smoke towered toward the darkening sky.

As the storyteller of the host group, Singing Wolf rose to begin the evening festivities. The storyteller need not be the holy man, but it was often so among the People. He positioned himself to best advantage, choosing the most impressive combination of light and background and shadow. He would use both spoken word and hand signs, for the benefit of his mixed audience.

"In the beginning," he said solemnly, accompanied by hand signs, "the People lived under the ground, in darkness."

All things must begin at the beginning. So it was with the stories of the People. Creation . . . In this way two tribes or nations could begin to understand each other. Traditionally, the beginning of every story is with Creation. The listeners nodded.

"We came into the world of sunshine, grass, and buffalo through a hollow cottonwood log," he continued. "The Old Man of the Shadows sat astride it and struck it with a stick to get our attention. A man stuck out his head to see what was going on, and found that he could crawl out into the sunshine. It was warm and good, and he called to his wife to come on out. But she did not do it until Old Man whacked the log again with his stick.

"Then they kept coming. Each time Old Man struck the log, another of the People popped out into the open, and breathed the clean air of the prairie, and it was good."

Singing Wolf paused, waiting for a response. At this point there was a built-in joke on the listener unfamiliar with the story. The long pause was guaranteed to stimulate curiosity. Usually, some listener would break the awkward silence with a question. A good storyteller could be confident that it would happen, but usually had a backup plan. In a reasonable length of time, or if the listeners were becoming restless, someone by prearrangement would ask the obvious question in some form. *Then what happened?*

Tonight there was no need for the assistant to ask. One of the visitors, eager to hear more, made the inquiry, and in the best possible form.

"Are they still coming through?" he signed.

"Ah, no," Singing Wolf signed sadly. "A fat woman got stuck in the log, and no more could come through. We have always been a small nation."

There was general laughter at the expense of the questioner. Then the leader of the visiting Snake People posed a more serious question.

"You are a small nation? This band seems prosperous. How many bands have you?"

Now was a time for caution. This casual inquiry carried a deeper meaning, only thinly veiled. What is your strength? The answer would be very important. A show of pride and self-confidence, a little boasting, not too much . . .

"Six," Singing Wolf stated truthfully. "We have many horses. That is why we are Elk-dog People. Then there are our allies, the Head Splitters."

This was a boast to impress the strangers with the fighting potential of the People. A warning, perhaps. The reaction was immediate, but subdued.

"Yes, we know them."

Of course . . . The area occupied by the Head Splitters was to the south and west of the People. They would undoubtedly have been in contact with the Snake People. But there was a strongly implied attitude here which came through quite plainly. "We know them" was only part of the story. The rest said "as enemies."

It was an uncomfortable moment, and Singing Wolf tried to smooth over this disclosure. Maybe he had already thought of this possibility.

"We have no enemies," he signed slowly and plainly. "We have been at peace for a generation. It does not matter tonight who are your friends or enemies. We camp together, eat together, exchange stories, maybe hunt together if our scouts find buffalo. Is this not as it should be?"

It was important while talking peace to appear to be speaking from a position of strength. Both groups knew that there would be no trouble at this meeting, because of their mutual vulnerability. But next time it might be different, and that was understood.

The other leader nodded agreement. "Let it be so," he signed.

Singing Wolf tried to lighten the mood of the gathering. "Now, tell us of your Creation."

There was a long pause. Finally, the visiting leader shrugged. "We, too, came from beneath the earth, but by a different path. It is no matter. You have yours, we have ours."

This was not going well. It would be good to salvage something from this meeting if possible.

"Shall we race horses tomorrow?" asked Singing Wolf.

It was a good move. The other leader, who had become distant and haughty, now brightened with interest.

"It is good," he signed. "We will let our young men decide who is the more skilled, no?"

The prospect of a day of racing and gambling was pleasant. Much more so than the uncomfortable way that the story fire had been going. That was odd. No one was certain what had caused the evening to fall apart. Many times in later years the People would spend pleasant evenings with the Snake People. But on that first camp together, it was not so. Maybe there was a distrust, a hesitancy to be entirely open to the newcomers.

Whatever the reason, it was largely overcome by the prospect of a day of activity, games, and contests.

Early the next morning the young men were preparing for the races, exercising up their horses or strutting for the benefit of onlookers. Even granting that the Snakes would flaunt only their best animals, these appeared to be horses of fine quality. The People were impressed.

But so, too, were the Snakes. A small group, the leaders of both groups, sat on a partly shaded knoll and watched the younger warriors.

"Where did your people first see the horse?" inquired Blackbird, leader of the Snakes.

"Ah, it was long ago," Walking Crow answered. "Our wolves

saw a man in a shiny headdress, riding on an animal. They told that it was a dog as big as an elk, and that it wore a turtle on each foot."

The other man chuckled. "The Elk-dog! Of course."

"And your people?" Crow asked.

"We do not have so clear a story of our first sight. But it was a little different with us. We were in contact with the Spanish hairfaces, and saw many horses."

"Your horses are good, and your young men ride well," Crow noted.

"Yes. We get many horses by raiding the Spanish herds . . . see?" He pointed to a gray mare that happened to be passing at the moment. There was the plain mark of a branding iron on her flank, a beautifully curved symbol.

"What is that?" asked Crow.

"A mark used by the Spanish. It says whose horse."

Ah, a mark of ownership, thought Crow.

"Like the paint markings on an arrow, to identify whose kill," he said to Singing Wolf, who sat beside him.

The holy man nodded. "I have heard that the Spanish mark horses in this way. These are good horses!"

"That is true. And they ride well."

"We will see how well, no?"

It was an almost frantic day, of innumerable races, wagers, trading, and festivities. In many respects the day resembled the secular activities surrounding the annual Sun Dance.

The Snake men proved to be excellent horsemen. Most of them were fairly short in stature, in contrast to the tall and slender Elk-dog People. Their legs were short, and their appearance while walking was odd, almost clumsy-looking. But once on horseback, *aiee!* These young men could perform feats that appeared little short of magic. Turning, twisting, dropping from one side or the other of a running animal, shooting to either side and even under the necks of their mounts . . .

The taller, longer-legged young men of the People found it difficult to duplicate the antics of the visitors on horseback. This was somewhat overcome by the skill of the People in handling their horses in a race. In straightaway racing their showing was better, with their slightly larger, more heavily muscled animals.

"Our grasses are better," explained Singing Wolf simply, "so our horses grow better."

Shadows were beginning to grow long when one of the wolves of the People loped into camp and pulled his horse to a stop before the assembled leaders.

"The buffalo come." He pointed into the unseen distance to the north. "Big herds."

Almost at the same time, one of the Snakes' scouts arrived with a similar message. The two groups of leaders turned to each other with broad smiles.

"Buffalo!" signed Walking Crow. "It is good. Tomorrow, we hunt!"

7

»» »» »»

It was a glorious hunt, which would be told in story and song in
the legendry of both nations for many generations.

No doubt it began as a contest. Two groups with similar ways
and similar needs had encountered each other unexpectedly.
There was a certain doubt, a distrust in the air. Both bands felt a
need to prove their strength, yet the circumstances prevented
outright fighting. Perhaps the races and contests might have dete-
riorated into a brawl, but it was not to be. Instead, the spirits
smiled, and the buffalo came. Huge herds, in numbers not seen
for many seasons. Now there was a common objective, that of
supplies for the winter. And what better way to demonstrate the
manhood and skills of young warriors than in the hunt?

The holy men of both nations predicted a great success, though
there must have been some question in both camps . . . Would
there be a problem with interference from the other hunters?

It was apparent to the observers from the start that there were
differences in the manner of the hunt. That of the People was

more structured, with a general plan of approach. A leader had been elected to announce the major decisions and plan the tactics.

By contrast, the visitors had a tendency to ride wildly in complete disregard for safety of hunter or horse. Any judgment seemed to be overshadowed and lost in the thrill of the hunt itself. This might have resulted in an abortive hunt, had the herds been small. Frightened buffalo, stampeding away from yelling, screaming riders, might have been gone before the hunt fairly began.

Today there was no such problem. The immense size of the herd was a thing of wonder. There were more animals than anyone had ever seen before. Even with the noisy charges by the hunters of the Snake People, there were still so many hundreds of undisturbed animals that no problem resulted.

There were the initial kills, necessary to obtain the minimum supply of meat for the coming winter. Then the men of the People began to use the opportunity for other purposes. The training of a new horse . . .

"*Aiee,* I had hoped to use this horse as a buffalo runner, but he wants to run to the left!"

"And you use a bow?"

"Yes. He is no good to me."

"But he runs well, does he not?"

"Of course. He carries the blood both of the Fire Horse and of the gray First Horse of the People."

"Spotted Dog, there, uses the lance. Talk to him."

A hunter using a bow must approach the *right* side of a running buffalo. A rider finds it virtually impossible to shoot to his right if he is right-handed, because the bow is in his left hand. A hunter who uses the lance, however, must approach his quarry from the *left*, because the weapon is in his right hand.

While it might be possible to train a horse against its natural tendencies, it is easier to select a mount whose habits correlate with those of the rider. Therefore, a horse which naturally approaches the running animal from the left is more suitable for a hunter who uses the lance.

"Let me try him," Spotted Dog suggested. "Maybe we can

trade. He doesn't look like much, though. Maybe you can trade him to the Eastern band."

"*Aiee*, you have never owned a horse as good as this! Try him! But you do not expect me to trade for that bag of bones under you, do you? You have others?"

The trading began, with each horseman downgrading the offering of the other and upgrading his own. Many horses changed hands that day.

The reference to the Eastern band was a long-standing joke among the People. The Eastern band had been considered foolish people since Creation, probably. There were many jokes, and it must be admitted that there were those among that band who seemed to act foolishly by intent, to enjoy the notoriety.

One who suffered a minor misfortune, then, might be the butt of a joke. A rider who was unhorsed and was forced to walk home might be subjected to an unkind remark.

"Too bad . . . you know his grandmother was of the Eastern band."

Or perhaps a jibe at the success of a great accomplishment of a friend: "*Aiee*, can this be? Was your family not Eastern band?"

Thus, the perennial jokes around the trading of horses. A lame or useless horse might bring a bit of tongue-in-cheek advice.

"Better keep him. Maybe you can trade him to the Eastern band next year at the Sun Dance."

In this hunt there was the added factor of the hunters of the Snake People. These spectacular riders seemed to break all the expected rules, shooting or lancing to either side and even behind them. They used a short, stout bow, and were as adept with it as they were with the horse. There were some spills and injuries, and more when the young men of the People began to try to duplicate the stunts of the Snake men.

"Father, may I try the hunt?" asked Wolf Pup eagerly.

Dark Antelope paused for a moment. He was about to say "No, you are too young," but gave it a little more thought. The boy *was* approaching manhood. He *had* done well with the horse herd. Well, the day must come sometime . . .

"Get your horse, your bow . . . You must stay with me."

"Of course, Father."

"Is this wise, my husband?" asked Gray Mouse anxiously.

"It must happen soon," Antelope assured her. "This is a good day, and he will be with me."

Antelope had returned to the camp to exchange his buffalo horse for a young mare he was training. He waited, warming up the young animal while still trying to calm her excitement. Wolf Pup returned, nervous but ready to ride.

"Good hunting," called Mouse. "Be careful!"

The two riders approached the area of the hunt. The hunters had been unusually successful in inducing a portion of the herd into a circling, milling mass. Though only a few hundred animals, the circle was large enough to keep running. Riders around the perimeter had so far managed to turn most of those which broke out of the mass back into the herd. At any moment, there could be a major break for open country, but it had not yet occurred. The occasional escapee was quickly pursued, and here and there sounded the pop of a musket.

"Stay with me," Antelope cautioned as they loped with the circling herd, drawing cautiously closer. "Now . . . See the yearling cow, there? Ease back, let her run . . . She is about to . . ."

The fat young cow broke away at a full gallop, and Wolf Pup kicked his horse into a hard run, fitting an arrow to his bowstring as he did so. Antelope tried to ride up on the other side of the quarry, but his inexperienced horse was fighting the rein. Wolf Pup would have to be on his own.

It was perhaps a hundred paces before the boy drew alongside the cow and loosed his arrow. It was like a dream. Dark Antelope watched as the missile leaped across the short space to plunge deep into the animal's flank. Only the feathers could be seen, protruding from just behind the ribs . . . a skilled shot . . .

The running cow stumbled, ran a few more steps, and collapsed to lie kicking in the dusty grass. Wolf Pup turned his horse and rode back, smiling triumphantly. *His first buffalo!*

"Do not get down," his father called. "It will be there, and marked with your arrow."

They started to circle again, looking for another shot. Before they could select one, however, a horse some distance ahead of them shied away from the running herd. The rider lost balance . . . He had not yet regained his seat when a huge bull thrust out of the dusty herd and lowered its head for the charge. The massive horns swung low, under the belly of the horse. The stricken animal screamed in pain and terror as it was tossed high. Antelope and Wolf Pup gasped as the rider flew even higher, somersaulted, and plunged back into the cloud of dust. The bull charged away, followed by a horde of running animals. They thundered over the fallen horse and rider, breaking toward open prairie.

"Back!" yelled Antelope. "Get away from them!"

Father and son reined away from the herd, which now began to expand and spread, each animal trying to follow the established direction toward escape. The riders reached a safer vantage point, and paused to watch the exodus of the vast river of brown, flowing toward the distance through a fog of dust. The thunder of hooves died to a dull rumble in the distance.

"Who was it?" asked Wolf Pup. "The bull . . ."

"I do not know," his father said. "One of the Snake men, I am made to think. Whoever, he is dead!"

They turned their horses back toward the scene. The animals were excited, scenting blood and death, and were unwilling to approach. They dismounted and walked forward. Two mounded, shapeless masses lay before them, one much larger than the other. Both were pounded into the dust of the prairie, and white shards of bone thrust up through battered skin. The man's face was indistinguishable.

"*Aiee!*" said Wolf Pup softly.

People were running from the camp now, and there were excited cries of question.

"This," observed Dark Antelope, "is why any hunt may hold danger."

He knelt and picked up the feathered end of a splintered arrow, examining the painted stripes. This might be the only way to identify the body before them. Except, of course, to see who did not return to his family after the hunt.

8
>> >> >>

Each young person, in any society or culture, goes through a sobering experience. At one time or another, the fact of one's own mortality looms before him.

It is virtually impossible for a child to imagine a world in which he (or she) does not exist. People come and go. They move on, they die and are seen no more. Even so, they are *others. Such things do not happen to me,* the child believes, though possibly not in words. It is unacceptable to think otherwise.

But there must come a time in the process of becoming an adult when we are forced to look at a disturbing possibility: *That could have been me!* It is to be hoped that this experience does not happen too early, during one's tender years. Presumably, one who has reached adulthood is able to handle such a realization more smoothly. This may not be true, but it is more comforting to believe so, for those who have already seen their own mortality.

For Wolf Pup, his first buffalo hunt was also his time of awareness. He had seen the death of a young man only a little older than himself. For a long time he would see the scene again in his dreams . . . The charge of the great bull, the hapless horse gutted by shiny black horns . . . The rider hovering for a moment above the dusty melee before plunging to his death. It bothered Wolf Pup to realize that the youth had been permitted that moment . . . a space of three or four heartbeats . . . to see his own death rising up to meet his fall. *It could have been me . . .*

Even so, it was no one that Pup had known. The unrecognizable heap of bloody rags had been identified as a youth of the Snake People. The sound of a plaintive, wailing dirge, rising and falling, floated across the valley from the other camp. Wolf Pup took note that they, too, had a song for mourning, as did the People. Everyone, he assumed, must have such a song. He had never thought about it much. He was aware that Head Splitters mourned in this way, but now . . . *It happens to everyone sometime,* he thought.

These serious realizations were not enough to spoil the triumph of his first horseback hunt. He was proud to have everyone know that he had made a kill. There were two sides to this day of his maturity, as there are two sides to . . . well, to almost anything. To a fire, which has heat and smoke. Usually it is used for heat, but there are times when the smoke is wanted. For the curing of meat, when the weather is too damp to dry it . . . For the tanning of skins, after working in the mashed pulp of brains from the same animals.

The world is divided, he thought. *There are hot and cold, wet and dry, light and dark, men and women, summer and winter . . .*

And living and dying . . . Are these also not part of the same thing? The purpose for living may be easier to see, but in death there must also be a purpose. What . . . ah, yes! Its purpose must be to cross over to the Other Side. He must ask his grandfather about that. Singing Wolf would know.

It was another day or two before Wolf Pup found an opportunity to approach his grandfather. There was much to do following the hunt. The processing of the meat and skins was largely under the supervision of the women. However, it had a tendency to involve everyone. Husbands and young men helped wives and mothers with the turning of heavy carcasses.

"Red Dog, bring a horse! This one is too big for us to roll over."

Children were assigned tasks of carrying. Anyone old enough could carry some small bundle, and in doing so, learn the ways of the People. And even the smallest could sit near a rack of drying meat to shoo away flies, birds, and curious dogs. The dogs were not much of a problem, because the leavings of the hunt, after the butchering and skinning, were theirs. These spoils would be shared, although reluctantly, with their wild cousins the coyotes, and with the vultures. The dark birds were already gathering. They soared high above on fixed wings, drawing invisible circles in the blue of the autumn sky.

In a matter of days, all of these who had shared in the bounty would have finished their respective functions. Men, dogs, coyotes, vultures . . . Possibly also bears, and almost surely the small scavengers such as raccoons and opossums. A few scattered bones that remained ungnawed would be cleaned and polished by insects, and the prairie would return to its former state. The harvest of its produce had been gathered.

It seemed to Wolf Pup that he had felt before that he understood. But this autumn there was somehow a sudden broader understanding. *All things,* he thought . . . *everything has meaning for everything else. It is all one . . .*

Would this be the sort of revelation that one would learn . . . would *realize,* on a vision quest? He was sure that it would be much the same. Even more enlightening, probably. He wondered when he might be considered ready for such a step . . .

Shadows grew long, and coyotes began to call to each other. From the surrounding hills their chortling laughter seemed to mock the dogs, who barked back at first, but then gave it up and quieted. They were too well fed today to contest anything.

A nearly full moon rose a little while before dark, and there was excitement in the air. The extra-successful hunt was stimulating. Even though the work had been hard, people were slow to retire.

They gathered to smoke, to socialize, to talk over the events of the past day or two. And it was good.

Wolf Pup approached the camp of his grandparents, a bit reluctantly. He wished to have a serious talk with Singing Wolf, but was afraid that there might be other adults who would be there to socialize. Well, he could only go and see.

A few more families had erected lodges now, since it was apparent that they would be here for a little longer stay. They might as well be comfortable for the time it would take to accomplish the processing of the meat and skins. This time of year brought undependable weather, and any sudden change . . . Well, a rush to salvage racks of drying meat would not be helped by trying frantically to set up lodges in the face of a rising storm.

The lodge of Singing Wolf and Rain was one that had been erected. Dark Antelope had seen to that, so that he need not worry further about his parents' comfort and safety. Wolf Pup found his grandfather leaning on his backrest beside the doorway, placidly smoking and gazing at the rising moon.

"I would speak with you, Grandfather," Wolf Pup began respectfully.

The old man nodded agreeably and took a puff on his pipe.

"You have made a buffalo kill," he stated. This was common knowledge, of course. "It is good."

"Thank you, Grandfather. But it is not of that."

The holy man's expression changed hardly at all, but his eyes widened a little.

"Something *more* important?" he asked.

"Yes . . . no . . . well, maybe."

The old man's eyes crinkled at the corners in amusement. "Ah, I see . . . Tell me of this."

"*Aiee,* I do not know where to begin!" Pup said.

The holy man waited.

"A man was killed, Grandfather."

Ah, so that is it, thought Singing Wolf. He nodded. "I heard of it. One of the Snake men, no?"

"That is true. I watched it, Grandfather."

"It bothers you that you could do nothing? Nothing to help him?"

"No, no. It was not that. I saw that . . . No one could have. But I . . . Grandfather, it might be me. They mourn over there . . . It could as easily be that my mother sang tonight the Mourning Song."

"That is true, my son. It is always so. We are born, we live, we die. It is all one. Like the grass, the trees, the buffalo. All are here for a season, or a few seasons, and then cross over."

"But . . . his parents mourn . . . *We* mourn for those who die. The People do."

"Ah, of course. But we mourn for *our* loss, do we not? It is not for him, the young hunter whose wife sings tonight, that she mourns. It is for herself, for *her* loss. And in her grief, she honors him, no?"

Wolf Pup nodded, still somewhat confused.

"What of the Other Side, Grandfather? Is it good or bad?"

"Does it matter?" The holy man paused, drew on his pipe, and blew a cloud of fragrant smoke toward the darkening sky. "Is *tomorrow* good, or bad?"

"We do not know."

"True. But do we worry about it?"

"Well, no . . ."

"That, too, is true. Here we have good times and bad, and we do what we can, and do not worry about the rest. Why should it be different on the Other Side?"

"Grandfather," Wolf Pup said suddenly, "will I understand these things after my vision quest?"

"*Aiee*, I do not know, Pup. Some things are not meant to be understood, but only felt. Why, are you thinking of going on a quest?"

"Someday."

"Good. Not quite yet, maybe. But a vision quest is as it says: a quest, a *search*. One seeks to meet his own spirit-guide."

"And the guide explains?"

"Maybe. Usually not. The guide is a *guide*. A spirit who helps by pointing a *direction*. Then we listen to our guide, and search for the trail with the help of the guide."

They talked a little longer, and Wolf Pup walked out of the camp to be alone. He must think on this . . .

It was not long before Dark Antelope stopped by to talk with his father. Antelope lighted his own pipe with a stick from the fire, spoke to his mother, and sat down.

"Wolf Pup was just here," the holy man said.

"Oh? What did he want? He did well in the hunt, Father."

"So I heard . . . He is searching, Antelope."

"Yes. He is at the age to do so. He saw the Snake man killed, you know."

"So he said. He asked about a vision quest."

"*Aiee!* He is too young!"

"Of course. He knows he is not ready. But he wonders if that will answer some of his questions."

"Ah, he has always had plenty of those!"

They chuckled together, and then the holy man spoke, in a very serious tone.

"Antelope, his questions are good. I am made to think that your son has a very powerful guide, who is trying to get his attention."

"You have always felt something special about him, Father. What must we do?"

"Nothing. He and his guide must find each other. Oh, one thing . . . We once spoke of showing him the Story Skins. I am made to think that he is ready for that."

9

>> >> >>

Wolf Pup sat in his grandparents' lodge, staring at the objects around him. He had been here, in this lodge, many times before, but somehow was seeing everything in a new light. Even the stylized figure of a wolf which adorned the outside of the lodge skin beside the door seemed to catch his attention. Seated on its haunches, nose pointed at the moon . . . singing. Singing Wolf. *How,* he wondered, had the holy man, his grandfather, earned his name?

His main thoughts, however, were somewhat different. His father, Dark Antelope, had casually suggested to him that they stop by to visit Singing Wolf and Rain. However, the atmosphere was anything but casual. Pup sensed a tension in the air. Not a threatening tension, but one of excitement and expectancy, like that at the annual Sun Dance, when the day has been announced but has not yet arrived. He was not sure why he felt so, and could hardly have expressed it in words, but this feeling told him that this was a special day, as the day of the hunt had been.

His gaze wandered around the lodge, as the two older men

made small talk and enjoyed a social smoke. Since this was only a temporary camp, the lodge lining had not been hung. It was rolled and tied, and piled with the other baggage against the slanted wall. Usually, he remembered this lodge for its paintings on the vertically hung lining. Without them, his attention wandered to other things.

Singing Wolf sat in the place of the host, directly across the lodge from the east-facing door. His guests were seated to his left, but very informally. This was merely a family visit. Behind the holy man, a few objects hung by thongs from the lodge poles. From their position, he knew the importance attached to these things. Small bundles, bags, and cases held the many substances and objects that had to do with the profession of the holy man.

A little way above these things, but still below the smoke-blackened upper part of the lodge, hung two objects which were of utmost importance to the Southern band. One was a pipe case of white buckskin, lavishly decorated with brilliant quillwork. Wolf Pup had seen it used, and was always impressed by the ceremonial honor involved. This was the resting place of the medicine pipe, handed down to Singing Wolf from *his* father. Many of the pipe cases among the People now were decorated with beads instead of quills. Trade with the French had brought this, along with the use of the "thunderstick" muskets.

Singing Wolf was not one to hold back progress. He had been one of the first young men to own and use a thunderstick, it was said. Still, when it came to something as important as the medicine pipe and its case, the holy man had always clung to tradition. A medicine pipe case should be adorned with quills in the time-honored way, no?

As a youngster, Wolf Pup had chuckled to himself about this. The glass beads which were now available must be much easier to use, he thought. He had seen his mother and his grandmother sewing them to shirts and moccasins. Quills would require much more work. However, his grandmother seemed even more concerned than her husband that anything to do with his office as holy man be done in the traditional way. The small cases and rawhide boxes that held the mysterious objects of his profession were decorated only with quills.

Wolf Pup's gaze wandered on, to another object. It was of metal, beautiful in shape. Tiny dangling bits of silver sparkled in the dancing firelight like the flash of sunlight reflected from minnows in a clear stream. He had seen this object worn ceremonially around the neck of his grandfather. It was probably the most revered talisman of the People, that which had given them their name: Elk-dog People.

Wolf Pup was a bit uncertain about that part of the story. This object was said to have been worn by the First Horse. In its mouth, somehow . . . He had heard the story, but had paid little attention. Only now, with his newfound feeling of maturity and solemn responsibility, he wished that he had listened more closely. He could not quite see how it could be put in a horse's mouth . . .

"You wish to see the Elk-dog Medicine?" Singing Wolf asked. "Here!"

The holy man reached to take the Spanish bit down from its peg.

"You know its story?" he asked Wolf Pup.

The young man nodded, gulped, and finally murmured an answer. "Some of it, Uncle."

He was embarrassed, here in the presence of his grandfather's wisdom. Strange, on this day when he felt that he was about to be accepted as a man. He had thought that he was ready, during the hunt. His first buffalo kill . . . *aiee*, the thrill of it! But it had been a sobering experience to watch the death of the other hunter. Now he was unsure. Was he really ready to become a man, to assume the responsibilities that were implied? At times it seemed that it would be much safer to remain in the role of a small boy a little longer.

But that thought passed quickly. "Tell me of these things, Grandfather," he requested.

"Of course. Here, you may touch it."

Singing Wolf held the Spanish bit toward the boy. It was deco-

rated with bits of fur . . . otter and ermine, and several dangling
ornaments of beads. Not the glass trade beads of the French, he
noted, but beads of shell and bone, drilled with the whirling point
of a craftsman's bow drill. A single eagle feather hung from one
shank. The entire object was equipped with a looped thong of soft
buckskin so that it could be worn as an amulet around the neck of
the holy man.

Wolf Pup reached out to gently touch the smooth metal. It was
warm.

"Its spirit is good," he said softly. "At least, I am made to think
so."

"It is good that you feel it," Singing Wolf agreed.

"How was it used, Grandfather?"

"Ah, yes! For many lifetimes, it has been worn as you have seen
me wear it. Hung around my neck on the thong. But its power is
to control the horse, the elk-dog. There was a time, you know,
when there were no horses. The People walked."

"I have heard so, Uncle."

"Yes, it is true. Then came a man with fur on his face, riding on
a gray mare. The First Horse! This bit was in the mouth of that
animal. Our wolves who first saw this came to tell the People of it.
They had seen, they said, a dog as big as an elk, wearing a turtle
on each foot. The People thought they were lying, of course. Especially since they insisted that a man was sitting on its back."

"Our ancestor, Heads Off!" exclaimed Wolf Pup. He remembered that part of the story. The stranger had been wearing a
shiny headdress, round and smooth. The scouts who watched him
saw him remove this hat, and for a moment it seemed that he had
removed his head. The name stuck, even after he had been
adopted into the nation of the People.

"But how was its power used?" Wolf Pup asked eagerly.

"Oh . . . You see this circle?" The holy man ran his finger
around the iron loop that was hinged to the center of the bit's
curb. His touch was almost reverent. "This circle holds the
power. It surrounds the lower jaw of the horse, and gives the rider
control."

"I see. As we tie a thong around the jaw, no?"

"That is true. A circle of rawhide to remind Horse that the power to control him is here, in this circle of iron."

The thrill of excitement was a powerful thing. Wolf Pup could hardly sit still.

"Tell me more of these things, Grandfather," Wolf Pup requested.

The two older men exchanged glances. Across the little fire pit in the center of the lodge, Rain looked up from her cooking and caught her husband's eye. She smiled and nodded, pleased.

"Did you know," Singing Wolf asked the boy, "that my father, Walks in the Sun, wore this Elk-dog Medicine on the journey Too-Far-South?"

"*Aiee!*" whispered Wolf Pup. The story of that disastrous expedition, a generation before Singing Wolf's time, was still an impressive tale. There were only two or three survivors.

"I am made to think," Singing Wolf said, "that without it, my father might have died with the others." He rose and replaced the bit on its peg. "But now . . . What I wanted for you to see are the Story Skins."

The holy man rummaged among the bundles and packs at the wall, and began to lay aside some long objects wrapped in soft buckskin. His wife rose and came over to assist him.

"Here, another one. There."

"Is this all?" Singing Wolf asked her.

"I am made to think so," she answered. "See if these are what you need."

"It is good!"

He sorted among the half-dozen rolls and selected one, ceremonially untying its wrappings to unroll it on the floor.

"Here, hold the edge, Antelope," he pointed.

Dark Antelope complied, and they began to examine the pictographs, painted on the smooth surface of the skin.

"Yes, this is the one I wanted," Singing Wolf said, half to himself. "Now, Pup, see this picture? Each picture tells of a year, the most important event of that year. Here is Heads Off and the First Horse."

Wolf Pup was fascinated. "But here are more horses," he observed, pointing to the next pictograph in the spiral.

"Yes. The People saw that with horses we could hunt better, defend ourselves better. Then here . . . that year we were at war with the Head Splitters. We could not hunt, and we had to eat some horses. It was The-Year-We-Ate-Horses."

"But the Head Splitters are our allies!" Wolf Pup protested.

"That is true. But it was not always so. Much later . . . Here, this one!"

He unrolled a different skin and pointed to a complicated pictograph showing several buffalo pushing mounted riders over a cliff.

"See, these warriors wear blue paint. They were invaders. Enemies from the north. The People and the Head Splitters had to join together to defeat them."

"*Aiee!* How was this done?"

"Two young holy men, one from the People, one from the Head Splitters . . . see, here they are! Their combined gifts allowed them to bring a great herd of buffalo to Medicine Rock and push the enemy warriors over the cliff."

Wolf Pup's heart was beating fast.

"And the story of the People is all here, on these skins?" he asked.

"Yes, most of it."

"Does it tell of *Creation?*"

The holy man smiled. "Not entirely. There might have been such skins once, but even skins rot with age. Some of the old stories have been painted again. Mostly on lodge covers, decorations on shirts. You have seen them."

"Yes. But Uncle, the pictures are not enough. You must know the story that goes with each."

"That is true, Wolf Pup. That is part of the duty of the keeper of the Story Skins. He must pass the stories down with the skins."

Wolf Pup was silent a little while, examining the paintings of long ago which told the story of the People.

"Ah! What is this one?" he asked.

It was another scene with many buffalo, and a hapless victim wearing a white buffalo cape, tossed high by a great bull.

"Ah, yes, that one!" Singing Wolf said sadly. "The man is Three Dogs, an evil impostor who claimed to be a holy man. His misuse of power killed him."

"But he wears the white cape . . . *your* cape!"

Singing Wolf chuckled. "Not mine, Wolf Pup. It belongs to the People. I only care for it just now. But yes, this one in the picture was lost, destroyed. It was recovered many lifetimes later. Another young holy man's quest. That is in one of these other skins."

"Enough for now," interrupted his wife. "It is time to eat."

10

>> >> >>

The People moved on into winter camp, and the Snake People did likewise. There was a last council, at which the leaders of each group stated publicly the general area where they intended to winter. There was not yet complete trust, despite the favorable contact and the favorable results of the hunt.

But it was good to state their plans openly. It lent an atmosphere of trust, and implied an ongoing peaceful relationship. Unstated, yet understood by both groups, however, was an obvious factor. It is virtually impossible to conceal the location of a band composed of some forty lodges, hundreds of horses, and innumerable dogs. It is more practical to exchange information in advance. A potential enemy can learn it anyway, and a friend is saved much bother.

The Southern band of the People, then, elected to move only a little farther to the southeast, where the oaks would give better protection. The Snakes announced that their council had decided to move back to the southwest, into more familiar country. As a southern nation, even the more adventurous of their people were cautious about a winter on the open prairie.

The day of departure came, and the lodges were struck and packed. Two columns headed into the rolling hills, ready to prepare for winter in their own ways, but both well supplied with food. The coming Moon of Hunger had become almost a joke. It was hard for Wolf Pup to realize that it had once been called the Moon of *Starvation*. The old Story Skins told that tale. It was easy to see how the coming of the horse had made hunting so much more efficient.

Singing Wolf had pointed out many things to him as they studied the skins. Others he saw for himself. Heads Off, on the First Horse, had used a lance in the hunt. Other hunters in later pictures favored the bow.

Wolf Pup had been amazed at how many bits of information it was possible to glean from the skins. People were identified by means of a smaller, separate pictograph above the main scene . . . A man called Red Feather, apparently, from such a symbol above his picture, connected to his figure by a line. Broken Knife, Wolf's Head . . . Sometimes the interpretation was obscure.

"Ah, that is where the stories help," his grandfather assured him. "They are handed down with the skins."

This entire experience held great meaning for Wolf Pup. He would always look back on this autumn as the time of his coming-of-age. He was still unsure what he intended to do about it. The thought crossed his mind, of course, that it was possible for him to aspire to the honored position now occupied by his grandfather. Just now, he did not want to think about it. After all, there was no sense of urgency. Besides, he had other things on his mind.

Possibly the one that he considered most important was that of a vision quest. The season was too late, too unpredictable for him to carry out a quest now. But possibly after the Sun Dance. Maybe even before, as the spring season wakened the earth. Either way, he felt that he should seek the advice and consent of not only his parents, but his grandfather. Surely a holy man, especially one as wise as Singing Wolf, would have things to tell him about the quest. How to start, *what* to seek.

There was no question that since the day when Wolf Pup was shown the Story Skins and the Spanish bit, the Elk-dog Medicine, he had changed. He felt an excitement in learning of his past, of the ways of the People. There was also a closeness to his grandfather that he had never felt before. Singing Wolf, with his vast knowledge and experience in things of the spirit, had always seemed somewhat aloof. Now the young man was made to see that much of this may have been the ceremony required by the holy man's office. Singing Wolf was not only a devoted family man too, Pup now saw, but more. He was a kindly, understanding Grandfather with sympathy and a keen sense of humor. They had chuckled together over the pictographs of the hairfaced outsider who appeared to remove his own head. There was joy in the love of Singing Wolf for his calling. Wolf Pup began to take greater interest in the activities of his grandfather in the fulfillment of his duties.

Perhaps this interest would have become apparent more rapidly if it had not been for another occurrence. There was a distraction, one that he could not have described at first. It was heralded at first by the gradual appearance of a soft downy fur on Wolf Pup's upper lip, and along the line of his jaw. Dark Antelope saw, and commented to his wife, Gray Mouse.

"Yes, I had seen," she answered. "He is nearly a man. He has grown so quickly, Antelope! *Aiee,* a mother has babies for only a little while. Already his voice changes. And he has taken part in the hunt!"

"But that is good, Mouse! He will be a good man. Strong, respected, no?"

Gray Mouse smiled, a little sadly, and leaned her head on her husband's shoulder.

"That is true. But sometimes I am made to think that there should be a song . . . not of mourning, exactly . . . but a song of sadness for a mother to sing when she loses her babies to the world that will be theirs."

Dark Antelope put his arm around her waist. "That, too, is true. But we have a few years yet before he seeks his own lodge. And we have Swallow, there!"

The two of them smiled at the little girl, singing to her doll. She would soon reach four summers.

"Yes," agreed Mouse. "I will enjoy that. But Antelope, tell me . . . does Pup not have heavier fur on his face than some?"

"Maybe. Some men of the People do have. It is said that there have been some who could not even pluck their faces, they were so hairy."

"Of the *People? Aiee,* I would not want to make love with such a man!" she teased.

"Some of the French are bearded," he reminded.

"Or them, either!" Then she became more serious. "Antelope, I do not know of such things. I grew up in the lodge of my grandmother, Running Deer, where there was no man. Who teaches him? About the beard, I mean."

"Yes, of course. I will show him how to use the clam-shell tweezers, Mouse. But let it go a little while. This is a man-thing. This fur on his lip tells that he carries the blood of Heads Off. That was more important before the traders came in with their fur-faces. But let him enjoy it a little while, and then he will decide to pluck it."

Wolf Pup, of course, knew nothing of this conversation, but he was quite aware of the changes in his body. And in his mind. There were girls in the Rabbit Society, and he had grown up with them. They had learned the athletic skills together, in competition. A woman of the People must be able to use weapons in defense or in the hunt, when necessary. Some of the girls were quite skilled with the bow, as well as in throwing the small ax. Some excelled at running or swimming.

There had come a time, however, when girls his own age had undergone a change. There was a sudden spurt of growth, some two seasons earlier than that of the boys. They not only became taller, but their bodies changed. Places that had been flat and uninteresting now bulged provocatively inside the soft buckskin dresses.

There was a stirring in the loins of Wolf Pup as he noticed these things. He did not quite understand. He could see that his playmates in the Rabbit Society, those with whom he had raced and wrestled, were no longer children, but *women!* Their movements and mannerisms, the swing of the hips and body as they walked, were those of more mature women.

The boys giggled and joked among themselves about this, and there were lewd remarks. In a sense, they understood what was happening, but were not yet equipped to do anything about it. This did not prevent them from watching and enjoying the transformation, of course.

Women of the People had always been considered attractive. As a group, they were proud of their bodies. The dress of the women of the People was often quite short, and sometimes slit up the side. This was ostensibly because their daily duties required much activity. A long or tight skirt would be a great hindrance in the tasks of butchering, dressing skins, and tending cooking fires. Another advantage, however, was that such a garment afforded opportunity to display a shapely leg to prospective suitors or potential husbands. Shapely legs did not go unnoticed.

As the girls of Wolf Pup's age developed, then, they drifted from the close-knit association of the Rabbit Society. Older women took them aside to teach of the changes in the power, the medicine of a woman's menstrual cycle. Among some of their neighboring tribes, women spent those days of each moon in a separate menstrual lodge. The People merely taught caution for the days of menstruation. A menstruating woman's power was such that she must not touch a favorite weapon of her husband's, for instance. It was well known that a bow might never shoot straight again. Likewise, an object of spiritual significance might easily lose power if it were handled accidentally.

In all of this, the women of the People, considered more advanced than some, remained in their homes. Should not a woman have the intelligence to avoid such accidents? Plainly a superiority was implied. *Maybe the women of other tribes must be removed to a menstrual lodge. Ours are clever enough not to pick up such an object or become a threat.*

Wolf Pup was not thinking in such terms, of course. He appreciated the growing attraction of a well-formed leg. Odd, he thought, that he had never noticed before. A leg had been only a leg. Everyone possessed a pair. But now, many female legs had become objects of exquisite beauty, some more than others.

Among those that he watched with interest were a pair belonging to a childhood friend, Otter Woman. Her long legs had begun to change their shape last season. The calves became fuller and rounded gently, making ankles appear more slender. Knees, too, were trim and well formed, and the glimpse of smooth thighs through the slit in her skirt as she walked . . . *Aiee!* He was not certain when or how it had happened. At about the time her buckskin dress became tighter across the hips and the chest maybe. Or was it only that now *he* had changed and had begun to notice?

Otter Woman had become a bit aloof. Haughty, almost. It seemed that she now looked down on the boys with whom she had been friends. True, she was taller than most of them. So were several of the other girls. They had become *women*. Their male counterparts were still children.

There was much jealousy on the part of the immature young men. The ripeness of the girls' puberty attracted the attention of older youths with more size, strength, experience, and maleness. It was extremely frustrating to Wolf Pup and his peers to watch the young women who had been their friends pair off with older men. Some were talking of marriage, even. A couple of the young women just a season older had actually established their own lodges. One girl married a widower old enough to be her father, and became a mother to his children only slightly younger than herself. Of course, her new husband had a lodge of considerable size, and many horses . . . Her mother was proud.

Otter Woman seemed interested in a young man called Spotted Horse. This was a source of much disappointment to young Wolf Pup. He felt the hurt of jealousy and of rejection.

It was in the Moon of Greening that he was walking outside the camp and heard the plaintive song of the courting flute. It came from a clump of willows near the stream, a sheltered place where he had been before. He had nearly reached the clearing, where he wished to be alone to think, when the first notes of the flute began to sound.

Wolf Pup stopped still. He did not want to intrude or to eavesdrop. Neither did he want to make his presence known. He stood for a moment, wondering if he could turn in the leafy tunnel to retreat without discovery. Then he realized that he could, by moving his head a little to the left, see the couple in the clearing.

The back of the man who played the flute was toward him, but he recognized Spotted Horse by his size and muscular build.

The other figure was looking past her suitor's shoulder and almost straight into the willows that concealed Wolf Pup. He was staring into the dark eyes of Otter Woman. Even worse, he saw her sense his motion and the lovely eyes focused on his.

He turned and fled, almost certain that he had not only been seen, but recognized. Now she would think he had been snooping after her like a child. *Aiee!*

Wolf Pup's heart was very heavy.

11
» » »

The loss was hard to bear. Wolf Pup did not want to see Otter, or even think about her. So, naturally, he could think of nothing else. It was sheer torture to think of his friend in the arms of another. He tried not to think of her facial expression in the embrace of Spotted Horse. Would she gaze into the man's eyes with that pleasant, friendly expression that he knew so well? Would the corners of her dark eyes crinkle with pleasure as she smiled over some private joke that they shared? He wanted that expression on the lovely face to be his, his alone. He had felt that it *was* his, in friendship before the complicating factors of man and woman were introduced.

Now, in the depths of his despair, he did not see any relief from the torment that was constantly with him. In the past he had felt that a little time alone was usually helpful. He enjoyed such isolation. To withdraw from the hustle and bustle of the camp with its noises, sights, and smells was always a calming thing. A short walk over the hill or along the river, just out of sight of the distracting sameness of daily routine . . .

But now it did not seem to help. Whatever Wolf Pup tried to think of, his thoughts wandered. Always they returned to happy childhood times, and a part of that innocent past was, of course, his childhood friend Otter.

He would absently gaze at a cottonwood leaf, and recall times at play. The leaf of the cottonwood, split at the tip and rolled into a cone, made a perfect lodge cover. Pup and Otter and the other children had constructed whole villages of cottonwood-leaf lodges. It had been a pastime of children for many generations. Since Creation, maybe.

"This will be my lodge, the largest and best in the band," someone would boast.

Then the other children would search for an even larger leaf. Wolf Pup had discovered that if he could find a tree which had been cut, the sprouts that grew from its stump always bore enormous leaves. Others would search for a big *tree* and try to knock leaves out of its top with a throwing stick. Meanwhile Pup explored areas where last year or the year before, the People had harvested lodge poles. He did little boasting, but he knew that the other children were aware that the lodge of Wolf Pup was usually to be envied. It was a matter of pride.

Part of that pride, he now realized too late, was the pleasure that it had brought to Otter. The girl had always shared his triumphs, and comforted him when things had not gone so well. They had been friends . . . Close friends, in a way that did not need to be voiced. Only now did Wolf Pup begin to realize that maybe they *should* have talked of it. Now he knew that he had simply assumed that the cottonwood-leaf lodge, shared with his friend, would someday be a real lodge of many skins. Otter, now Otter *Woman*, would take pride in that too. But he had assumed too much. Now she was courted by another.

Aiee, what could he have done differently? His tortured mind asked it again and again. The hollow, hopeless answer always came back the same. *Nothing*. Otter had changed from a girl to a woman before his eyes. His own body had not been quite ready. A year, a little longer . . . The thoughts, the stirring of desire had been there in his mind. But the bodily changes that would make him a man were slower. They were not complete yet, even now.

Why? he had asked himself repeatedly. *Why is it so?* He could see that among his male friends, the same thing had befallen them. Some began the process of maturation earlier than others, some later. True, he was one of those who developed later. Yet even had his voice changed and facial fur sprouted earlier, it would not have been enough. The boys of his age were still outdistanced in the transformation. The girls became women first.

Therefore they, now young women, were subjected to courtship and romantic approach by older males. Their own contemporaries, not yet ready, could only watch with jealous resentment.

Wolf Pup felt that this was a thing he could not discuss with his father or his grandfather. The other boys talked of it some, with giggles and smirks, but it was a serious matter for him. He could see the pattern of how it had happened, but had no thoughts as to why. He was too preoccupied with his loss anyway.

Eventually he realized, as young men do, the other side of the situation. As Wolf Pup and the boys of his own age reached toward maturity, so did girls somewhat younger than they. He could see evidence of ripening young womanhood in girls who had always been considered virtually infants by his peers. Some of his friends had matured physically earlier than Wolf Pup. They were now beginning to show romantic interest toward girls younger than themselves by two or more seasons. This, then, must be the way of things, Pup reasoned. The girls become women first, and are paired off with older men. For the boys *now* reaching manhood, the eligible women were those somewhat younger. It must be that it had always been so, but he had never noticed until now.

Having reasoned out the way of things, Wolf Pup found that it did no good to understand it. His primary problem had not changed. He was not interested in the nubile young women whose dark eyes fluttered seductive glances in his direction. They were attractive in their newly acquired shapeliness, but . . . *Aiee*, he could still think of none but Otter Woman.

He watched the long lines of geese high overhead, beating their way north with the changing of the season. Most were the great white birds with black wing tips. Some were blue-gray, the young of the flock. Their cries from far above reminded him of the distant barking of dogs.

Where do you go? His thoughts reached out after the birds. As a child he had wished that he could follow the geese, to see new sights and learn new things. Now this longing returned, more severe than any he had experienced before.

He knew why, of course. It was becoming intolerable to be in the same camp as his lost love, Otter Woman. He avoided her as best he could. Even in doing so, he felt foolish. It was ridiculous to be slipping furtively among the willows or even among the lodges, attempting to avoid a confrontation. A time or two he had unexpectedly encountered her, and the embarrassment was unbearable. That once in the thicket, when she was with her lover and her eyes met those of Wolf Pup . . . *Aiee*, it was painful to remember! How small, how helpless, and how foolish he must have looked to her.

Another time, the two had met near the river, but with many people around. They stopped, looking at each other, and it seemed for a moment that Otter Woman was about to speak. Then she appeared to change her mind, and brushed on past him with the firewood that she was carrying.

Wolf Pup felt more foolish than before. He started to call after her, but what would he say? Flushed with jealousy and embarrassment, he turned to go on, and found that he had forgotten what he had started to do.

Maybe the worst reminder of all the events that were happening that spring was the plaintive sound of the courting flute. He had always thought of it as a pleasant sound. It was a hollow tone, not unlike the mating call of the gray doves as they paired off to nest. He had felt that as a pleasant coincidence. Now it was a dreadful, hollow reminder. He could not seem to find a place to avoid the sound of courting. Not only Spotted Horse was playing the flute, but others. It did not matter to Wolf Pup. The sound itself, no matter what the source, sent him into the depths of despair.

Once he took a horse and rode out into the greening prairie just to get away from the sound of *any* courting flute. It felt good, to feel the horse under him, to breathe the clean air and look into the far blue distance.

He stopped to rest and to let the horse drink at a hillside spring. It was pleasant here. He lay back on the new grass while the horse grazed eagerly and the water murmured a song of comfort. Then that, too, was spoiled. His drowsy reverie was shattered by the coo of a dove in the tree above the spring. Wolf Pup opened his eyes to see the gray pair consummating their courtship on a branch overhead. It was too much. For a moment his anger flared and he reached for a rock to throw at the doves. Then he realized the stupidity of such an action, and tossed the rock aside.

"Grandfather, I would seek my vision quest," Wolf Pup stated.

The holy man raised his eyebrows slightly, but said nothing. He took a slow draw on his pipe and puffed a little cloud of fragrant bluish smoke.

"Why?" he asked.

Wolf Pup had not expected such a question. Or any question, for that matter. He did not know what he had expected from his grandfather. Advice, perhaps, but not questions.

"Well," Wolf Pup stammered, "I . . . I have made my first buffalo kill, I am becoming a man . . . I need to get away, to think."

"Ah!" nodded Singing Wolf. "To 'get away.' There are things that trouble you?"

"No! Yes . . . maybe. *Aiee,* Grandfather, that is the problem. I do not know."

"I have seen you walk out or ride out alone. To think?"

74 » DON COLDSMITH

"Yes. Sometimes." Pup had not realized that his grandfather had noticed.

"It is good, to be alone to think," the old man observed, puffing again on his pipe. "What troubles you, my son?"

"I am not sure. Others . . . my friends, are courting."

Singing Wolf waited quietly, but his thoughts were racing. Could it be that Wolf Pup was considering becoming a woman-man? The family had never considered that. Was that Wolf Pup's problem? True, he had always been quiet and sensitive, but *aiee!*

"You are not courting?" he asked.

"No. I . . ." Wolf Pup stopped and was silent.

His grandfather then decided to try another approach. "Did you not have a friend in the Rabbit Society, Pup? What was her name? Beaver?"

"Otter. Otter Woman. Yes, Spotted Horse courts her."

The holy man studied his grandson's face. The dejection. *Ah, yes! This is it!* he thought. *The boy is in love!*

"I see. And there is no other woman in the Southern band?"

The face of Wolf Pup reddened. "None that would interest me!" he blurted.

"Ah! So, Wolf Pup, you would go on a vision quest to get away? To forget?"

Wolf Pup was quiet for a moment. It sounded childish, even foolish, when stated that way. His grandfather was right, of course. He would have to admit that such a motive was wrong.

Singing Wolf thoughtfully saved him from such embarrassment. "I am made to think," the holy man mused, "that this problem might interfere with your quest. It might be better . . . Look, Pup, the band will soon move, and you will be needed to help. We will go to the Sun Dance . . . Yes, after the Sun Dance! That is a good time for a vision quest, anyway. The Moon of Roses!"

Wolf Pup thought about it for a little while. He could not argue the wisdom of this suggestion. It might be possible to avoid Otter Woman until that time. The travel . . . He could busy himself, herding horses. Maybe he would be allowed to act as one of the wolves. Then, the mingling with the other bands. It would be easy

to avoid contact at the Sun Dance, with hundreds of the People
and their allies who would attend. Then, off on his own for prayer
and fasting.

"It is good," Wolf Pup said.

But he knew that it was not.

12

>> >> >>

There were times during the days of the Sun Dance and its surrounding events when Wolf Pup was almost able to forget his depression. It was an exciting time.

It had begun with the arrival of the Southern band. It was apparent from a day's travel away that there were already people at the selected site. Large numbers of them, judging from the pall of white smoke from the cooking fires that hung over the valley.

"That will be the Northern band," Dark Antelope said.

He was riding with Wolf Pup for a little while. Pup had been assigned as one of the wolves several times, and needed no supervision. But sometimes Antelope enjoyed the chance to get away from the dusty confusion of the main column. He had actually asked his son's permission to ride with him.

"Of course, Father." It was flattering to be asked.

It was Wolf Pup who had first seen the distant haze over the low ridge to the northwest, and had called attention to it. Antelope was pleased. Yes, the boy would make a good scout and tracker.

Now they had stopped on a high, flat-topped hill, to search the area with their eyes. Below them, the column wound through the valley along the river, following one of the time-worn trails. Far ahead lay the dark line of hills that would mark the site of Medicine Rock. That was the landmark, and the agreed-upon place selected for the Sun Dance.

It was understood by all bands, of course, that the camp would not be near the Rock itself. It was too forbidding a place, too populated with the spirits of ancient events that had taken place there. Their presence, while probably not actually a threat, might interfere with the structured ceremony of the Sun Dance. The camp and the Sun Dance pavilion would be on the more level area some distance downstream. That was to be assumed, even though it had been six, maybe seven seasons since Medicine Rock had last been selected as the gathering place.

"But will the Eastern band know?" someone had asked the night before.

There was general laughter.

"It does not matter," said an old woman. "They are always the last to arrive."

"Of course," observed another. "It takes them longer to find their way."

The first group to arrive was always the Northern band. The Real-Chief of the Elk-dog Nation was a member of that band, and had been now for many generations. It was the responsibility of his family to select the location of the dance pavilion and begin its construction. The young men would also be searching for the largest and finest buffalo bull they could find, to be used as an effigy in the ceremonies. By this time much of the preliminary planning would have been done. Poles would have been cut for the open-sided, brush-roofed arbor of the pavilion.

Wolf Pup could hardly remember the last time that the People had met here for the Sun Dance. It was nearly half a lifetime ago for one his age. But every season was exciting, with the mixing of the bands, the pageantry, singing and dancing. There would be much visiting with friends and relatives from other bands, trading of horses, racing, and gambling. Every Sun Dance was exciting, but there was an extra excitement about this location. The heavy, brooding spirit of the gray stone cliffs of Medicine Rock lent another dimension.

"Father, tell me of the Rock," Wolf Pup said suddenly as they started on.

"*Aiee,* you have heard of it all your life!" Antelope answered.

"Yes, but that was when I was younger," laughed Pup. "Besides, as Grandfather says, a good story bears repeating."

"That is true. Which story of the Rock did you want?"

"Any of them. Is it true that one of our ancestors wintered there?"

"Yes, so it is said. A young man named Eagle was pushed over the cliff by buffalo. His horse and many buffalo went over too. Eagle had a broken leg, and wintered there. The People had thought he was dead, trampled in the stampede. There was an old man who helped him."

"Oh, yes, I remember that part. And afterward, he became a great storyteller. He was lame?"

"Maybe. It is said that he limped. But I am made to think that it was his spirit that was changed, more than his leg," Antelope explained.

"From the spirits of the Rock?"

"I do not know, Pup. Ask your grandfather of this."

"But are there not others who have been changed there?"

"Yes, maybe . . . Yes, that is true."

"And was it not here that our People became allies of the Head Splitters?"

"*Aiee,* Pup, you remember the stories as well as I do. Yes, that is true. Two young holy men, one of ours and one of the Head Splitters, combined their powers, their spirit-gifts, to defeat . . ."

"The Blue Paints! It was on the Story Skins!"

"Yes. See, you know of these stories! What is it, Pup? What are you asking?"

"Ah, I do not know, Father," the young man muttered, a little frustrated.

"It is good," said Dark Antelope, somewhat to the surprise of

Wolf Pup. "You are searching. Have you talked to Singing Wolf of this?"

"No. Not since we started to travel."

"It would be good to talk to him again, maybe."

The opportunity did not come immediately to talk to his grand-father. That afternoon they met a party of young hunters from the Northern band. There were five of them, from the family of the Real-Chief, searching for the Sun Dance bull.

"The Mountain band is already here," they informed the new-comers. "A few Arapahoes with them. We saw dust to the west this morning. Probably the Red Rocks. You are going on in tonight?"

"Probably not," Antelope answered. "The column moves slowly. We will camp soon, and arrive by noon tomorrow."

"It is good!" the young hunter exclaimed. "We will tell every-one!"

They cantered off.

Just before sunset, with the advantage of Sun Boy's position in the west, the wolves of the Southern band saw dust to the north of their line of travel.

"Probably the New band," Antelope guessed. "Too early for the Eastern band."

His guess proved true the next morning. As they crossed a low ridge, they could see the other column some distance away, crawl-ing over a similar rise like a great caterpillar. Scouts from the two groups met and exchanged news and greetings.

There would be no hurry to arrive first, because camping areas for the different groups were already assigned by the protocol of tradition. The position in the circle of scattered lodges around the pavilion corresponded exactly with the seating of the band chiefs in the circle of the Big Council. The New band, outsiders who had joined the People a few generations ago, had been accepted to the extent that they now had an assigned place in the circle, next to the empty spot reserved in memory of the Lost band from ancient times.

The column of the Southern band was approaching one of the low rises ahead when a band of armed and painted riders suddenly appeared over its flat crest. Yelling, screaming the throaty war cry of the People, and brandishing weapons, they charged directly at the approaching column. A few fired muskets in the air. It was always a frightening experience for a moment, this mock charge of welcome by the young men of the other bands.

The riders veered away at the last moment, and continued to race along the column. Young men of the Southern band joined in the demonstration, racing with the others, yelling in wild abandon. They circled the rear of the column, and back up the other side. Wolf Pup joined them, kicking his horse into a hard run, riding like the wind, his heart racing and the roar of excitement in his ears.

The leading riders pulled to a sliding stop back near the head of the column.

"Come on!" someone yelled. "Let us welcome the New band!"

Wolf Pup glanced around, looking for his father. He could not see him in the dust cloud kicked up by the thundering hooves. An old woman was yelling threats and obscenities at the exuberant youngsters for raising such a dust. Wolf Pup was about to follow the leading riders across the ridge to "attack" the other band when he happened to glance at the rider beside him. It was Spotted Horse. Even worse, the rider beyond was another that he knew well. It was Otter Woman.

It was not unusual for a few of the young women to join such a celebration. Young wives, before they began the responsibilities of motherhood, might accompany their husbands. Girls hoping to be noticed by a potential husband might do so to attract attention. But *aiee!* Otter Woman? How could *she* do this?

The day was spoiled for Wolf Pup. He had managed to avoid contact with Otter during the journey by volunteering to ride with the horse herd when he was not acting as wolf. He had tried to stay so busy that he would not think of her. It had actually been partially successful. He had tried to think not of her, but of the upcoming event of which he and his grandfather had spoken, his vision quest.

There had even been periods of time when he did not think of Otter Woman. Not very long periods, it was true, but it did prove that such a thing was possible. There *could* be a life for him after this great loss. He avoided the thought of any other woman, yet. For *that* step, he was still not quite ready. But he could at least see that it might be possible.

Until now . . . All the hurt and all the heaviness in his heart returned when he saw her. Her cheeks were flushed and her eyes wide with excitement as she quieted her dancing horse, ready to sweep away with the young men in the mock attack on the approaching New band. With *her* young man . . .

Spotted Horse, muscular and handsome, was smiling broadly at Otter Woman, laughing and showing his strong white teeth. The excitement of the day was in him. In them both.

But it was gone for Wolf Pup. The day which had been bright and optimistic and exciting had lost its attraction for him. The acrid odor of the dust, overlooked or even enjoyed when he had raced around the column with the others, was now different. It was unpleasant, bitter, like ashes in his mouth.

Otter Woman turned her mount and raced away, Spotted Horse following closely. She threw a backward glance over her shoulder, and her eyes met those of Wolf Pup for an instant. There was a moment of recognition that became the greatest hurt of all. He turned his horse away, back into the dust of the column.

13
» » »

Wolf Pup stood, looking up at the face of the cliff, and was torn by his mixed emotions. He was eager to get started, to begin his fast and to experience the long-awaited thrills of his vision quest. Still, the looming rock face above him seemed so massive, so overwhelming . . . He had a feeling that he had been guilty of overestimating his own importance in the vastness of the world.

Closely akin to this was a feeling of guilt. Maybe he should not have talked so strongly. It had not been easy to convince his parents and his grandfather to allow him to seek his vision quest. He realized that his grandfather might suspect his motives. The holy man had questioned him at great length about it. Pup was certain that Singing Wolf felt his grandson's grief in the loss of his childhood sweetheart.

"But Grandfather," Wolf Pup had pleaded, "is it not good, to have no distraction, no woman to worry about?"

The old man nodded. "That is true," he said thoughtfully. "The vision quest must have your whole attention."

He may have suspected, Wolf Pup thought, that this was what

Pup wanted desperately. It would take something of great magnitude and power to make him forget. The soft yet mischievous eyes of Otter Woman, the sheen of her hair, the graceful curves of her incomparable body . . . *Aiee!* How *could* he forget her?

Now he stood before the massive power of the brooding Medicine Rock and wondered how he could have considered his own problems of such importance. He felt as if he had been scolded for misbehavior. He took a deep breath and studied the rocky face. It was irregular in shape, much more so than it appeared at a distance. There were ledges and crevices and large stones perched precariously where they had fallen through the ages to land on some outcropping of the cliff. Some of the gashes and crevices, especially the higher ones, appeared cave-like. He thought of the legends of his ancestor, Eagle. Yes, one of those gaping holes above, staring like empty eye sockets, could be the very one where the injured Eagle had wintered.

In some places at the base of the cliff were jumbled piles of stone, some blocks as large as his parents' lodge. One crevice across the stream appeared to be filled with these broken stones, as if some giant hand had poured them there like grains of sand. Pup wished to climb to the top and make his camp there. It would have been easier to cross the stream below, nearer the Sun Dance camp, and approach the rock from the level of the cliff's top. Somehow, that had not appealed to him. He wished to look up, to climb its face and reach for the top, where he would make his ceremonial fire.

The thought crossed his mind that he *could* remain at the rock's base, near the murmuring stream. He quickly rejected that idea. He felt a need to be nearer the sky, to reach upward for what he sought.

"Grandfather, I am made to wonder," he had asked. "Is the spirit of the Rock a good one, or a danger? Many of the People fear it."

Singing Wolf had puffed his pipe for a little while before he answered. "I am made to think," he began, "that it is neither. I see it as a place of many spirits. Some may be good, some bad. But all together, they make up the spirit of the Rock. Maybe it is not always the same. But again I am made to think that it depends much on the heart of the one who goes there. If his heart is good, it makes him stronger. If it is bad . . ." The holy man shrugged, as if this implied some dire calamity that would be unavoidable.

And now, Wolf Pup wondered for a moment if his heart really *was* good. He *had* thought of how fortunate it might be if something were to happen to Spotted Horse.

He shrugged off such thoughts and walked toward the riffle where he must cross to approach the Rock's face. White gravel clattered beneath his feet and the sound seemed loud to him as it echoed back from the wall of the cliff. He felt like an intruder here. He paused, listening, though he did not know for what. There was only the murmuring voice of the stream, and the high-pitched cry of a red-tailed hawk high above the rock.

A strange thought crossed his mind. In the stories of long-ago times, it was said that the mischievous Old Man of the Shadows, one of the deities of the People, could understand all languages. Not only those of humans, but of all the animals. Even more . . . he spoke the tongues of the whispering breeze and the murmuring water. When the cottonwoods rustled their leaves, the story-tellers said, they were conversing with the Old Man. *Good day to you, Uncle,* the whispering voices would say, and Old Man would answer, *And to you!*

In this moment, Wolf Pup felt a strange affinity, a closeness to that ancient story. It was a comfortable, calming experience.

"And a good day to you, Uncle!" he said aloud to the murmuring ripple of the stream.

Pup knelt and drank from his cupped hand, filling his belly. He had begun his fast when he left the People. He crossed the riffle and moved on, stepping to a strip of grassy shore a few paces wide on the other bank. A dense thicket of prairie dogwood grew between him and the cliff's face. But there . . . yes, to his left, a dim trail, winding upward along a narrow ledge. A path used by animals, maybe. Yes, it was wide enough for a deer. Or a man. Wolf Pup began to climb.

The trail was easy in some places, steep and rocky in others. He stopped to rest, leaning on a boulder that lay on the ledge. Below him in a gash that was choked with great stones, he could see some whitish patches. It took him a moment to realize that these were bones. Yes, there was something in the story of the defeat of the Blue Paints. The powerful medicine of the two young holy men had turned a herd of buffalo over the cliff, pushing the enemy warriors to their deaths.

Aiee! Among those white objects deep in the crevice might be not only the bones of buffalo, but of horses and men . . . Blue Paint warriors. It was not a comfortable thought.

He reached the top and stood to look back. The stream seemed small below him. His most remarkable sensation at the moment, though, was that of looking *down* on the tops of giant trees. Cottonwoods, oaks, and sycamores rustled leaves in their afternoon conversation. (*Aiee,* an odd thought.) But their appearance from above was so different! *This,* Wolf Pup thought, *is how the eagle sees such things.* Yet another thought came back at him . . . *how the eagle sees the whole world!*

He chose a spot for his fire, near the edge, but not too near, and laid his pack and his sleeping robe there. Now, some fuel. The sun was low, and purple shadows already filled some of the distant canyons and valleys.

Wood was scarce, here at the top of the cliff. He walked along the rocky shelf and broke dry branches from the fragrant sumac and small trees which struggled to find a footing there. Well, he could gather enough for tonight, but he realized already that he must look elsewhere. The chore could interfere with his quest. He remembered a dead tree on the cliff's face a little way down. Maybe . . . He glanced at the sun. Yes, there was time.

He hurried back down as far as the dead tree and broke enough branches to feed the fire through the night. It would not be needed for warmth during this summer weather. Likewise, since he would be fasting, it was not needed for cooking. The function of the fire was purely ceremonial, a notice to any spirits who might inhabit the place. *Here I will camp,* it said. There was an implication of asking and receiving permission. But above all, the fire was essential, to establish spiritual communion in a new place.

Wolf Pup took out his fire-sticks and previously prepared tinder from his bag, and methodically constructed his little cone of twigs with a handful of dry grass beneath. *A lodge in which the fire will live,* he had thought as a child.

Now, a turn of the thong of his fire-bow around the spindle of yucca . . . a foot on the notched fire-board . . . In the space of a few heartbeats, the twirling spindle was producing a brownish powder. It began to spill through the notch, falling into his pinch of tinder beneath the board. Smoke began to rise and the powder darkened. It was almost black now . . . There, a glowing spark! Carefully, he laid aside the fire-sticks and cupped the little ball of cedar bark in his hands, wrapping it gently around his precious spark. He lifted it toward the sky and began to breathe life into it with his own breath, a soft steady stream from below. The smoke became more dense and just as the tinder burst into flame, he pushed it carefully into the little lodge of twigs.

The dry grass ignited, and orange flames crept up through the cone. Pup added more sticks, and a pinch of tobacco to appease the spirits. Then he stood and sang the Song of Fire into the deepening twilight. Somewhere below the cliff, a hunting owl called to its mate. A coyote sang on a distant ridge, and a night bird began its hollow greeting to the time of darkness. The sounds of night-creatures were replacing those of the day.

He took a sip of water, sparingly for now. He had filled his waterskin at the stream and could fill it again. But it would be better to avoid the distraction of climbing up and down the cliff. His primary goal was to avoid *all* distractions and concentrate on his vision quest.

There was a rumbling in his stomach, partly from the expected protest during the first day of his fast. Partly, he had to admit, from pure excitement. Never had the stars seemed so bright, the breeze of the summer night so filled with promise, or the glowing disk of the rising moon so red.

Now what? He had looked forward to this for so long, had been so eager to start his quest. Now it was here and there was nothing happening. He pushed the unburned ends of a few sticks into his fire and added a couple more. There should be just enough fire to keep it alive . . . In light of that, he looked carefully at his supply of fuel. Yes, there was probably enough here for the entire time of his vision quest. In the morning he could gather a little more fuel, just to be sure. Then that would free his thoughts for whatever was supposed to happen next.

Wolf Pup did not expect to sleep tonight. He was far too excited. Still, he spread his robe and lay back, watching the Seven Hunters move slowly in their nightly circle around their lodge at the Real-Star. From long habit, he looked to the second hunter from the end of the line . . . Yes, there as always was a smaller star beside him, the star which represents the hunter's dog at his heel.

He closed his eyes for a moment, and opened them some time later. Much later. The moon stood overhead now, and his bladder was uncomfortably full. He rose to empty it, replenished his fire, and lay back down on his robe. Again, he did not expect to sleep, but the next time he opened his eyes the first glow in the east was announcing the rising of the sun. It was the second day of his vision quest.

14
>> >> >>

Wolf Pup had thought that he would be unable to sleep that first night. The excitement of actually having started his vision quest seemed to eliminate all possibility of sleep.

He was somewhat prepared for the effect of fasting. The first day of hunger pangs, then the clarity of the senses as the hunger would recede. He had heard it described many times. Descriptions were always vague, and he was not certain how he would recognize the symptoms. How does one know that he is seeing better than ever before? Or hearing or smelling?

On top of this uncertainty, the thrilling wait for the unexpected made his palms moist and sent his heart racing. Sleep was unthinkable. He was astonished then, when the rising sun found him just awakening from a deep slumber. He dimly remembered dreaming, but the details were gone. As he continued to come awake and to become oriented to his surroundings, the last vestiges of his dreams faded. He could remember nothing, not even the main situations of his dream scenes. He was uncomfortable, as if something had been taken from him. He tried to tell himself that it was something he had never really had anyway, but that was poor consolation.

Wolf Pup built up his fire, blowing a few glowing coals into flame with small dry twigs and adding larger sticks. He sang the song of greeting to the morning sun, and that to the fire, and was unsure what to do next. He felt that he should be doing something, but what? Praying, more songs? Some sort of improvised dances? He thought of offering another pinch of tobacco to the spirits of the place, but was not certain that it would be right. Some of the ceremonies of his grandfather did not allow the holy man to touch tobacco until after the ritual was completed. Was the vision quest such a ceremony? He did not know. *I should have asked more questions,* he told himself glumly. But how could he have known what to ask? And, as he looked back, any questions that he *had* tried to address to his grandfather had met with very vague answers.

Maybe that is part of the experience, he thought. *Maybe one must make his mind completely open, empty so that the thoughts can enter.*

That was a strange thing to contemplate, and even harder to do. He tried to concentrate on thinking of nothing and his thoughts began to wander. He thought with a pang of regret of Otter Woman, and wondered what she might be doing now. Rising to greet the day, probably, like the others of the People. For them it would be a day of travel. He studied the distant prairie. Yes, there to the south, a smudge of smoke that probably marked their night camp. Women would be building up the fires to cook a quick meal before they departed.

He would follow the band after his quest was completed. It would be easy, because the prairie sod would be scarred by the hundreds of lodge poles and the pole-drags used for transporting baggage. *Travois,* they were called now, through contact with the French. Several new words were in use, since more trading of furs had brought more French influence. Pup had heard his parents discuss that situation.

The rawhide pack used by the People was called a *parfleche* . . . The temporary storage of goods that they often employed was a *cache*. He tried to think of other terms . . . *Plew!* Yes, the skin of a fur-bearing animal, especially a beaver. And he had heard a trader refer to the symbolic prayer stick which recounted the honors of a warrior as a *coup* stick.

Wolf Pup shook his head. *What am I doing?* He felt guilty, thinking of such things, when he should have been concentrating on his quest. He shifted his gaze to other areas of the vast prairie before him, wondering where the other bands might have stopped for the night. Yes, there to the north . . . That would be the smoke of the cooking fires of the Northern band.

The Eastern band, to the northeast, was much closer. As usual, they had gotten a late start, and had covered less distance. He could not make out the smoke of the New band. The country was more broken in that direction, and he was not certain whether that strip of blue-gray was smoke or a distant ridge.

To the west he could see, or thought he could, the smoke from the night camps of both the Red Rocks and Mountain bands. He wondered if they could see each other . . . Probably not. He had an advantage here on the Rock, the highest spot in the area.

What am I doing? he asked himself irritably. *I should be thinking thoughts of the spirit!* Again, he felt guilty at his lack of concentration. Maybe he could control his wandering thoughts by concentrating on the simplest of observations. His father had taught him those skills, the skills of a tracker.

He glanced around him, close at hand. There was a yellow-breasted lark a few steps away, singing his chortling song from his perch on a fist-sized stone. The nest of its mate would be near, but hard to see, so perfect would be her coloration, blending with the dry grasses of last season.

Near where he sat, a shiny beetle rolled a ball of buffalo dung. Now *there* was a thing that had always made him wonder. The beetle, no larger than the last joint of a man's finger, was able to build and roll a ball much larger than itself! How could it be so strong? He had watched the creatures many times, and still could not understand. The size and *weight* of the dung-ball was often twice that of its maker.

The ball would be rolled into some hidden crevice, away from the dangers of the world, and a single egg deposited in it. At least, so his father said. That, too, was a matter of wonder for Wolf Pup.

He watched the beetle pushing, rolling the dung-ball with its back legs, frustrated by a pebble, maneuvering around a clump of grass. *Why?* Could the egg not be simply placed in any buffalo chip?

The answer came to him . . . buffalo chips are used for fuel. Even if not picked up by humans for that purpose, many chips were burned with the almost annual burning of the prairie. The next generation of beetles would be protected from the wildfires by being buried! Could that be the reason for all the hard labor of the creature? Maybe he would ask his grandfather. But Singing Wolf would probably only smile, puff his pipe, and observe that "It is their way."

Wolf Pup looked up from his reverie about dung beetles, and cast a glance around him. Nothing had changed very much. The long slanting rays of Sun Boy's torch were striking the south face of the cliff below him. The acrid fragrance of sumac warming in the sun mingled with more delicate scents . . . Was it not the Moon of Roses? Below him somewhere was a grapevine. He had not noticed it as he climbed, but now he was aware of the fragrance of its blossoms, small and hardly noticeable, but whose delicate sweetness was perhaps the best of all.

He looked down, wondering where the vine might be in the tangle of vegetation that clung to a crevice in the Rock below him. A flash of motion caught his eye, and he focused on three crows in pursuit of an owl. *Kookooskoos, you hunted too long,* he said to himself, in the words of an old children's rhyme. He smiled as the silent hunter sailed majestically into a fringe of cedars on the Rock's face and disappeared. Its lodge must be in some cranny there. The disappointed crows sat on a dead branch and protested the unfairness of their quarry for a few moments and then departed.

Below him and a little way upstream, a doe stepped cautiously out of a clump of willows and moved toward the stream to drink. Her fawn followed her closely . . . *Aiee!* Another one . . . twins! *It is good,* he thought. It was well known that in a season which is more favorable, the deer have more twinning. *How do they know?* he wondered.

A bow shot downstream from the deer, a large black bird moved out of the bushes and stood for a moment, surveying the area, then another, and another . . . in all, nearly thirty of the turkeys walked majestically into the open, searching as they went for insects in the grass. Two or three hens, it seemed, with their combined hatches of half-grown poults. A strong band . . .

The People did not hunt the great birds to any extent, except when circumstances dictated. But it was good to see. That, too, a thriving flock, was a sign of a good season.

Wolf Pup stopped in his line of thought, startled. He had been enjoying the morning, and the living pictures that were spread before him. He had noted in passing that these signs were good, but *aiee,* they were important, too. *This was his vision quest.* A hawk far above him shrilled its sharp cry and he looked up. Yes, the sky was bluer and wider than ever before. The green of the oaks and sycamores along the river was a more pleasant shade than he had ever noticed. The deer, the turkeys . . . all signs were good.

This is it! he wanted to shout. He had not recognized it, the expected clarity of the senses that came from his time of fasting. His glance swept the horizon. Was it only his imagination that he could see more clearly, see *farther* into the blue of distant hills? Was this *really* the most beautiful morning of all those since Creation?

He could not be still. He walked back and forth along the rim of the rocky shelf, improvising a song that was a prayer of thanks and of wonder at the grandeur of the world. So this was how a vision quest felt! He saw that it could not be described, only experienced. He must tell his grandfather . . . no, it could not be told. Well, Grandfather would understand, surely.

Another thought came to him. This was only the second day of his quest. The best was yet to come, the visions.

15

>> >> >>

When his vision came, it was in a completely unexpected way. Thinking back on it later, Wolf Pup did not see how it could have been otherwise. It *would* be in some unfamiliar manner. If the experience were to be predictable, the vision quest would hardly be needed, no?

He had been deeply drawn into the entire ethereal mood of the quest, losing all sense of time. He slept, woke, sipped a little water, renewed his fire, and sang the songs of prayer. Even with the clarity of the senses, time seemed to lose meaning. He would sleep and wake, and wonder whether this was the same day or if he had slept the night through. This wonder was merely idle curiosity, however, because time did not seem to matter. It was simply unimportant.

So, he was never completely certain when it happened. The second night? The third? *Was* it night, or did he merely dream during the day, the visions coming while he was awake? Later, looking back, there were many things that he did not understand.

Of one thing, he was certain, however. He had come to realize that there are many things that are meant to be *experienced,* not understood. This enabled him to feel a freedom, a joy in all of the daily things of the world. He had seen them all his life, but felt that he had never really appreciated them until now.

The process of this vision was certainly like nothing he had ever experienced before. He had thought that the revelation would come to him in a blaze of glorious celebration, somehow. Instead it was gradual, and happened to him so quietly, so slowly, that it was almost unnoticed.

It was like the changing colors of a sunset, imperceptible in their movement as the scene unfolds. Or the silent fall of fat snowflakes on a quiet night, sifting down on the world like the soft breath-feathers of *Kookooskoos,* the owl. Each flake in itself makes little difference, but soon there is a blanket of white.

So he did not know *when* the time of visions began or ended. Probably the process was well along when he realized that his senses had become more acute. He simply did not realize it until later. And he was never certain how much of the experience was vision and how much was dream. Or is there any difference? Maybe *all* of the life experience is merely part of the same contin-uum. It seemed so to Wolf Pup.

After he began to see and hear more acutely than ever before, he found that by concentrating, he could reach out with his thoughts and touch the thoughts of the creatures he saw and heard. He played with that for a little while.

The red-tailed hawk that circled above was searching, seeking for something . . . Yes, food. A rabbit? A mouse? Any small crea-ture, to feed her young in the nest at the top of a giant oak near the river. He could not see the nest, but could have described it in great detail, so strong was his feel for the bird's spirit. Three young, not quite ready to leave the nest.

A sense of fear caught his attention . . . Ah, yes, *there!* A rabbit, crouched beneath a tuft of grass. It had seen the hawk, and was frozen, motionless. It would remain completely still until the hawk moved on.

Some of the spirit-thoughts were vague and only partly formed. The sensation of the cottonwoods was merely one of warm sunlight and soil filled with satisfying nutrients, and of cool clear water at their feet. There was a teeming background of that sort, mixed with the poorly delineated sensations of the crawling things that burrow in the ground. Wolf Pup shifted his spirit-search to other things.

A fox trotted into the open from the thicket below the cliff, and his spirit reached out to touch it. There was the spirit of the hunter. It was much like that of the hawk, searching for the same quarry. But there was an extra dimension here. While the hawk was relying mostly on sight, the fox was also using scent. And Wolf Pup found that he could *use* the miraculously acquired ability to experience the *senses* of the creatures he saw. He could reach out to them, know what they were thinking, could get inside their heads for a little while. Just now he could actually *smell* the warm scent of the frightened rabbit in the grass clump. *As the fox smells it!* he thought. What a wonderful experience!

A dark thought interrupted his reverie, a thought that bordered on terror. He glanced around, and saw a large black snake climbing toward a nest in a sumac bush near his little camp. A frantic bird fluttered and scolded, uncertain whether to defend her eggs or to save herself. She finally retreated, barely in time. *It is good,* thought Wolf Pup. *She can lay more eggs.* And his grandfather's saying came to him: *It is the way of things.*

There had been a time when he might have worried about the bird's loss. Even now he felt a pang of regret. But with this new understanding that he need not understand, it was easier. Tomorrow the incident would be forgotten . . . No, not forgotten, but placed in its proper perspective as part of the way of things.

He thought of the Apology, the brief prayer that a hunter of the People makes over his kill. Especially over the first kill of a season, or of a hunt. And especially over the buffalo.

"We are sorry to kill you, my brother, but upon your flesh our lives depend, as yours depend upon the grasses . . ."

And as the life of the snake depends upon the bird's eggs, and the bird's upon some smaller creatures . . . he thought. *It is all one, and the way of things.*

As he slept that night, a dream came to him. It was as if he knew that he was asleep, and that the experience was a dream, but could not waken. Or did not want to waken, maybe. It was as if he sat beside his little fire there on the Rock, yet also *watched* himself sit by his fire. It was daylight, just after dawn, and there was another nearby. It was a coyote, long and lean, yet with thick fur and a muscular appearance. An *old* coyote, but still healthy.

Wolf Pup's newfound ability reached out to feel the animal's thoughts, but he was startled to find that he could not do so. There was some impediment that prevented it. Just as one sometimes cannot run in a dream, he could not use the gift of insight that had been his the previous day. There was another impression or two which he now felt very plainly. One was that the coyote was laughing at him. There was actually an amused expression on the animal's face and in the yellow eyes. Wolf Pup was somewhat irritated, because he felt that he had missed the joke, and the joke must be on him. He took a deep breath and studied the coyote, which now cocked its head to one side and continued to study *him.*

This is only a dream, he told himself irritably. But then it occurred to him that yes, it *was* a dream, but a part of his quest. He should take it seriously. This changed his attitude somewhat, and he wondered what he would be expected to do. Almost instantly it came to him. A greeting . . .

"Good day to you, Uncle," he said aloud.

That was the appropriate form of address to any adult male of the People older than one's self. Wolf Pup could not have explained why it seemed appropriate now. Except it was a form of respect for age, experience, and knowledge. Perhaps this dignified creature conveyed the impression of wisdom. At any rate, it seemed appropriate to address it with respect.

Now, though it had seemed good for him to address the coyote, there was no reason to expect an answer, even in a dream. It was similar to the way in which one utters a prayer and expects or hopes that it will be heard. Yet, in sending that prayer, one realizes that he is consigning it to the world of spirit, and does not expect an answer to come back in words. At least, not usually.

Wolf Pup was astonished, then, when he did receive an answer. It was not in words, but any answer at all . . . *Aiee!* The manner in which he received it was not as a series of sounds like spoken language. (Would the spirit-world speak the tongue of the People?) The mouth of the coyote did not move, yet words . . . no, thoughts seemed to form in the mind of Wolf Pup, as if they had been placed there by Coyote.

And a good day to you, Wolf Pup, came the answer to his greeting.

But it is a dream! he thought in protest. Before he could put the thought into words, an answer came back to him.

Of course. Is that not why you are here?

Again, he had the strong impression that the animal was laughing at him in his ignorance.

"What must I do?" he demanded aloud.

The coyote chuckled, this time aloud, but the answer formed in Wolf Pup's head.

Ah, that would be too easy. You must think on it.

Irritated, Wolf Pup found himself beginning to rouse from the dream. The scene was fading, but he needed more.

"Wait!" he cried. "I do not understand."

Think on it!

The coyote's form was fading. So was the fire, the fringe of brush beside his little camp . . .

He woke and sat up, startled. It took a moment to reorient himself to reality. His fire was nearly out, and it was dawn. Yes, the surroundings were the same, except that he had thought it was night. Well, it *had* been night, but it was morning now.

He tossed a few sticks on the coals, blew them to a bright glow, and watched the flicker of flame lick up and around his fresh sticks, replacing the white smoke of rekindling.

Aiee, what a dream! he thought. *A coyote, over there. I talked to it!*

He glanced around to the spot where the dream-creature had sat on its haunches. There, sitting and staring at him, head cocked to one side, sat a large, muscular coyote.

Wait! he thought. *Am I still in the dream?* He studied the coyote a little longer, and decided that it did not really matter. Where does the dream end and reality begin anyway? Was he being tested, somehow?

"Good day to you, Uncle," he said aloud, with respect.

This time there was no answer, as there had been in his dream. The coyote simply rose, stretched, and turned away, walking methodically, completely unconcerned. It was perhaps twenty paces away when it paused, as coyotes do, for one last look over its shoulder.

Wolf Pup was still watching, confused and irritated at his inability to sort out the things that were happening to him. The coyote looked straight into his eyes, and for just an instant . . . Was there that expression of amusement, as there had been in the eyes of the coyote in his dream? A silent laughter at the ignorance of mere mortals? Wolf Pup felt as if there were some inside joke, which had been flaunted before him, but which he had not been permitted to share.

Suddenly the truth struck him. He was never certain how it happened. Was it that he had "thought on it" and had reasoned it out? Or was he assisted by the thought-communication that he had experienced in his dream? He jumped to his feet.

"Wait!" he called after the retreating figure. But the coyote was gone.

He sat back down, dejected. How stupid he must have appeared! *Aiee,* to have talked to one's spirit-guide, and not to have realized . . . Ah, no wonder the guide was amused! But the heart of Wolf Pup was very heavy.

16
>> >> >>

He had hoped that during the coming night he would dream again. Maybe he would be permitted to apologize for his ignorance. But it was not to be. The only coyotes in evidence were a pair on a ridge across the river. He did not even see them, but heard their chortling cries, sounding like laughter. Maybe they *were* laughing at him, he thought glumly.

He slept, but did not dream, and when he woke, he felt that his vision quest was over. He was disappointed, because he felt no different now. He feared that he had been offered a gift of the spirit and in not recognizing it, had refused it. It is no disgrace to refuse the responsibility of the spirit-gift, of course. But it is no great honor, either. He must talk to his grandfather, who would understand such things.

It was three days before Wolf Pup caught up to the evening camp of the Southern band. He sought out his parents, and ate the food that his mother urged upon him. He was not really hungry, having chewed strips of dried meat as he traveled to break his fast.

His muscles were tired, his feet sore from walking. But to take a horse on his quest would have been a distraction. It would have been too easy for the animal to wander off while Wolf Pup's entire attention was focused on his fast and his visions.

The vision . . . He had thought much about that since he left the Rock. There was an urgency now, to share it with his grandfather and try to interpret its meaning. As soon as it seemed reasonable to do so, he rose and told of his intent to visit with his grandparents.

"It is good," his mother agreed.

The camp of Singing Wolf and Rain was only a few steps away, but darkness had fallen now.

"*Ah-koh,*" Pup called to announce his presence as he approached their fire. He had spoken to them briefly when he had arrived.

"Sit!" offered his grandfather. "It is good to have you back!"

"Have you eaten?" asked Rain.

"Yes, Grandmother, at my mother's fire. But thank you."

The young man seated himself, unsure how to begin this conversation. Since the vision quest is a very private thing, to ask about it would be a breach of manners. Singing Wolf said nothing. Finally Wolf Pup managed to begin.

"Grandfather," he said hesitantly, "I must ask about something. Tell me . . . is it permitted to speak of one's vision quest?"

He knew that it was seldom done. Many people publicly announced the identity of their guides. One might wear or display an emblem or fetish, such as an eagle, indicating that this was his guide and the source of his power. Wolf Pup could not remember, however, that he had ever heard anyone describe the vision which had brought about such a relationship. Maybe it was forbidden to do so.

His grandfather looked at him quizzically.

"Sometimes," he observed. "You wish to talk of it?"

"Maybe. There are things that I do not understand."

A look of pleased amusement crossed the face of the holy man. He nodded. "It is good. That is as it should be."

"It *is?*" blurted the astonished youth.

"Of course. Now, the speaking of it . . . One's vision is a very private thing, you know. Most do not tell it widely, for then it would no longer be private. Is it not so?"

How simple it seemed, from the lips of the holy man.

"But I would ask you . . . There are things about it, Grandfather!"

The old man nodded. "Oh, *that.* Of course. It is your choice, to tell your vision or not. But it may be wise to do so, in this case. And this does *not* make it public, of course."

A great sense of relief came over Wolf Pup. Complicated things seemed to become so simple in the light of his grandfather's wise observations.

"Maybe," Singing Wolf continued, "we should walk."

Wolf Pup had always enjoyed walks with his grandfather. They had shared such walks many times since before he could remember. Sometimes they had talked, sometimes only shared together the beauty of a sunset or a leaf in autumn. But it had been good, always.

The old man rose and the two made their way out of the smoke and confusion of the camp. Neither spoke until they reached a low rise overlooking the scattered points of light from the campfires below. They sat on blocks of stone still warmed by the afternoon sun. Still, Singing Wolf did not speak, but waited. There was still a rosy glow in the west, and the sounds of the creatures of the night were beginning to replace those of the day. In the distance, a coyote called, and this stirred Wolf Pup to speak.

"Grandfather, I would tell you my vision. I . . . I think I might have refused a gift."

Singing Wolf's eyes widened in darkness, but he showed no other reaction.

"Why do you . . . No, let us hear the story first. Go ahead."

Wolf Pup's story came pouring forth now, like the rushing waters of a flash flood from a distant rain upstream. He told of his hunger pangs, his forgotten dreams, his realization of the in-

creased clarity of the senses. The holy man said nothing, but nodded in understanding.

When he began to describe the dream of the coyote, Wolf Pup
became unsure.

"I do not know, Grandfather. Maybe a dream, maybe a vision,
but then I saw it after I woke, too!"

"Wait, wait, Pup. Back up. Tell what you saw."

"The dream, or . . . ?"

The holy man shrugged. "Who is to say there is a difference?
Go on."

"Well . . . I was asleep. Or so I think. I dreamed that I
dreamed, maybe. *Aiee!* It was as if I knew that I dreamed, but saw
it from outside myself."

He waited for a moment, but his grandfather said nothing.

"Then the coyote was there," he went on. "We talked . . . no,
I talked. Coyote talked to me without words, somehow. In my
head, maybe. He said . . . or told me in my thoughts that I
should think on it."

Wolf Pup stopped again, and waited. Finally his grandfather
spoke.

"What do you think this means, Pup?"

"I . . . I thought later that this might have been my guide,
Grandfather. I was stupid not to see it. But I saw him later, when I
was awake. Does a guide come . . . ?"

"Wait, wait now. A spirit guide is of the spirit, Pup. It is not
limited to night or day, sleep or awake, as we are."

"So this *was* my guide?"

"It would seem so. *You* thought it to be?"

"Yes, later. But I did not see it at the time, Grandfather. I must
have refused, and the guide left me."

"What was it that he said? What stays in your head about it?"

"He said nothing in words, Grandfather."

"Yes, yes, I know."

"What I remember was that I must think on it. But I was not
sure what. The message was just *you must think on this.*"

"Yes . . . On the whole thing. I am made to think, Wolf Pup, that your guide is trying to get your attention."

"But he *had* my attention!"

"Yes, but . . . Pup, maybe you are trying too hard."

"And I have ruined it?"

"No, no. Look, I am made to think that you are being offered a gift of the spirit. What sort, I cannot say. But you saw your guide, once asleep, once awake. This may be a very powerful guide, my boy."

"But did I not refuse?"

"Oh, no. To refuse such a gift, you must know that it is offered. You did not yet know."

"Then I am stupid!"

Singing Wolf chuckled. "No, no. The spirits are very patient. You were not quite ready. Now I am made to think that you are. That is what is being told to you."

"But I thought the purpose of the vision quest is to do this! Should I not understand now?"

The holy man chuckled. "*Aiee*, Wolf Pup, some things we may never understand. We do not need to, only to experience, to enjoy. What has happened to you is that your eyes have been opened. Your guide has caught your attention and prepared you to see."

"Then what do I do now?"

"Just watch, to see what will be shown to you."

"How will I know? *What* do I watch?"

"You will know, my son. Your guide will not let you stray very far. When it seems right, thank him for his help. Oh, yes! This time, you did not know when your guide was with you until after he was gone. It may be that way again."

"But I will recognize him now, Grandfather!"

"True, if you see him. But you may not. There may be times when you say to yourself, '*Aiee!* My uncle the Coyote must have been here to help me!' *That* is when to thank him."

"That is all?"

"Nothing is ever *all*, Pup. It is a journey that has no end, but a wonderful journey. *Enjoy* it. Now, what do you think your guide wants you to do? 'Think on it,' he told you. On what?"

"I was about to ask *you*, Grandfather. On *what?* Things of the spirit?"

"Maybe. Are you made to think so?"

Wolf Pup was hesitant. He did not want to appear presumptuous. And the experience at the Rock had made him feel very humble.

"Grandfather," he said timidly, "could it be that I am to follow the way of a holy man?"

In the near darkness, Wolf Pup could not see the broad smile of satisfaction on the face of his grandfather. That was probably just as well.

Singing Wolf brought his joy under control and spoke again, somewhat sternly.

"That is a rocky path sometimes. Are you sure?"

"No. But I am made to think that it is possible. If, of course, you think I could be an apprentice to you."

Wolf Pup was still hesitant. Such a declaration was a big step, the biggest of his lifetime, maybe. It would require many moons, many years, even, of instruction. Responsibility, and considerable personal sacrifice. To declare that he was ready to do so, to admit that he had received the call, meant that there could be no turning back. It was a decision that meant a severe limitation of his life choices. And in truth, he was still unsure.

"Maybe you should think on this a little while longer," suggested Singing Wolf.

It was just at that moment that from far off in the distance came the rippling, chortling cry of a coyote. The sound, familiar to Wolf Pup through his entire life, seemed to take on a special meaning at this time. Maybe it was the excitement of the night and the stimulation of the conversation with his grandfather. Maybe it was that his eyes had been opened to things of the spirit. He smiled in the darkness. *Thank you, Uncle*, he said silently.

He turned back to his grandfather and took a deep breath.

"No, I am sure," Wolf Pup said with confidence. "When may I start?"

17
>> >> >>

The next day found Wolf Pup on top of the world, ready and eager for whatever his apprenticeship might bring. He was quickly sobered by collision with day-to-day reality.

"We cannot begin such an important thing while we are traveling," his grandfather reminded. "Maybe a little in summer camp, if it is not too hot."

Wolf Pup clenched his teeth in frustration and embarrassment.

"Of course, Grandfather. I was . . . that is . . . I wondered whether there is anything that I could begin to do meanwhile."

That was as valid an escape from his embarrassment as he could find on a moment's notice. *How stupid,* he thought, *for me not to think of that! Of course there is no opportunity to learn while we travel!*

As if in reprimand to this thought, Singing Wolf spoke again.

"Certainly," the holy man answered. "You can learn while we travel. Observe, watch what you can see. We will talk sometimes, maybe."

That was very little help. Merely a reminder to pay attention.

Aiee! Did his grandfather not realize that he would do that any-way? Wolf Pup was irritated and distressed, and there seemed to be no one to whom he could turn.

It became even more frustrating. He was returning to camp one evening with an armful of wood for his mother's cooking fire. He had found an old cottonwood near the stream, which had suffered the loss of several large limbs. A "wolf tree" . . . One past its prime, and in its declining seasons, yet able to leaf out each spring for a little longer. But near a wolf tree there are no new seedlings. Its spirit is strong and defiant still, forbidding others to take its place. *Not yet,* it warns. *I am not ready to go.* So it sheds a limb here, another there, another next season, unable to provide nour-ishment for them all.

Fuel is scarce on the prairie. The People had been using mostly buffalo chips for the past few days. These were excellent fuel, but smoky. He was pleased to find this evening's supply of dry cotton-wood. It was a good feeling to be able to find something that would please his mother.

Absorbed in such thoughts, Wolf Pup did not even see the ap-proach of the young woman until they practically collided. And his vision was partially obscured by the load of sticks in his arms.

"*Aiee,* watch where you are going," laughed Otter Woman, step-ping aside.

He was caught off guard. He had tried to avoid her since he rejoined the band, and it had not been easy. Mostly, it had been possible to ride with the horse herd, or to volunteer as a wolf. The hurt at her rejection was beginning to heal. But he knew that this encounter would start it all over again. He could tell because he had not remembered how bright and sparkling were her eyes, how beautiful her smile. The sound of her lighthearted laugh made his own heart heavy.

Had she come here on purpose to torture him? No, that would not be her way. Then he realized that others seeking fuel would have noticed the old wolf tree downstream. They would come seeking, as he had.

"I have not seen you, Wolf Pup," Otter was saying.

"I . . . I . . ." he mumbled uncomfortably. "I have been on a vision quest."

"Oh! It is good! I was afraid that you were trying to avoid me."

What can one say in such a situation? The truth of her statement was apparent, and Wolf Pup was at a loss for words. Then his anger rose.

"How would you know?" he snapped. "You were busy with Spotted Horse!"

Otter Woman stared at him for a moment. He could have sworn that her eyes filled with tears at his accusation. A flash of anger flitted across her face and then receded.

"*That* was it?" she asked quietly. "*Aiee,* Wolf Pup . . . Did you not know that our friendship, yours and mine . . . *Aiee!*"

Her voice trailed off as her eyes became misty again.

"You mean, you are not . . . I thought you were to marry him!" Wolf Pup blurted.

"No, no! Horse is only a friend. He asked me, yes. But have we not . . . You and I . . . ?"

Yes, yes, he wanted to shout.

"Of course," he managed to say, though his voice was tight. "I was not thinking well, Otter. And my vision quest led me aside."

"I understand. Tell me, Pup! How is it with the quest? It is good, no?"

He was somewhat startled. In a few short moments Otter Woman had restored the intimacy of their friendship. Now her eyes were sparkling, eager to share his innermost thoughts about his experience. This was too fast, maybe. There was still something between them not yet healed. Wolf Pup drew back. Not physically, just in spirit.

"I cannot tell you all, Otter. It is . . ."

"Yes, I did not mean to intrude, Pup. Forgive me." Her face fell.

Yes, he thought, *this is my friend. It can be good again.* And of course there was a part of his quest that would be public. He could share that now.

"I have been made to decide," he told her, "that I should follow my grandfather's way."

"Ah! That of the holy man?" Her eyes sparkled with excitement. "I have always known that you were special, Pup! You have been given the gift of the spirit!"

"No . . ." He was embarrassed to have it said aloud, when his own view remained so unsure, so humble. "Only that I study it, Otter," he mumbled. "I am not sure that I will be worthy of such a gift. What if I misuse its power?"

Otter Woman smiled. "Your guide will not let you."

There was much in that short statement. It offered reassurance, but more. It said that Otter Woman knew that he had established contact with his spirit-guide. Also that she did not intend to question further about the guide. Such things are very personal, and this showed her intention not to intrude. He felt his respect and admiration . . . his *love* for this woman growing, spreading warmth over him, body and spirit. And he could now carry on a courtship! His spirits soared like the eagle.

"I would begin courting, Otter," he told her. "I have not learned to play the flute, but I will begin."

She smiled, and the warmth of that smile made his knees weak. Then the look faded from her face and was replaced by one of concern and sadness.

"What is it?" he asked in alarm.

"I . . . I am not sure, Wolf Pup . . ."

"*About us?*" he blurted. What was happening?

"No, not that. I was thinking, though. I do not recall a holy man's assistant who had a wife!"

Panic struck him. "Nor do I!" he said thoughtfully. "But Otter, we have not seen many. That owl prophet in the Northern band . . . His wife *is* his assistant."

"I am made to think that is different," Otter observed. "Your grandmother assists Singing Wolf too."

"True. She beats the drum for his songs and dances."

"Yes. But what about the holy man of the Eastern band? His apprentice is single, is he not?"

"But Otter, you cannot judge anything by the Eastern band. You know how *they* are."

"That is true. But do *you* remember any married apprentice?"

"Well . . . no."

"*Aiee,*" Otter Woman said sadly, "I am made to think, then, that you must take a vow of chastity! How long is your learning period?"

She had voiced that which both dreaded to mention. If what they suspected was true, they could not marry until after his time of apprenticeship. And how long . . . ?

"I do not know," Wolf Pup admitted. "I suppose that is decided by my grandfather."

He looked into the depths of her eyes and the thought crossed his mind that this was more important than to be an apprentice to the holy man. *Yes!* He could simply refuse the gift of spirit, and follow his father's ways. A great weight was lifted from his heart.

"Look, Otter," he blurted. "I can refuse the gift! That is not a disgrace. Then we can marry."

"No," she said firmly. "I would not let you give up such a call for me. But I will wait."

He thought about that for a moment. *Aiee! Can I wait?* he thought.

Otter Woman broke through his pondering. "Find out how long," she suggested. "But I will wait."

Wolf Pup was unsure. The risk of having Otter Woman single and available while he was otherwise occupied presented a real threat. His trust was not completely restored. Not yet.

"I will ask," he told her.

Singing Wolf watched him approach, and noted the look of concern. Something was bothering the young man. Well, that was understandable. Wolf Pup was eager to begin his training. It would be a few sleeps yet before the band arrived at their summer camp site. Maybe, though, he could begin to tell the youth about some of the responsibilities involved. Yes, that would do.

"Grandfather, I would speak with you," Wolf Pup began after the greeting. "It is about the learning to assist you."

"Yes, yes," Singing Wolf said in a palliative tone. "I understand.

Let me tell you of it. First, you will need to move into our lodge. Then you will be at hand when I need you. Your grandmother will teach you some of the simple things. You and I will talk and you will learn. It is good that you have no wife to distract you, no?"

The holy man had no idea that at this point Wolf Pup very nearly told him that he had changed his mind. Still, the young man looked troubled. Singing Wolf waited.

"Grandfather," Pup said suddenly, "how long is the time of learning?"

"Why, all of one's life, my son. Is it not so?"

"Yes, but not that. I mean the apprenticeship."

"It does not matter, does it? Two years, three?"

"It *matters*, Uncle. What if I want to marry?"

Ah, so that was it! Well, good to have to make such a decision now. This would test the boy's sincerity.

"*Aiee!*" the holy man exclaimed in mock surprise. "You cannot do both. Not at the same time. There is a time of chastity, you know."

"But how long?"

Singing Wolf shrugged. "Who knows? We will see."

"It is yours to decide, Uncle?"

Singing Wolf thought about it for a moment. He must know more of this, because there could be no major distractions in the training of an apprentice. Well, they would begin. It would not take long. It would soon become apparent how sincere was the desire of Wolf Pup to become a holy man.

"That is true," Singing Wolf answered, "but only partly. *You* are the one who decides. I only observe and interpret."

Wolf Pup nodded, obviously uncomfortable.

"Who is it?" asked his grandfather. "Otter Woman? I have not heard any announcement of her coming marriage."

Wolf Pup nodded, still uneasy.

"It is good," said Singing Wolf. "That one is worth waiting for."

The young man seemed to feel a little better. But not much.

18
» » »

It would certainly be a test, Singing Wolf knew. It was good, maybe. This would quickly show how determined Wolf Pup would be to learn. If the boy was actually as dedicated as he *must* be, that fact would be apparent.

On the other hand, such determination would be tested. The holy man had begun to quietly observe the situation with Otter Woman after the conversation with his grandson. Yes, it was as he remembered . . . This young woman was, in form and figure, all that a woman of the People should be. The exquisite legs, long from knee to hip, well displayed by the dress of the People . . . Short skirt, slit up the sides . . . It was no wonder that the Head Splitters, whose body build was shorter and stockier, had long ago stolen girls of the People for wives. That was before they became allies. Things were better now.

But *this* girl . . . As he noticed her again in light of Wolf Pup's problem, he realized that even in the past few moons Otter Woman had changed. And it was all for the better.

Singing Wolf had wondered as a young man how that change

takes place. A little girl, almost overnight, becomes a woman. Her childish shape begins to bulge in graceful curves. Where she was square, flat, and straight, she becomes firmly rounded, yet invitingly soft to the touch. Her walk is different. The motions of a child in walking or running are efficient and graceful, but they are childish. And while they are pleasant to watch, there is no comparison to the movement of a young woman. Somehow, the growth of the bones, the increase in height, creates a different *quality* of motion. The sway of the hips, the swing of the long legs, and the gentle twist of the waist. These things all combine in a dance of beauty like the sway of the willow in the cooling breezes of summer.

Singing Wolf had spent much time in observation of these things, and it was good. It also helped him to understand the problem now faced by his grandson. His own courtship, long ago, had not been easy. Rain had been interested in another young man. At least, he had thought so. He smiled to himself as he thought of it. His friends had been cruel in their jokes. *How does it feel, Wolf, to be bested in love by a man of the Eastern band?*

But that was long ago. Rain had not been seriously interested in the other suitor, as it turned out. She was only teasing him. Possibly, he thought, the situation had been much like that faced recently by his grandson. Another suitor, who seemed to be favored. Wolf remembered well when *that* weight had been lifted from his heart and Rain came to him.

Still, he had not had to face the choice that Wolf Pup now faced. His own period of apprenticeship had not been at the same time. He and Rain had already established their lodge before he was offered the gifts of the spirit. And his apprenticeship had been with his father, who was much younger . . . *Ah!* That was the thing which had been eluding him. It might have been possible for Wolf Pup and Otter Woman to go ahead and marry. Then in a year or two, Pup could begin his training, when the newness and excitement of the couple's own lodge had quieted.

But Singing Wolf felt a sense of urgency. He was not getting any younger. The snows of many winters lay heavy on his head.

He was forced to wonder how many winters were yet to be. He must pass on the knowledge and skills of his position to a successor, if possible. The stiffness in his bones on chilly mornings told him so. Sometimes he felt as if he were a young man, trapped in an aging body. *Aiee*, especially when he looked upon such beauty as that of Otter Woman.

"What is it, my husband?" Rain interrupted his thoughts as she came to sit beside him.

He put his arm around her. It was uncanny, the way Rain could always tell when he was troubled. And her thoughts were always good.

"Ah, Rain, I was thinking of our grandson. He has a great decision."

"I thought he had decided. He will study your medicine?"

"Yes, but he has just learned something else. The girl . . . Otter, you know?"

"Yes. Otter Woman now. What of her?"

"Ah, Wolf Pup thought that she was to marry Spotted Horse."

"She is *not?*" Rain asked.

"No. She and Wolf Pup . . ."

"*Aiee*, this *is* a problem!" Rain was always quick to see such things.

"I am made to think so. It is important for me to begin to teach him."

"Of course, my husband. Yet you will have many years to do so."

He smiled at her. "I hope so. Many with you, Rain. But we must consider . . ."

"Yes, I know, Wolf. Yet I am made to think that . . . Is this not *his* choice? That of Wolf Pup?"

Singing Wolf considered for a little while.

"Yes, that is true," he said slowly.

"That is why it bothers you," Rain teased. "There is nothing that *you* can do about it."

He was irritated for a moment, because he knew that she was right, as usual. It must be the choice of Wolf Pup. But what a choice! To begin a long and difficult period of self-denial and demanding education, with heavy responsibility, or . . . The vision of the lovely ripe womanhood of Otter Woman flitted through his mind.

Aiee, he was glad that such a serious choice was not his! He was not certain whether at that age his own sincerity could have withstood the test. What if he had been faced with the choice? Sharing warm robes with Rain, or committing himself totally to the demands of the holy man's instructions. And when both he and Rain had been at the height of their desire for each other . . . That was *still* good, but to have been faced with the choice when the flames were at their hottest . . . Singing Wolf was not at all certain how he would have been able to make such a choice.

"Yes," he agreed thoughtfully, "it must be his to choose."

And maybe it was good. If Wolf Pup chose to start his training, it would surely show his dedication to the career and responsibilities of the holy man.

If the worst happened, and Wolf Pup chose to marry now . . . Well, maybe in a year or two Pup could begin, if he felt the call. There might still be quite a distraction for many years. Any man would envy the husband of such a wife as Otter Woman. Maybe that would be *worth* refusing the spirit-gift. There was certainly that possibility. Either way, the choice was Wolf Pup's.

Singing Wolf was pleased that there seemed to be no hesitation on the part of Wolf Pup. Of course he would begin his training, the boy said. It was obvious that Wolf Pup was not completely happy about the sacrifice. His questions regarding how long the initial trial might last revealed that. But it would also be an excellent evaluation of the boy's sincerity.

One thing did bother Singing Wolf a little bit. That was the desirability of the girl. One who looked like *that*, whose every movement was sure to stimulate the male desire, would not be immune from attempts at courtship. In fact, there would probably be crowds of young men following her, like dogs after a female in season. Ah, well, it was no concern of his. If that was meant to be, so be it! It would be a shame, though, if Wolf Pup's very sincerity did cause him to lose the woman. *Aiee*, what a woman!

But, he told himself, it would be a test for her too. Yes, if this girl, no matter how stunning her beauty, could not discipline herself to wait a season or two for her intended husband . . . Well, she simply lacked the dedication needed for the wife of a holy man. And after all, what is a year or two in the larger way of things?

It is a very long time at that age, when the juices of youth are coursing through one's loins, he realized. *But no matter*, he argued with himself. *If they are sincere, and it is meant to be, it will be so.* In this way, he thrust the problem aside, and absolved himself of responsibility.

The training of Wolf Pup began with familiarization with the objects of importance to the People. Especially those important to the Southern band. Of course, some of the significant objects related to the personal medicine of Singing Wolf. His medicine bag was so personal that even his wife did not know its contents. The medicine pipe . . . It was understood to belong to the band, and the holy man was merely a temporary custodian for this generation.

Wolf Pup seemed especially impressed by the pipe, in its protective case with intricate quill-work. It possessed a spirit of its own, a warm, alive thing that was hard to describe. The holy man allowed his pupil to touch and feel the smooth warmth of the red fire-bowl.

"One of your duties," he explained, "is to honor and respect this pipe. It is to be protected from harm. You will keep it clean and ready, and hand it to me for the ceremony when it is time. Its pouch, too . . . both its case, the lodge in which it lives, and the pouch, here, tied to it. That holds the tobacco, of course. You will learn to prepare it, mix it, everything about it."

He could tell that Wolf Pup was taking all of this very seriously.

"Now you know of the bit, the Elk-dog Medicine," he went on, taking the object down from its peg.

"Yes, Uncle, I have seen it in the Story Skins, but I do not understand how it was used."

Singing Wolf nodded. "Well, you know that our ancestor Heads Off was riding the first horse seen by the People."

"Yes . . ."

"This object was in that horse's mouth when he came to us," the holy man went on. "It contains the power to control the horse. See, this circle, around the lower jaw."

"But we use a thong . . ."

"Yes, of course. The People had only this one medicine bit. They learned to make the circle not of iron, but of rawhide, when they got more horses. I am made to think that many different materials could be used. The circle and the part in the mouth only remind the horse that the power over him is ours."

"And the bit, the Elk-dog Medicine, is a symbol, a ritual? That is why you wear it?"

"Yes. That is why. Mostly, only for ceremonies that involve horses."

"What of the feathers, the fur?" Wolf Pup pointed to decorations tied to the bit.

"To honor it. See, it has its own medicine bag too." Singing Wolf pointed to an ocher-smeared buckskin pouch no larger than his thumb, tied to the object. "The pipe, too, has one, you know. These two things, the pipe and the Elk-dog Medicine, are our most important objects. They carry our power . . . Power of spirit."

"What of the Story Skins, Uncle?"

"Important, yes. They tell of the People. But there is a difference, Pup. They have no spirit of their own, but only help us remember when we tell the stories of the People."

"But you do not use them at the story fires."

"Of course not. The stories are *learned.* The Story Skins help to tell what has happened up to this present time. And we do not have Story Skins all the way back to Creation."

"Did we, once?"

"Maybe. I do not know. These go back many lifetimes. They tell one or two important things of each year. Good years, bad years, battles."

"And the coming of Heads Off and the First Horse."

"That is true. Now, let us look at some of them . . ."

And the lessons went on . . .

19
»»»

There is no single word in most languages that can express all of the different ideas implied in the American Indian's use of the word "medicine." To a European, medicine has to do with healing. But in this context, it covers much more.

The holy man of the People, or of any other People native to North America, whatever their tribe or nation, *is* a physician. His expertise includes many other functions, however. He has gifts of the spirit that border on the supernatural, transcending science. He is a prophet, in the old definition, one who speaks for God. But he is sometimes granted gifts of the spirit which give him special powers of prophecy, an insight into the future. His is also a priestly function, as a religious leader. Misuse of any of these powers may result in loss of the gifts, or even in death.

"Medicine" in this context, then, must be seen as a mixture of religion, healing, magic, and instruction. Sometimes it even includes storytelling, adding the function of historian.

. . . . .

Wolf Pup settled into the hard work of his apprenticeship with confidence. There was excitement and expectation. He would now begin to learn forbidden truths, and would be taught the secret rituals and signs, the medicine of the holy man.

There was no doubt in his mind that he had received the call of the spirit to do this. It was exciting and pleasing to learn that Otter Woman was still available and willing. That was a distraction, of course. A conflict . . . not really a conflict, he decided. Merely a distraction. And after all, he had been given an option. He could marry, and then undertake his apprenticeship later. He had discussed it with Otter, and she had urged him to go ahead.

"It would be harder," she suggested, "to be separated for a time after we are together. And I will wait."

His grandfather had seemed pleased at this choice. That was always the way with Singing Wolf, direct and to the point. Even with the ceremonies and rituals, there was a firmness and surety that lent confidence to the observer. The storytelling of the old man, too, was delivered in the same way. When Singing Wolf told a story, one could hardly doubt that it *happened*, and exactly that way. And if his grandfather was pleased with Pup's choice, the whole endeavor must be considered good.

Wolf Pup moved into the lodge of his grandparents. That was no great change. The big lodge with the painted symbols of the holy man's medicine had been erected near that of his parents for all of the young man's life. Every time the band moved, or traveled to winter camp, it was so. Pup was moving to a lodge which had always been only a few steps away. He had, in fact, spent many nights in that lodge through his childhood years.

His grandmother smiled a greeting, and pointed to the area that would be his for some time. Across from the east-facing doorway, and just to the left . . . The bed of his grandfather was directly opposite the door, in the traditional spot for that of the head of the lodge. Visitors entering would greet their host as he was seated on his robes, beyond the fire, facing east.

"You will be on his right," Rain explained as she pointed.

She had removed all the assorted items which accumulate in a lodge to make a place for Wolf Pup to throw his robes. He had few other possessions. His bow and quiver of arrows, his knife . . . His mother had presented him with a new buckskin shirt in honor of this new beginning. He knew, too, that she would see that his moccasins were replaced when needed. His medicine bag, of course, but that would usually be worn on a thong around his neck.

Now his grandmother spoke again.

"For most of his ceremonies you will be at his right," she explained. "You will hand him what is needed."

"But how will I know?"

"He will teach you. I will help, of course."

"You do much to help him, Grandmother?"

"Yes. Well, some. His medicine . . . you know, he can let me use it sometimes."

"How does he do that?"

"*Aiee*, I do not know, Pup. Ask your grandfather. I only know that he does it sometimes for a little while. I suppose he will tell you."

Again, he felt the thrill of unknown excitement at the wondrous things he was to learn.

It was quite a letdown, then, when he began to realize that mostly, this period as the holy man's understudy was nothing but hard work. There were innumerable plants to learn to identify, gather, and prepare. Sometimes it was the leaf, sometimes the flower, the seed, or the root. They must be handled and prepared in different ways. Some were dried in bundles and hung from the lodge poles, others stored in rawhide packs. Some were dried and then ground, to be mixed with other ingredients at the time of use.

As the band moved into winter camp the activity intensified. Many of the medicine-plants or their parts are seasonal, and it was time for gathering. The mixed scents of drying plants permeated the lodge with pungent fragrance. Wolf Pup realized for the first time that this was the source of such a scent.

The smells of childhood bring back forgotten memories more

easily than any of the other senses. How often a faint scent of a fragrance or an unpleasant smell brings an unexpected recall of a childhood scene. We are transported instantly to a place and time remembered dimly from long ago.

In the case of Wolf Pup, still in his teens, there was not the nostalgic return, but a different excitement. He was learning the sources of the smells of his childhood, when he would enter the dim space of his grandparents' big lodge. It was good to be able to verify the odor of sage, of fragrant juniper, catnip, and others. *Ah, yes, that is sumac,* he would think to himself. It was all an exciting introduction to a new world. That offset the fact that even the things of the spirit are sometimes associated with hard work.

He was permitted to assist in the mixing of the holy man's tobacco, and this was a great honor.

"A smoke is for two purposes," his grandfather explained. "The most important is to honor the spirits. Sometimes, though, it is only for pleasure . . . You know, when we visit in the lodges of our friends, to talk or play the games in winter."

"This is different tobacco, Uncle?"

"Sometimes. You know, everyone has his favorite mix."

"Yes, but you use a special mix for the medicine pipe?"

"Oh. Yes, that is true. Even so, most holy men have their own mix. It tells the spirits who is calling." His eyes twinkled. "Usually, that mix has more tobacco. Tobacco is pleasing to the spirits."

"And the other plants are not?"

"Well, yes, but . . . *Aiee,* Pup, you ask too many questions!"

Wolf Pup's face reddened. "Is that not why I am here?"

His grandfather seemed lost in thought for a moment, then gave a deep sigh.

"That is true, Pup. I was about to say that you will learn all of this later, but . . . *Aiee,* later is *now.* I will tell you of this. Tobacco does not grow in the Sacred Hills, no? Neither does sweetgrass, also pleasing to the spirits. These things we get from traders. Sweetgrass from the north, tobacco from Growers mostly to the east. Now, such things that are scarce cost more dearly in trade, no?"

Wolf Pup nodded.

"So," the holy man continued, "when we use tobacco for pleasure, we can mix it with something to make it go further. You have seen people smoke the hairy tuft from an ear of corn? But we are not Growers, and usually do not have that. Some like red willow. Not leaves, but bark and shavings. I like that myself. A red willow stick, shaved and toasted over the fire, the browned chips brushed into the pouch and the stick shaved again . . . I will show you, but that is for a rainy day. A little tobacco can go a long way."

"But that for spirits has more tobacco, less other things?"

"That is true. Of course, it is all for the spirits, no? Like all things, Pup. All that we do, they notice. But sometimes, we need to call attention, do something that is mostly for them. For us, as well, of course."

"Like the lighting of the first fire when we camp?"

"Yes! Exactly! I always use a pinch of pure tobacco for that. It gets their attention better."

"How do you know, Uncle?"

Singing Wolf gave him a critical look. It said plainly that the question was inappropriate. It also appeared that the holy man thought that this was going too fast, and that the lessons for today were at an end. He frowned.

"Enough for now. Go and get your grandmother some wood!"

Wolf Pup jumped to his feet and hurried outside. His grandmother watched him go.

"I did not really need any more wood," she noted.

"You can use it. Anyway, he asks too many questions."

"*Aiee!*" exclaimed Rain in mock surprise. "Is that not why he is here?"

"But he cannot have it all at once!" the holy man snapped.

"That is true. Yet were you not eager when you began to learn?"

"Of course, woman! But there are things not meant to be told, only to be experienced, no?"

"Then what would be the harm in telling him *that?*"

"But he must not get it too fast."

Rain chuckled. "Ah, my husband, you are jealous of all the wonder that lies before him."

Singing Wolf softened. "Maybe. It is a wonderful trail that he begins to travel. But much hard work!"

"He knows that. You have told him."

"That is true. But he is so young, Rain!"

She nodded. "So were you, once. And I, of course."

He smiled, rose, and came to put his arm around her.

"Rain," he said quietly, "I have hoped for one who would learn my medicine. It gives me great pleasure that this is the one. I must be sure that I do it well. What if I . . ."

She placed a finger on his lips.

"Such things are not to be said. Anyway, your guide would not let you do this in any way but the best."

"That is true. But the *responsibility*, Rain!"

"Ah, you agreed to that long ago! Singing Wolf, your heart is good, or you would not even have the gifts now."

"Yes . . . Ah, Rain, you have always been able to make me feel better."

He enfolded her in his embrace, and drew her to him, but she pushed him gently away.

"No, Wolf," she teased. "I cannot make you feel any better right now. Pup will be back soon, and besides, I must finish cooking." She slipped from his arms, and glanced back over her shoulder. "But I appreciate the thought. Remember it for later!"

He chuckled. "*Aiee*, Rain, it has been a long time since we have had such a thing . . . A young person in our lodge."

"That is true. But it is good, no?"

"Of course! Well, except for the inconvenience."

Both were still chuckling when Wolf Pup returned with his armful of wood. The young man did not understand at all, but it was apparent that this was no time to bring up such a subject.

He was grateful that the mood of his grandfather was improved. He was still unsure exactly what it had been that caused the irritation. He had asked about the spirits . . . No, had asked how one *knows* about the spirits. Well, he would try to avoid that subject.

He was left with a quandary, however. How would he know what questions to avoid? He glanced at his grandmother, and received a friendly, understanding smile. An idea occurred to him. Rain had always seemed just a bit softer, more approachable. Maybe he could contrive to ask *her* what to ask of the holy man. He smiled at her, and there seemed to be an understanding of a sort he could not define. Yes, it made him feel better, and yes, he was sure that he had an ally in his search for knowledge. Yes, he was certain that his grandmother could help him when Singing Wolf seemed out of sorts.

And it was good.

20

» » »

Wolf Pup was restless. It was the Moon of Greening, and a restless time of the year anyway. He had managed to concentrate fairly well on his learning during the winter months. There were times when he had hardly left the lodge for days on end except to attend to bodily functions.

Now it was different. With the weather moderating, the People were emerging from the winterized lodges into the sunshine. Sun Boy's torch was still somewhat pale and yellow, but it was plain that its fire was growing stronger. Once again, Sun Boy had persisted, and was now driving Cold Maker back to his cave-lodge in the frozen mountains of the North.

And with the warming of the earth and more human contact, romance was in the air. Just as the life-giving juices rise in the awakening trees and grasses, there is a stirring of excitement in the loins of humans. The hollow, haunting notes of the courting flute were heard around the camp, and couples could be seen hand in hand, or walking together with obvious intentions.

For Wolf Pup it was sheer torture, because he could do nothing about it. He could speak to Otter Woman if they chanced to meet, but could not carry on a courtship. There was little opportunity, anyway. His time was almost totally occupied with small tasks assigned by Singing Wolf. Sometimes it seemed to Pup that his grandfather deliberately tried to find things to keep him busy. Was it to keep him away from Otter Woman? Maybe. But possibly just to impress the young apprentice with the importance of his tasks.

And I know the importance! Wolf Pup thought, fuming with resentment. *He does not need to convince me.*

He had spent most of the morning grinding red ocher for paint, a boring task. There was enough red ocher in the gourd where it was stored to last for many seasons, Pup thought. Why more? In fact, why not grind only a little at a time, as needed? It seemed to him that his grandfather was going to a great deal of trouble to make him miserable. In his mind, he knew that it was not true. His grandfather would not deliberately do such a thing. But in his heart, it was hard to convince himself. He found himself burning with resentment.

His grandmother had arbitrarily suggested that he go for a walk. She was wise in such things. Already he felt better as his anger cooled. He had climbed the slope behind the camp. Now, still breathing a little harder from the exercise, he sat on a ledge of white limestone and looked across the valley below. The bright green of new grass lay across the hills like a robe. Along the streams and gullies, the willows were beginning to leaf. Their color was yellow now. Soon they would appear a darker green than that of the prairie grasses.

It was only a few days since the hills had been stark and black. The warrior societies had burned the dry grass as part of the new season's beginning. Singing Wolf had explained to his apprentice the significance of the ritual.

Since he was old enough to remember, Wolf Pup had been impressed with the spring burning of the prairie. It was such a spectacular sight, the long lines of fire snaking across the hills. He had a general idea as to why the fire was a part of their world, but now he was to learn in detail.

"You have seen the buffalo go south for the winter," Singing Wolf began.

Wolf Pup nodded. "Like the geese."

"Yes. Something like that. But *why* do they go?"

"Well . . . it is warmer?"

"That is true, yes. But think now, Pup. What do they eat?"

"Grass, of course."

"Ah! And *when* do they go south?"

"When . . . Yes! When the grass dies!"

"Right!"

"But Uncle! They eat the dry grass."

"True. But as with our horses, who also eat dry grass, it is not as good. They become thin, waiting for the time of greening. Then Sun Boy makes his new torch, and the sun returns, bringing warm weather, the grass, and the buffalo."

The old man paused, packing his pipe with a pinch of his favorite mix.

"Pup, hand me a stick from the fire there!"

Wolf Pup did so, and waited while his grandfather drew on the pipe and blew out a puff of pungent smoke.

"Now, where was I? Oh, yes! How do the buffalo know where there is grass?"

"To the north?" guessed Pup.

"Yes, of course. Maybe where and *when!*"

"I do not understand."

Singing Wolf looked impatient. "What are we talking about, boy?" he demanded.

"Buffalo . . . the grass . . ."

"The *burning! Aiee,* Pup! Think!"

Wolf Pup, feeling chastised, nodded. "Yes, the burning," he mumbled.

"But if they are far away," the holy man went on, more charitably, "the buffalo cannot see or smell. So, we must *bring* them back. That is a part of being a holy man of the People. The holy man decides when to burn. The smoke rises up to the spirit-world, and the spirits tell the buffalo *'it is time.'* So, they come."

"The smoke, then . . ."

"Yes. The spirits are pleased by the smoke. Just as the smoke of a pinch of tobacco at a new camp, you know?"

"I can understand that, Uncle. Its fragrance . . . But the bigger burn . . . How does that please the spirits?"

"I cannot say, Pup. Only that it does. Maybe it is seen as good that we prepare the way for the buffalo."

"So the spirits tell them, send the herds to us?"

"Yes. You have seen how thick and green the grass comes after the burn. That is what brings the buffalo. The eating is better in the burned area."

Wolf Pup nodded. "But how do you know . . . How does the holy man know when it is right to burn?"

Singing Wolf appeared pleased. "Ah, yes! That is what you were supposed to ask. I will show you."

The two had walked some distance out from the camp, where the dry winter grass still stood. Much of the fall color had faded now. The pinks and reds and golden hues of the various grasses had faded. The stems were dry and lifeless, all a pale, neutral color. As uninteresting as the lack of life-giving nutrients which make them unpalatable to the grazing animals at this time. Even so, the young man recognized clumps of different varieties. Plume grass, real-grass, the shorter feathergrass, which still held seed heads like the breath-feathers of a bird.

"Now look," said the old man, stooping to pull aside the dry stems in one of the clumps. "See . . . ?" Deep in the dry clump he had exposed a few sprigs of green. "This is why you have learned to know the grasses one from another. To tell when to burn, you find a few good clumps of real-grass. 'Turkeyfoot,' I hear the children call it. Plume grass will work too. Now when the new green shoots are about this tall"—he indicated on the tip of an index finger—"it is time to burn. Too soon, the earth is naked, and suffers. The grass is poor. Too late, the new growth suffers. The grass is poor."

"And the buffalo will not come?"

"Sometimes. But think of it. If you were a buffalo, you would seek the best grass, no?"

Wolf Pup nodded. "And the spirits will tell them where the grass is best?"

"That is true. And that is why we must be careful *when* we choose the time to burn. Now, you see the green leaves there. Is it time?"

The young man considered thoughtfully for a little while. The obvious answer appeared too easy. There must be something else, but he could not find it. "It would seem to be so," he said finally, and somewhat reluctantly.

"No!"

Singing Wolf appeared pleased that his pupil had missed his guess.

"You have forgotten the wind," he admonished. "It would be dangerous today."

Of course, thought Wolf Pup. *I should have known.*

One of the dreaded occurrences in the grassland is wildfire. Sometimes it had been used by the People in war, but even so, a dangerous weapon. A shift or change in the wind might send an inferno roaring through dry grass as tall as a man, and faster than a horse can run.

"We must wait for a still day," Singing Wolf was saying. "You see, if something goes wrong, the medicine man is often blamed. He should have seen it coming."

"But if it goes right, Grandfather . . ."

The old man chuckled. "Yes, they sometimes remember. Usually, it was just expected to be so. But remember, it is wise to include a warning."

"What do you mean?"

"Have you ever noticed, Pup, when I cast the bones and say that the hunt will be good? Even then, caution that for some there will be danger."

"*Aiee!* It is not the bones that tell you that?"

"Of course it is! But they cannot tell all. If they could, there would be no need for me to interpret. Anyone could do it."

"But the caution, the danger . . ."

"Wolf Pup, did you ever see a hunt in your lifetime where someone was not killed or injured, or a horse gored?"

"Well . . . no."

"So! That must be included. A warning. Now, back to the burning. I will study the sunrise, the bones, wind, anything that I can. The grass is ready and we must burn within a few days. When the time comes, I will know."

"But I thought that your guide tells you when . . ."

"And so it does. But my guide does just that. *Guides.* I must do all that *I* can first, and then ask the help of the spirit-guide."

"So, much of your medicine is of your own knowledge, not a spirit-gift, Uncle?"

"Of course! Would I try to bring rain when my observations tell me that it will *not* rain tomorrow?"

Wolf Pup was confused now. "When you make rain, that is not your spirit-gift, your medicine?" he asked in astonishment.

"Yes, of course it is!" snapped the old man irritably. "The gift helps me to look and to *see* where I am looking. The gift tells me how to use what I see, what I know, and when to do so." He paused and smiled. "Of course, it is good to keep a little mystery in it, so everybody does not want to try it for himself. That would lessen the power."

Pup was silent. He would never have thought of this quiet man as one who would seek power. Singing Wolf had never sought political prestige, merely using his gifts as needed. But in so doing, he was honored, of course.

"Power?" asked Wolf Pup quietly.

"Not the way you are thinking, Pup. The power of the gift. Spirit-power. It is respected more if there is a little bit of mystery. You will learn."

They had burned the grass two days later. For the next two days the People watched the fiery snake loop across distant hills, as far as the eye could see. By night the sky was red with the reflection of fire on low-hanging smoke. It disappeared in the blue of a distant ridge two days' travel away, but the white clouds still boiled up from beyond for another day.

"Yes," observed Singing Wolf. "It goes well."

21

»»»

"**A** good burn," Singing Wolf observed to his wife, as he looked through the doorway across the greening prairie.

It had been scarcely ten sleeps since the burn was carried out, and the stark, blackened hills were already covered with the lush green of new grass.

"That is true," answered Rain. "You chose the day well, my husband. But it helped, maybe, that warm shower two days later."

He smiled. "You think I did not foresee that?" he teased.

"Maybe. Maybe you were lucky."

These were private, inside jokes, born of long association, trust, and understanding. This was the one human being with whom Singing Wolf could occasionally drop his dignity. Even that had been less often with their grandson living in the lodge as an apprentice.

"Where is Pup?" he asked.

"I sent him out for a walk," Rain answered. "You are working him too hard, Wolf."

"Nonsense! He must be impressed with the responsibility."

"Huh!" she grunted. "At his age, were *you?*" She smiled at him seductively.

"That was different. I was not an apprentice until later. We were already married, no?"

"That is true. But how can he learn, Wolf, if everyone else is courting?"

"He has more important things to do. He must show his sincerity."

"It seems that I remember," Rain mused, "a time when you thought nothing more important than courting. You were jealous, too! That young man from the Eastern band . . ."

"Well, I . . ." he mumbled. "But you were not really interested in him."

"But you did not know that at the time."

"Well, Otter Woman has told Pup that she will wait, no?"

"Yes. And she thought so, then. But it is spring, Wolf. Others are courting, and Otter is a very beautiful girl. I saw Spotted Horse looking at her this morning. He still sees a chance."

Aiee, thought Singing Wolf. *What man would not look?* Maybe he should rethink this.

Aloud, he was firm. "No. His learning comes first. I must be sure that he is not distracted."

"He *is* distracted, Wolf," she warned. "Push him too hard, you will lose him."

It was not a pleasant thought. He was about to retort angrily when there came a tap on the lodge skin beside the door.

"It is Otter Woman," the visitor called. "May I come in?"

Rain held aside the doorskin and the girl stooped to enter.

"Wolf Pup is not here?" she asked, blinking to accustom her eyes to the dim interior of the lodge.

"No," answered Rain.

"You wished to see him?" asked the holy man.

"No. I had hoped to talk to you, Uncle. I thought I saw Pup leave the camp."

Singing Wolf ran his eyes over the lithe body before him, trying

not to be too obvious about it. *Aiee,* Wolf Pup *did* have a problem.
And there would be other suitors, to be sure.

The girl interrupted his thoughts.

"Uncle," she began hesitantly, "I would, meaning no disrespect,
ask of you a question."

"Yes, child, what is it?"

"Does Wolf Pup's learning go well?"

The holy man was completely surprised. He did not know what
he expected, but it was surely not that.

"Yes . . . yes, quite well," he stammered, off guard.

"It is good. Then maybe it could be that you can tell me when
he can marry."

Unnoticed, Rain smiled to herself in amusement. This one
would do!

"He has asked you to find out?" asked Singing Wolf suspiciously.

"No, no!" The girl looked embarrassed at such an accusation,
and perhaps a little angry. She drew herself proudly to her full
height. "Pup would not do such a thing. He does not know I am
here. I ask for myself!"

"I only asked, Otter. It is good."

There was a moment's pause while the tension began to ebb.
Otter Woman turned to Rain.

"You assist with the holy man's medicine, do you not, Mother?"

"That is true."

"And it is a help, no?" She directed the question to Singing
Wolf.

"Yes," he agreed. "Much help."

"It is good. Then would a wife not be a help to Wolf Pup, to
learn the ways of the spirit-gift with him?"

Singing Wolf saw that he was trapped.

"I could learn while Wolf Pup does. I am made to think, Uncle,
that his learning would be made even better with my help."

Young woman, the holy man thought, *I am made to think that
there are many things which you could make better for him!*

Aloud, he spoke gruffly. "What you say may be worth considering. I will think on it."

The girl flashed him her marvelous smile, which would melt the hardest of hearts.

"It is good! Thank you, Uncle."

She turned and stooped to exit the lodge. As she did so, the eyes of the two women met for a moment, and there was a brief understanding that passed between them. Such are the ways of women.

The doorskin fell into place behind the graceful figure, and Singing Wolf took a deep breath.

"*Aiee!*" he said softly. "What happened here, Rain?"

His wife chuckled softly. "I am made to think, my husband, that you have decided that your apprentice needs a wife."

The old man smiled, and she came to sit beside him. They knew each other well.

"Oh," he said. "Was it *I* who decided that? When did I decide?"

"Thank you, Wolf," she said, snuggling against him.

Such are also the ways of women.

Well, after all, the apprenticeship was well started, Singing Wolf reasoned. The pattern of concentration and dedication was established. And their grandson *was* doing well. He seemed to have an understanding of that which is important. Part of that, however, is that one must realize at some point that it is not necessary to understand all things. Sometimes it is best not to try.

Those who learn this are the happiest. They realize that many things are so merely because that is the way they are. This is not to say that there is no virtue in an inquiring mind. The ability to wonder is one of the greatest gifts of the spirit. But there is a point (*aiee,* who is to say where?) beyond which further question seems useless. Then one who has been blessed with the gift may feel a sense of calm acceptance. It is possible to relax, to go with the flow of things, to enjoy. Common sights and sounds take on new meaning, and the world becomes a place of awe and wonder. And it is good.

Singing Wolf had felt that his pupil was learning well, making great progress. He had had in mind that perhaps in the autumn Pup might be permitted a more active part in the holy man's duties. Care and protection of the medicine pipe, perhaps. He had started to instruct in the importance of that object, its history and its special functions. The boy was interested and attentive, but easily distracted. Singing Wolf had tried to keep his attention by assigning more work, but that was not working well.

The holy man realized, of course, that the postponed romance was a factor. He had not fully realized just how important a factor. But yes, as he thought about it, the young woman was right. With whatever help from Rain . . . He smiled at the thought. Ah, there was a woman! Their marriage had been good, and it was like her to try to help the young couple in their romance.

It was the Moon of Greening, soon to become the Moon of Growing. Moon of Planting, for the Growers, farming tribes along the rivers. His mind moved on toward summer.

The Moon of Roses . . . Yes, that might be a time for the marriage. The entire nation would be gathering for the Sun Dance . . . Yes, a good time. Wolf Pup would be completely distracted and preoccupied for a while. As it should be, of course. But by the time of the Fall Hunt, with its many duties, Pup might have regained his senses. At least partly.

"I am made to think," he said to Rain, "that the Moon of Roses would be a time for the marriage."

"It is good," she said, smiling. "Where will they live?"

"We must talk of this," he agreed.

Normally among the People, the young couple would stay temporarily in the lodge of the bride's parents, until they could manage to acquire their own lodge. That could probably not be before the Fall Hunt, when there would be enough skins available for a lodge cover. Some would be from the kills made by the new husband. Most would be gifts from family and friends.

This marriage, however, would present special circumstances. The custom of living with the bride's parents was challenged by the custom of the holy man's live-in apprentice.

"How did we do that?" asked Singing Wolf. "I do not remember it as a problem."

"We already had our own lodge," Rain reminded, laughing. "Remember, we would set it up next to the lodge of your parents? Your father would need his assistant and come tapping on the lodge cover at inconvenient times."

He smiled. "Ah, yes. We wondered if he did that on purpose."

"Maybe. But what of Otter and Pup?"

"*Aiee,* I do not know!"

"Maybe you should let them decide," she suggested.

"But I need him near me."

"Could they . . . could you let him go for a few days?"

"I suppose so. Yes, that might be a way. Let them take the edge off their passion, then back with us. *Both* to learn the ways of a holy man's lodge."

"It is good! Will you tell him when he returns?"

"Yes, why not?"

It was not long in coming. The young man tapped on the lodge cover and stepped inside, nodding a greeting.

"Ah! You have been watching the grass return?" asked Singing Wolf.

Pup glanced around anxiously, as if to see if he was to be scolded. Seeing nothing threatening, he spoke.

"Yes, Uncle, I was. The whole earth is greening, no?"

"Yes. A good burn."

"Uncle, I have wondered. How far does the fire go?"

The old man shrugged. "Who knows? Until it reaches a stream that it cannot cross. Until it rains. Why?"

"No reason. I only wondered."

"It is good to wonder, sometimes. But Pup, I would speak with you of your learning."

Wolf Pup turned in alarm. "I am not doing well enough?" he challenged.

"What? Oh, yes. It is not that. But it is springtime. Others are courting. I am made to think that your thoughts are often on romance."

"Grandfather, have I not done everything . . ."

Singing Wolf held up a hand to stop the tirade.

"Hear me out, Pup! *Aiee,* you talk too much!"

Wolf Pup waited impatiently.

"I am made to think," said the holy man, "that it is time for you to take a wife."

There was an anxious look on the face of the young man. "And stop my learning with you?"

"No, no. Marry, maybe at the Sun Dance. Then come back. We can talk of the details. But go and ask her parents. There are plans to be made."

Wolf Pup was already moving toward the doorway. He must find Otter and share this wonderful news with her. Then he must be thinking of a suitable gift for Otter's father. That in itself would be a problem, he thought as he stooped to leave the lodge. The doorskin fell into place behind him.

"It is good," murmured Rain to her husband.

22
>> >> >>

"**R**emember, your marriage is not until the Moon of Roses," Singing Wolf admonished.

He may have been half joking, but his tone was gruff and Wolf Pup knew that the message itself was serious. He would be expected to carry out all the duties of his apprenticeship. Then, as time permitted, he could spend a little while with Otter Woman. Singing Wolf had plainly stated that the two would be allowed a little while to themselves after the marriage. Then they would move into the lodge of the holy man for the duration of Pup's training.

This in itself was of no concern. Young couples, when first wed, were expected to start their life together in someone else's lodge. Usually, that of the bride's mother. There were ribald jokes about it. A young husband of the People was prohibited from speaking to the mother of his wife. This tradition precluded any threat of incestuous romance between the two. So in a way, it would be much easier to dwell at first in the lodge of Pup's grandparents.

His most pressing problem, aside from his duties with Singing

Wolf, was to approach the father of Otter Woman for permission to marry. He must offer a gift to compensate the parent for the loss of his daughter. Pup dreaded this a little. He did not feel that he knew or understood Otter's father very well.

Black Fox was one of the senior warriors of the People, a member of the old conservative Bowstring Society. He was a man of many winters, and held great prestige. He had shunned politics, but his wisdom was sought by many. He could have been a sub-chief, perhaps band chieftain, but had never aspired to such office. His area of skill was in such things as leading a hunt or a scouting mission. Fox and Dark Antelope, Pup's own father, had often functioned together in planning the hunt. Antelope's tracking skills and Fox's wisdom and organization worked well together. Pup had always been in awe of the man, because of the high regard in which others of the elders held him.

Otter Woman was amused by all of this. "You do not know him," she told the uncomfortable Wolf Pup. "He is only gruff on the outside. He is soft and loving, really."

"But I only see the outside," protested the young man.

Otter was the youngest child of the lodge of Black Fox. Basket Woman, Otter's mother, was a young wife, a pretty thing. She had been widowed while still childless, and she had no family, except for an older sister who was the sit-by wife of Black Fox. Their children were nearly grown, and Fox graciously agreed to take in the sister of his wife. This was not uncommon among the People, who looked after their own.

Then came a child to that union. Otter, child of Fox's old age, became his pride and joy. For this reason, Wolf Pup dreaded asking for her hand. It was not unheard of for a father to refuse, if the value of the gift offered was deemed unworthy of the loss of his daughter. And a daughter such as Otter, known to be a special favorite of one of the band's most respected men . . . *Aiee!* How could a poor young man, a struggling assistant to the holy man, offer enough to warrant serious consideration?

Since the time that the People acquired the horse many life-times ago, horses had become a symbol of wealth. More than a symbol, actually. Their entire world revolved around the cycle of the seasons, the grass, and the buffalo. For the People the buffalo provided food, garments, homes, and tools. One might boast of a larger lodge than his neighbor, made of more skins. But ultimately the *means* of acquiring those buffalo skins was represented in the horse. One cannot kill enough buffalo on foot to furnish much of a lodge. Therefore a person's affluence, to a great degree, was determined by his *potential* to acquire buffalo. This in turn translated to a simple method of estimating one's potential: *How many horses does he have?*

So it had become a common thing for a young suitor to prove himself to his prospective in-laws with a gift of horses. The more the better, because the number of horses owned by a young man indicated his affluence and prestige in the band.

The Southern band of the People had been the first to see and acquire the horse because of their geographic range. The ancestors of Wolf Pup had sometimes been called the Elk-dog band. Now that term was used by their neighbors to mean their entire nation.

The importance of horses on the plains had increased so much that now it was not uncommon for young men to raid neighboring tribes for horses. So far, this had not caused much trouble. The closest allies of the People, the Head Splitters, had honored the alliance so far, as the People had. But it was known that the Snake People to the south were stealing Spanish horses from the settlements. It was suspected by the Head Splitters that they were losing a few horses to the same raiders. It was hard to tell. The herd of a single band would number in the hundreds of animals. Who would miss three or four or ten? Some would often wander off anyway, when loosely herded by the young men.

All of this went through the mind of Wolf Pup as he pondered a suitable gift for the father of his would-be bride. He had a herd of his own, but only a few animals. No more than fifteen, probably. Maybe there would be some foals soon. But even if he offered every horse that he owned, it would seem to be a poor gift. Not fine enough to compensate for the loss of such a daughter as Otter Woman, child of the great Black Fox in his aging years.

During one of his brief and infrequent conversations with Otter, Wolf Pup raised this subject.

"My heart is heavy, Otter," he began. "What if my gift is not accepted by your father?"

She laughed. "*Aiee,* what have you to worry about? He will probably be glad to have me out of the lodge!"

"No, I am serious, Otter. Look, I have practically nothing of value. Only a few horses. Fifteen at most, even counting foals not yet born."

"You are serious, Pup," the girl said, sobering.

"Of course! This is the biggest thing of my life, Otter. What if Black Fox is not pleased with what I have, and says no?"

"But Pup, your family has always been known for its fine horses. My father has always envied their quality. Has he not traded for horses with Dark Antelope?"

"Yes, of course. But friends trade horses all the time."

"Pup, you do not understand. No one trades away the very best of his horses. Those, he keeps. There are horses in your family that Antelope would never trade."

Wolf Pup began to understand where this was going. "You mean, Black Fox has wanted horses that my father would not give up?"

"Of course. It would be beneath his dignity to beg from his friend."

Wolf Pup began to understand. It was a matter of pride.

"Fox has wanted a particular horse?" he asked.

"No, I think not. It is more . . . Did your family not have the First Horse?"

"Well, yes, in a way." He recalled the Story Skins. "First Horse, a gray mare, was ridden by the outsider, Heads Off, who became my ancestor. Otter, I am made to think that he was a Spaniard."

"Yes, yes, but the horse . . . You still have grays that go back to that horse, no?"

"So it is said."

"And then . . . was there not another horse, a Dream Horse among the People?"

"Yes. Not among the People, though. An ancestor of ours . . . that was many lifetimes later, Otter. A young man on a quest. Horse Seeker, he was called. He caught and trained a great horse, one he had seen in a vision. The Fire Horse, because of its color. But he released it. He had made a vow to do so."

"Yes, yes," Otter said impatiently. "But my father says that he probably bred all his mares first."

"That is true," agreed Wolf Pup. "A family story. Our horses . . ." He stopped short. "Wait! Otter, your father wants . . . *aiee*, not this or that horse, but the breeding. The blood-lines!"

"Yes! That is what I am trying to tell you. You have something that Black Fox wants. Others talk and boast of it, but only your family really has the horses that my father wants."

The world began to look brighter to Wolf Pup. Now that he knew, he could act on this information. Already he was thinking of individual horses in his band. His appeal would be to Black Fox as a horseman. Not quantity, but *quality*. He began to plan. His selection, his reasoning, even his speech when he would approach Black Fox to offer his gift in return for the hand of Otter Woman.

Should he proceed now to make his approach, or wait until the Sun Dance? He wanted badly to get the gift-offering and the subsequent permission to marry behind him. Somewhere in between, maybe.

His horses did not look their best. No horse does, in the Moon of Greening. The animals are thin, gaunt from scanty forage through the winter moons. Their heavy winter hair is shedding in patches, lending a moth-eaten appearance, like an old buffalo robe that has seen many winters. No, this was not a good time to brag about quality. He would wait, watch the animals carefully. They would begin to fatten on the lush new grasses, recovering weight and muscle. The nutrition of the new growth would waken the spirit of the green-starved animals. Coats would become sleek and shiny, as dull winter hair was replaced by healthy new growth. They would recover the light in the eyes, the "look of eagles."

Then would be the time to approach the father of Otter Woman, with the horses at their best in appearance and spirit. Some special grooming, some painted symbols, maybe. He would talk to Singing Wolf about it, because it might require all the medicine that he could ethically use to convince Black Fox. The old warrior must value the gift enough to give up his daughter.

23
>> >> >>

"**U**ncle, I would speak with you. It is Wolf Pup."

His palms were sweating and his heart beat wildly. Now was the fateful moment. He knew that the confrontation was not unexpected. Black Fox was aware that his youngest daughter, child of his older years, was of courting age, and had been for a season or two. The whole camp probably knew by this time that Wolf Pup and Otter Woman intended to marry. It was no secret.

Wolf Pup had attempted to select a time for this symbolic ritual that would show him to best advantage. It was nearly two moons now since he and Otter had conceived the idea of the gift of specially selected horses. During those two moons his horses had filled out, gaining weight and muscle tone. The last scraps of moth-eaten winter hair had fallen away, and the sleek and shiny coats of summer were things of beauty. Pup was proud of the quality of his horses. Surely, an experienced horseman such as Black Fox would see these qualities.

But he was unsure. He remembered a few seasons back when a young suitor had driven a band of loose horses directly through the camp to the lodge of his intended wife's parents. It had been a showy move. There were probably not more than twenty horses, but at a full gallop between and among the lodges it had seemed like many more.

That stunt had not been well received. It was a dangerous move, to drive horses at a canter through people on foot. Someone could have been hurt or killed. Aside from that, the nuisance of clouds of dust from the dozens of pounding hooves did not go unnoticed. Women yelled indignantly in righteous wrath as the gray cloud settled over their cooking fires and on the racks of drying meat.

"Go away, stupid one, back to your Eastern band!" shouted one old woman.

The young man was not of that lineage, but the accusation was appropriately delivered. People had talked for days about the event, even laughed about the suitor's incredibly poor judgment. His intended wife's father, coughing and choking in clouds of dust, had refused to even talk to him.

These were the thoughts that kept popping into the head of Wolf Pup as he waited for an answer to his greeting. Now it seemed to him that his offer of horses marked by quality rather than numbers was a stupid idea. He wanted to turn and slip away, to try to think of something else, but it was too late. He was here, holding lead ropes in his sweating hands.

The day had been chosen carefully. It must be soon, because the Southern band would soon break camp to start the trek to the Sun Dance. This timing had been chosen to allow the horses to fatten and shed winter hair. Yet to wait too long would be a mistake too. A horse, especially one of a dark color, looks his best in early summer, before the sun's rays burn and bleach the glossy coat, dulling its sheen. All of this seemed futile now to the waiting Wolf Pup.

He had almost decided that there was no one at home when the doorskin was pulled aside and Black Fox stepped out.

"*Ah-koh,* Uncle," Pup said respectfully, "I have come with a gift, that I might marry your daughter."

There, I said it. It is done, Wolf Pup thought.

The old man took a step or two outside, peered around both sides of the lodge, and then took a look behind the next lodge. He seemed puzzled.

"*Aiee!*" he said gruffly. "Only two horses? This is all that my daughter means to you?"

Wolf Pup's heart sank. He wanted to turn and run, but it was too late. He started to speak, but his voice was tight. Pausing, he took a deep breath, cleared his throat, and tried again, trying hard to maintain his dignity.

"Hear me out, Uncle," he implored. "I would explain."

Black Fox was looking curiously at the two animals that stood there. He gave a short grunt that could have meant anything. Wolf Pup took it to mean assent, and hurried on.

"I have thought long about this, Uncle," he began, ignoring the quick nod of agreement from the other. "I am a young man, and have only a few horses. Wait . . . Let me go on."

He took another deep breath. "I could," he continued, "get more horses. Some young men raid the herds of Snake People. Or catch wild horses, even. But horses that one may steal will not be the best. They would be those of not very good quality. Their better ones would be carefully guarded, no? And the same with catching wild horses. The easiest to catch are the slowest."

"So, what are you trying to say?" Black Fox demanded.

"Two things, Uncle. First, there are not enough poor horses alive to equal the loss of such a daughter as yours. Next, you are a great leader and warrior, and you have many horses. Most of them are better than any I could steal or catch for you. Besides, as you know, I would be a holy man, not a stealer of horses."

"So?" the old man asked.

"So I am made to think, Uncle, that what I could offer as a gift is a horse or two of the finest. I will tell you of these."

"This is not a horse trade!" Black Fox grunted irritably.

"That is true, Uncle. And I would not try to show anything about a horse, *any* horse, to such an able horseman as yourself. You can see them, and judge for yourself."

Black Fox nodded. "Not too bad," he said, as if to himself. "But what, then, did you want to tell me?"

"Of their breeding, Uncle. Let us look at the gray, there."

"I suppose she goes back to First Horse," the old man said noncommittally. "I have mares like that."

"True. Yours are some of the best," agreed Wolf Pup. "But . . . You recall the story of our ancestor, Horse Seeker, and the Fire Horse?"

"Of course. A wild stallion, no? Trained for one battle?"

"That is true. You know, then, that before Horse Seeker released the Fire Horse, he bred some mares?"

Black Fox chuckled. "I have always thought that he must have. *I* would have!"

Wolf Pup nodded. "This mare carries both bloodlines."

"There are many who say that in a horse trade," the old man said suspiciously.

"That is true. But Uncle, you know my family. My father is your friend. You know that if my family says this to be a descendant of Fire Horse, she *is.*"

Fox nodded absently. He was already walking around the young mare, noting her fine qualities. Her color was a deep blue-gray, with only a small white star in the center of her forehead. The head itself was beautifully shaped, broad between large soft eyes. The ears were short and slender, and the tips turned inward slightly. A refined, feminine head with an intelligent expression . . .

Black Fox turned his attention to the legs. Straight, square, well muscled . . . Powerful hindquarters. The hip was broad from front to rear, with heavy muscle evident. A short strong back that would not tire easily.

"*Aiee!*" said Fox suddenly. "She makes milk!"

"Yes. She will foal soon."

"Her first?"

"No. Her second. This is my best mare, Uncle. I hunted buffalo on her last season, and she is good. Worthy of such a horseman as yourself, even."

It was apparent that Black Fox was impressed, though he seemed to shrug off the flattery.

"I prefer a stallion for buffalo," he remarked.

"That is wise, Uncle. Many do. That is the reason for this other horse."

The two men turned to the slightly larger and stronger stallion. The animal's foreparts were a dark, shiny black. From the shoulders back the color was mostly white, with rosettes of black scattered over the rump.

"I have seen this horse." Black Fox said. "I did not know he was yours."

"He is yours, Uncle, if you will take him. A great buffalo runner."

"He runs to the right?"

"Of course." Wolf Pup had made certain that Fox's weapon for the hunt was the bow. To offer a horse that would approach from the wrong side for the proposed rider would be unforgivable.

"How is it," asked Black Fox suspiciously, "that you have such a horse?"

He was obviously interested.

Wolf Pup smiled. "He was born to one of my mares," Pup explained. "My first buffalo horse."

"She was spotted, like this?"

"No, no. She was a gray. I still have her."

"But the spots . . ."

"I am made to think, Uncle, that this goes far back among my family's horses."

"How so?"

"You know sometimes some of the horses of the People have some white on the hips?"

"That is true."

"My father says that his grandfather, Walks in the Sun, told him of this. In long-ago times when the People were still enemies of the Head Splitters, one of their young chiefs had a spotted stallion. It was white with dark spots over the entire animal. Oh, yes, there is a picture of it in the Story Skins. My father says that he is made to think that these markings go back to that stallion of the Head Splitters."

"But how . . . ?"

"Oh! The young chief who rode the horse was killed in battle by our ancestor, Heads Off, who claimed the horse."

It was apparent now that Black Fox was greatly impressed. Now it was time to reveal the final argument.

"This mare," Wolf Pup pointed out, "is in foal to the spotted stallion."

"Then . . . the foal she carries has the blood of First Horse, the Fire Horse, *and* the spotted stallion of the Head Splitters? All three?"

"That is true, Uncle. There may be other horses among the People with all three. There probably are. But all three were in our family, and . . . well, you know our horses."

"Yes . . . Wolf Pup, I am made to think that this is good."

"This lifts my heart, Uncle. Of course, if you wish, I can try to steal a hundred slow horses from the Snakes."

There was a guffaw of laughter from Black Fox.

"No, no. It is good, Wolf Pup. *Aiee,* you have done well. A very clever thing!"

"Then you accept this gift?"

"Yes, yes. It is a gift worthy of my loss. I know that Otter Woman will be well cared for."

"Thank you, Uncle. Otter has told you that we will live with the holy man while I continue to learn?"

"Yes, so she said. Her mother is not quite happy about that. But I am made to think that it is good. Now, you wish to wed at the Sun Dance?"

"That was our intent."

"So be it! Now, tell me more of this mare . . . When do you expect her foal?"

"Soon, my father says. See, her milk bag is filled."

"Yes . . . *aiee,* she drips a little . . ."

The two examined the waxy drops on the tips of the nipples.

"I am made to think," said Black Fox, "that it is no more than two sleeps!"

That is true, thought Wolf Pup. *And how could the timing be better?*

24
>> >> >>

To Wolf Pup, the world had become a much brighter place now. He could see ahead, could dream of his upcoming marriage. Singing Wolf had seemed to mellow somewhat too. It was as if once the decisions were made, there was no further problem. His demands on his young apprentice even seemed to become less.

The young mare given as a gift to Black Fox had indeed foaled a day later. Her colt was strong and straight, with an intelligent look and an active way of going, and the mare had plenty of milk. The colt's color was of the distinctive mouse-dun that told the true color underneath. When this fuzzy baby hair was gone in a moon or two, the animal would be black. Black Fox was pleased.

Now the day had been set for the move to the site of the Sun Dance. It would be three days after the announcement. There was a flurry of activity. No matter that everyone had known all along that the move was coming. There would always be some who were not ready. Women began to pack frantically. Children caught the excitement of the time, and the tempo of their games increased markedly.

For Wolf Pup and Otter, it was a major turning point. It marked the beginning of the events which would culminate in their marriage. It was hard to think of anything else. For once in their young lives, everything seemed to be going well and according to plan. It was difficult to believe that anything that might happen now could make a difference in their happiness.

But such is the deceptive way of the world, is it not? Surprises come when least expected . . .

In the bustle of excitement and preparation, no one had noticed a change in the weather. In truth, it had not yet happened. The sky was clear and blue, the sun warm, and the grass lush and heavy. The world was good, and there was the distraction of the impending move. Afterward, there was some whispered criticism of Singing Wolf for not having foreseen the tragedy, but *aiee!* How could any holy man anticipate such a thing?

It was late afternoon, and the two young lovers had stolen away from the busy camp and its chores to seek a little time together.

"My father is pleased with his horses," Otter said as they climbed the slope to the south of the scattered lodges. "You have seen the foal?"

"Yes. Otter, it is as I had hoped! Ah, that will be a horse!"

They reached the top of the ridge and sat down to survey the rolling prairie before them. The day was still, and a pair of buzzards circled endlessly high above, mere specks of black against the blue. In the rising air currents of the sun-heated afternoon, they required not a wing-beat to soar on and on. Wolf Pup watched for a little while. *What is their purpose?* he wondered.

"Pup," the girl spoke, "why do the buzzards soar so high?"

"What do you mean?" he asked, startled that the thought was so much like his own.

"Well, look at them . . . Do they need to be so high? Are they still looking for food, or do they soar because they *can*, and because for them, life is good?"

Wolf Pup chuckled. "I was wondering the same. How far can they see from up there? How would it look?"

Otter Woman watched another circle of the birds before she answered. "A girl of the Red Rocks band told me that her people see the mountains for several days' travel before they reach them. Do you think so?"

"Maybe. Look, off to the southwest, there. That first ridge is about a day's travel away."

"Yes. A short day."

"Right. Then the one beyond that, another half day. And it looks bluer. The farther ones look more blue."

"That is what the Red Rocks girl told me. The mountains look blue. You have not seen mountains, have you?"

"No. I would like to sometime. Maybe we can go there to visit your Red Rocks friend."

Both giggled at the thought of being together.

"We can see if mountains are blue," said Otter.

It was apparent in the scene before them. The closest of the rolling hills were as green as the grass around them. Each succeeding ridge became a different shade of blue-green. The more distant ridges were more and more like the blue of the sky. The last visible ridge of the Sacred Hills was hardly distinguishable from the sky itself. In fact, was that actually a range of hills, or a distant cloud bank? It was hard to tell.

Still, there seemed no urgency in the situation. They talked of other things, and watched an eagle soar across the valley to its nest in a giant old cottonwood on the river. Closer at hand, a pair of rabbits carried out the ritual dance of their mating ceremony. One sat, frozen and still, while the other charged from several paces away at breakneck speed. At the last instant, the unmoving rabbit leaped straight up, high in the air, while the other rushed past underneath. The young couple watched, laughing softly, as the ritual was repeated several times.

"Which is which?" asked Otter.

"I cannot tell," Pup admitted, "but surely the warrior is the one who charges."

"Maybe both are warriors," she suggested.

Otter was looking past him at the distant horizon, and her expression changed.

"Look, Pup! That *was* a cloud bank, not a range of hills!"

He turned, and was astonished to see how much closer it had moved. Now there could be seen the flicker of fire in that gray-blue cloud. Even as they watched, they could begin to hear the mutter of thunder, hardly distinguishable at this distance. Still, there was no cause for alarm. Both had watched storms come sweeping across the prairie before. It is an interesting and exciting show. One must only avoid being in a high place when Rain Maker begins to throw his spears of fire. Or, of course, under a large cottonwood. It is well known that cottonwoods attract the lightning-spears like no other tree.

But just now, there was no immediate danger. They could watch the storm develop, and retreat to the shelter of the lodges when it seemed advisable. It was quite possible, even, that the storm might miss the area of the Southern band's camp entirely. The young couple continued their conversation, enjoying the opportunity for a quiet time together with some degree of privacy.

Now the color of the rising cloud seemed different, somehow. It was still some distance away, but the hue was changing. No longer blue or blue-gray, it was now an ugly, dirty gray-green. There was a threat of a different kind here. The entire prairie was suffused with an otherworldly greenish glow. Not a breath of air stirred, and even the birds and the crickets were silent.

Below them in the village, no one seemed to notice anything unusual. The People were busy, preparing for the move. Wolf Pup turned to watch the advancing cloud front again. It was creeping forward like a living thing, appearing taller as it came nearer. Soon they were looking upward at the swirling mass, and then it seemed to rear above them, writhing and twisting.

It was frightening, like a dream in which one wants to run but cannot. The two were detached observers, as if what they were watching was not of this world and had no meaning for them. It was still quiet. There was no mutter of thunder now, and the flicker of lightning had subsided, as if frightened away by an even more sinister force. The distant hum of activity still rose from the camp below, oblivious to the approaching cloud. Pup realized that the People could not see what was happening beyond the ridge.

"Let us go," said Otter, in an unsteady voice that seemed loud in the stillness.

"A little longer . . ." Wolf Pup answered, entranced by the vast panorama that spread before them.

The dark cloud now seemed to rise in a layer, to ride up and over the heavy silence that lay about them. To the west they could see bright daylight at the horizon with the darker cloud lying heavily *over* it in a layer like a thick blanket. No, more like the layer of smoke that rises above the camp. On a quiet fall morning it finds its level and merges with other smokes to hang there motionless until a subtle shift in the air disperses it.

But this was different. There was an ominous feel to the evening, a feel of something evil. To the south the heavy mass hung low to the ground. Only to the west could they see the strange layered effect which marked the leading edge of the storm. Another glance below showed that the People still did not realize the danger. They could not yet see . . .

"We must warn the camp," said Otter Woman softly.

Wolf Pup nodded, but made no effort to go. He was fascinated at that which spread before them.

It was just then that in the distance to the southwest they saw the whirlwind start to form. The appearance was like that of a huge, thick snake which seemed to shake itself loose from the layer of cloud to dip downward toward earth. It was fatter at the end that remained attached to the writhing cloud above. The tentacle probed downward toward earth, searching, reaching like something alive and with purpose, growing thicker and fatter as it did so.

It was hard to tell how far away the thing might be, because of the strange light and the distortion of size of earthly objects. Huge trees along the distant river were dwarfed by the immensity of this evil thing. It appeared that the tentacle might be half a day's travel away, or maybe only a few bow shots.

Another probing snake shook itself down from above, groped around, and withdrew again, pulling itself back up into the cloud. Then another . . .

The first and fattest of the twisting snakes touched the ground and debris was sucked up into it. At the same time objects were thrown aside at its base, like water splashing from the impact of a thrown pebble. A giant cottonwood was twisted, shattered, and disappeared into the mouth of the ravenous creature.

"It is coming this way!" Otter Woman yelled. "Pup, it will hit the camp!"

That would be hard to tell, because its path was erratic, but there seemed to be a strong possibility. The thing swung back and forth, chewing up anything in its path. Oddly, Pup was reminded of a grazing animal, swinging its head from side to side as it crops the grass, then stepping forward.

They turned to run toward the camp, and as they did, the *sound* of the evil thing began to reach their ears. It was a rumbling roar that shook the earth, rising in intensity and pitch, a howl that raised the hair on the back of Wolf Pup's neck as they ran. Could they possibly outrun the monster? It was farther from them than the camp, but was traveling faster than they could run.

They began to yell as they drew nearer the camp. People looked up, startled, and then began to run toward the river.

"Down, behind the bank!" Dark Antelope shouted to the hurrying crowd.

Where the day had been still, it now became active. The wind whipped and twisted. Small pieces of debris filled the air, stinging faces and obscuring vision. Wolf Pup and Otter became separated in the wind and dust. He assumed that she had gone to help her family. He hurried toward the lodge of his grandparents and thrust his head inside. It was empty.

He turned to go, and the beaded case of the medicine pipe caught his eye. Quickly, he stepped across the lodge and lifted it from it peg. *The Spanish bit, too!* he thought. He grabbed that honored object also.

What about the Story Skins? No, he could not carry them all, and there was no time . . . He turned and ran, just as the monster struck the camp. He saw the big lodge lifted in its entirety, and flung himself prone, hugging the medicine pipe and the Elk-dog Medicine bit to his chest. His scream of terror was lost in the roar of the whirlwind as it swept through the village. Some flying object struck him across the head and shoulders, and blackness descended over him like a thrown blanket.

25
»» »» »»

It was all over in an instant, and the air was calm again. Singing Wolf poked his head up and over the cutbank where many of the People had reached relative safety. There was no safety, really, but one seeks the lowest spot available and lies flat until the Whirlwind passes.

He was a bit embarrassed that he had not had time to give more warning. He should have seen the signs. It was almost an accident that he had been able to give any warning at all.

The village lay in ruin before his eyes. There had been nearly sixty of the big lodges, so sturdy and tall in appearance. Now the area was littered with scraps of lodge skins, broken poles, and pieces of the lives of the People. The air was still again, and in the silence could be heard the cries of people searching for loved ones, mingled with the screams of the injured. A few lodges still stood at the east edge of the camp. The Whirlwind had spared a narrow strip there as it passed. There were oddities to be seen . . . a single flimsy lodge still standing amid all the ruin, with those which had stood adjacent completely gone, poles and all. An old man peered from its doorway, confused at the unfamiliar scene. People were wandering, dazed, not knowing what to do or where to begin it.

The holy man turned to his wife.

"Rain . . . are you all right?"

She nodded, her eyes wide with wonder.

"*Aiee!*" she whispered. "You?"

"Yes. But . . . our lodge . . ."

"Wolf! What about your medicine pipe? The Elk-dog Medicine? The Story Skins? *Aiee!* All gone!"

Dark Antelope came trotting over.

"Mother . . . Father . . . You are safe?"

"Yes," said Singing Wolf, "we are all right. Your family?"

"A few scratches. The lodge is gone. Where is Wolf Pup?"

"He is not with you?"

"No! We thought he was . . ."

"Maybe with Otter?" Rain asked. "They walked off together, earlier."

The thoughts of Singing Wolf were whirling. In all of his nearly sixty summers he had never seen such havoc. Whirlwinds, yes. Two or three times . . . Once as a child, again as a young man . . . One a few summers ago. But all had been at a distance, usually a great distance. He had seen the damage after the encounter sometimes. A row of trees with a huge bite chewed out of the middle of the row and swallowed by the monster as it passed.

There were strange tales. He remembered an old woman who in his own youth had told and retold her story. When she was a child, she insisted, she had been picked up by the Whirlwind. She described the view from high above, as she looked down on the village of skin lodges. She had been carried across the river and dropped gently in a grassy meadow, completely unscathed but stiff and sore. There had been many who feared the "Daughter of the Whirlwind" and called her crazy. There had been a time when Singing Wolf had thought so too.

Now he was sure that she had told her story exactly as she remembered it. It would certainly explain the one thing that her detractors had never been able to answer: if her story was not true, *how did she happen to be across the river?* She had had to swim back.

Now, too, fragments of memory came flitting back, remembered from other Whirlwinds. A flock of turkeys, plucked bare by the twister . . . Ripe plums, hundreds of them still on the trees, which had been impaled by grass stems, blown like tiny arrows . . . An old warrior's eagle feather headdress, still hanging on the pole in front of the spot where his lodge had stood, with not a feather ruffled. That, of course, could be attributed to the strength of his medicine.

All of these stories came to mind as Singing Wolf and Rain climbed up and out of the gully to join this search for whatever might be left of the Southern band. And for Wolf Pup . . . They started toward where they believed their lodge had stood. It was difficult to orient one's self when there were no longer any landmarks. The area seemed flat and naked.

Ahead of them a dazed figure stood swaying unsteadily, a number of objects clasped tightly in his arms.

"Wolf Pup!" His grandmother ran forward to take his elbow. "Are you hurt?"

"What? No . . . I do not think so . . . I . . . Uncle, the Story Skins . . . I could not . . ."

"It is good, Pup," Rain comforted him. "You are alive!"

"What . . . where is Otter?"

"We have not seen her," Singing Wolf answered. "She was with you?"

"Yes . . . Well, no. We were on the hill. Then we came down just when the Whirlwind struck. My parents?"

"They are safe. We saw your father."

"Good! Maybe Otter is with her parents. We were separated when the wind . . ."

"Yes, yes," his grandmother comforted. "We will look for her. Are you sure you are not hurt? Your head . . . ?"

She pointed to a bloodied spot on his left temple, and touched it gently.

"*Aiee*, a bump like the egg of a goose! It is fortunate you were not killed!"

"What are you holding, Pup?" asked Singing Wolf.

The young man was still clasping his arms tightly over his chest.

"What? Ah . . . I tried to save that which is most important. The pipe . . . the Elk-dog Medicine . . ."

He unfolded his arms carefully, and handed the beaded pipe bag to his grandfather. Then the Spanish bit.

"What is the other bundle, there?" asked the holy man.

"I . . . I am not sure," muttered Wolf Pup, still somewhat confused. "I grabbed . . ."

"One of the Story Skins!" cried Rain in recognition.

The heart of Singing Wolf began to swell with pride. In all the horror and confusion of the Whirlwind's strike, the young apprentice had kept his head. Wolf Pup had protected the sacred objects with his own life. The holy man found that his eyes were filling with tears. *This is not a Pup any longer*, he thought. *Today this is a man.*

Through the afternoon, Singing Wolf pondered the whimsy of the Whirlwind and its strange spirit. The People had always seen it as a powerful relative to the Little Whirlwind, who dances across the flat land in the heat of the day. Singing Wolf had always seen the Little Whirlwind as one of the forms taken by the Trickster when he is in a playful mood. The Old Man of the Shadows can take any shape he chooses, of course. A bird, fish, rock, or tree. Or a human. He can speak all languages, even those of the trees and the stream.

When he was a child, Singing Wolf used to imagine that he could understand their conversation. When the soft breeze rustled the leaves of the cottonwoods, they were speaking to the Old Man: "*Good day to you, Uncle!*" And the Trickster would reply, "*And to you!*"

But when the Old Man felt like dancing, he would take the form of the Little Whirlwind, skipping and bounding across the land. Singing Wolf was certain that this was one of the plainest examples of the whimsical spirit of the Trickster. Mischievous, but harmless when it came to the People. The heart of the Trickster must be good toward the People. Otherwise, he would not have summoned them from underground and led them through the hollow log into the sunlight at Creation. Is it not so?

It was for this reason that the holy man did not believe that the Big Whirlwind was closely related. The spirit was different. Old Man would not wreak such havoc on the defenseless, even in his anger. His acts largely revolved around a spirit of mischief and fun. Jokes at the expense of others, yes, but not with this spirit of destruction and evil. The Big Whirlwind, too, behaved whimsically, but also dangerously. Wolf thought that maybe Big Whirlwind might be a brother to Old Man. Or possibly, an errant son. Yes, that might be it . . . A strong son, with the sense of humor of the Old Man, but without his wisdom.

Their allies the Head Splitters sometimes saw the Big Whirlwind as a giant creature like a horse with the tail of a fish. He could not exactly understand that simile, though. He could see that the snakelike thing which reaches down out of the cloud might look like the pawing forefoot of a horse. Maybe . . . But the tail of a fish? Well, possibly they had seen one of the dark appendages flip downward and then back up into the cloud. But as the old saying goes, who knows what a Head Splitter is thinking?

One story of the Head Splitters' lay on his mind after the Big Whirlwind passed. It was said that a few summers ago a hunting party saw one of the largest Big Whirlwinds ever seen. They watched in terror as the giant appendage reached downward and touched the earth, turning *red* as it did so. *"A red sleeve,"* they had called it. Singing Wolf was sure that this was because in much of the range of the Head Splitters the earth itself is red. But no matter . . . The hunters then saw black creatures in the Big Whirlwind, writhing and squirming within the cloud. They thought these must be demons of some sort.

It was not until the next day that the party crossed the path of the Big Whirlwind and found it littered with the carcasses of hundreds of buffalo. What had appeared to be small writhing creatures in the cloud had been a herd of buffalo, lifted and devoured alive by the Big Whirlwind. The thought made his flesh crawl.

There was a council that night, of course. It was necessary to discuss the extent of the damage, and what would be needed to help those who were without shelter. There was even some question as to whether the Southern band would be able to attend the Sun Dance.

Nearly every family had suffered loss. By what seemed a miracle, there were only two deaths. One young horse herder, caught in the open, had been lifted and dropped. An old woman who stayed in her lodge . . . deliberately, some said . . .

Most of the injuries were slight, such as that of Wolf Pup. And Otter Woman had come searching for him almost as soon as the dust settled. She was unscathed.

Material things had fared poorly. Only a few horses were dead, injured, or missing, but other possessions . . . *aiee!* They were scattered from here to the horizon. The People had spent the afternoon salvaging what they could. Robes, pieces of lodge covers, even some unbroken lodge poles.

There were a few good omens. Most of the Story Skins lay in an orderly pile, still tightly rolled, where once the lodge of the holy man stood. One was picked up among the debris a few bow shots to the northeast of the camp. And Wolf Pup, apprentice to the holy man, had been hugging one tightly to his chest when he was found. That greatly increased the young man's prestige, since he had also saved other sacred objects.

So much so, in fact, that before the council ended, Singing Wolf made an important announcement. From this time on, his grandson would no longer be known as Wolf Pup.

"He is no longer a Pup," the holy man said solemnly. "This is a man who has shown his bravery and his dedication. He has saved the sacred medicine pipe, as well as the Elk-dog Medicine, from destruction or loss. From this day he is not to be called Wolf Pup, but *Pipe Bearer*."

And so it was.

There was another decision that night. The Southern band agreed to start for the Sun Dance, hunting along the way as they traveled.

"What more do we need?" an old woman joked. "We have our hunters, and our cooking stones did not blow away. At least, not yet!"

26
»» »» »»

Pipe Bearer . . .

Among the People, a man or a woman might have several names during a lifetime. There was the baby name, given by the parents at birth. At the ceremony of First Dance at the age of two, another name was given by an elder of the family, usually a grandfather. Most commonly it would be his own, to perpetuate the name. Since it is forbidden to speak the name of the dead, the very words could otherwise be lost from the language.

Yet it is not always so. If the name seems not appropriate for a child . . . Or, as in the case of Wolf Pup, his grandfather had not been willing to give up the name.

"I may have use for it yet," Singing Wolf had said, a twinkle in his eye. He had given another name, but few remembered what it was. They were Singing Wolf and the Wolf Pup, and so it had been. The entire band knew who they were, and of their close relationship as the child grew. What the boy was called seemed unimportant. He would probably choose his own name when he became a man anyway. It was common to do so, to commemorate a major event in one's life.

Or it might be that the People would bestow a name informally which would become the name of common use. It had been so with Woodchuck, the outsider who had become one of the People. His companion, Sky-Eyes, too, because of their physical appearance and characteristics. There was also the French chief Wormface, who wore a thin strip of hair under his nose like a caterpillar.

One could go on with examples. Sometimes names began as a joke, like that of Talks a Lot, or Magpie, named for the flashy, raucous bird whose name means the same in the tongue of the People. Not particularly appreciated, the name was nonetheless accurate, and it stuck.

One more way that a name might be acquired . . . It might be given as an honor by a ranking elder of the People. It was so in this case. Young Wolf Pup, apprentice to the holy man, had shown his bravery, and was recognized for it.

Pipe Bearer . . .

He was not comfortable with it.

"It was not bravery," he told Otter Woman privately. "I was there, and I saw nothing else to do!"

"That is true," she agreed. "But Pup . . . Pipe Bearer . . . No one plans to be brave. It happens. What you did makes Singing Wolf proud. It makes *me* proud too."

"But I do not deserve . . ."

"Ssh!" she interrupted. "Just enjoy the honor, Pup! *Aiee*, I said 'Pup' again! May I still call you Pup?"

She snuggled against him as they stood on the hill again. It was apparent that he need not answer.

"We leave tomorrow," he said.

"Yes, I know. We have never seen the Southern band look so pitiful, Pup."

"That is true. I was surprised that the elders want to attend the Sun Dance. There is some loss of pride."

"Yes, but *aiee,* Pup! Think of the opportunity to tell the story of the Big Whirlwind!"

They both chuckled.

"That is true," agreed Wolf Pup, now Pipe Bearer. "It would be hard to wait a whole season before telling the best stories we will ever have, no?"

There were still bizarre stories coming out of the aftermath of the tragedy. One woman told of a pair of new moccasins which she had placed in a rawhide pack carrier. After the attack of the Whirlwind her lodge was gone, but a few objects still lay about. One was the rawhide pack, still tied shut. But the moccasins, she insisted, were now standing neatly *on top* of the pack. No one tried to question her honesty or her sanity, for nearly everyone had such a story.

Another family had lost one of their most cherished possessions, a metal cooking pot. It was missing, along with most of their other household goods, and there were private jokes that the wife of that lodge was considering singing the Song of Mourning over her loss.

It was a few days later that one of the wolves, ranging far in the preparations for departure, found the pot, and realized to whom it belonged. Slightly dented, it was otherwise intact, and sitting upright. There was still some stew in the pot, though it was now moldy . . .

Perhaps the most remarkable thing about the whole calamity was that there was not more loss of life.

"The People may have some protection from Big Whirlwind," Singing Wolf told his apprentice. "We do not know. But maybe, if the Little Whirlwind is merely one shape of the Trickster, and Big Whirlwind is his brother or his son . . . I am made to think that Old Man might have some influence. Maybe Old Man says to Big Whirlwind, 'Look, my brother, let us not hurt the People too much. Let us play some tricks!' You know how the Trickster loves tricks. Oh! You heard about the moccasins on Cat Woman's pack?"

"Yes, Uncle," answered Pipe Bearer. "Did you believe her story?"

"Ah! It does not matter, does it, whether you or I believe it? *She* saw it, so it is real to her. It is her pack, her moccasins, her story!"

A small party of riders was sent to give the word to the rest of the tribe at the Sun Dance site. The Southern band had met with tragedy, and would be late in coming. The ceremony could be delayed until they arrived.

There were many messages given, to be delivered to friends and relatives in the other bands. Finally, the leader of the party threw up his hands in a helpless gesture.

"*Aiee!*" he cried. "I cannot remember everything! Look, we will tell them who are the dead and those badly hurt . . . not many, and that everyone else is safe, no? You will all be there within a few days."

So it was decided, and the messengers departed. They would be able to travel faster than people dragging a lodge pole *travois*, or carrying baggage on pack horses. It was estimated that they would arrive at the Sun Dance maybe three or four days before the rest of the band. Maybe more.

It was on the third day of travel for the Southern band that they crossed the track of the monster Whirlwind. There was a path of destruction about a bow shot wide which zigzagged across the prairie in a path that appeared as long as a day's travel. Great trees were represented only by torn and twisted stumps. Yet, a few paces away, out of the monster's path, clumps of daisies and but-terfly-flower bloomed undisturbed.

"Uncle," said Pipe Bearer, "could this be *another* Big Whirl-wind? I am made to think that the one which struck us was travel-ing in another direction."

"I, too," agreed Singing Wolf. "But you said there were several tails that flipped down out of the cloud and back up. Maybe," he paused with a twinkle in his eye, "maybe it had pups!"

"That this is a child of the other?"

"No, no. I was only joking. But if Big Whirlwind is a brother to our Trickster, the Old Man, think on this: Old Man can be everywhere or nowhere, all at the same time. He can be in two places at once, or three, if he chooses, or everywhere. Cannot Big Whirlwind do the same?"

"That is true," said Pipe Bearer thoughtfully.

"But," his grandfather continued, "we do not have to explain it, or even understand it. You remember. I once told you that if you think you must *understand* it, you have missed the point?"

Pipe Bearer smiled ruefully. "That is also true, Uncle."

"You have always wanted to know much, Pup, and that is good. But some things must be taken without question, no?"

Pipe Bearer nodded. He was inwardly amused and pleased at his grandfather's attitude. Singing Wolf was much more mellow and easygoing than he had been at the beginning of his training. It was not sudden, though now much more obvious than before. It had been gradual, he realized as he looked back. An acceptance, growing as they worked together. Their discussion today as they stood on a stony outcrop of rimrock was almost like that of colleagues. He would always remember the day, the warmth of the sun on his buckskin shirt, the smell of the prairie, the yellow butterflies on the orange flowers of the clump just below them . . . the twisted stumps of ancient cottonwoods below them at the river's edge, and the path where the very grass was twisted and torn up by the roots. For some reason he was reluctant to step into the monster's trail. This was the day that he had felt really accepted as a colleague by his grandfather. His training was not yet finished, yet he knew that this was the time of his arrival at maturity in the mind of his grandfather.

But it was also amusing to him to note that the holy man had just now addressed him as "Pup." Singing Wolf, who had *given* him the new name Pipe Bearer, still thought of his grandson as "Pup." Even more curious to the young man was this his own reaction was amusement and not resentment. There had been a time when he would have called attention to the error, and would have requested that he be called Pipe Bearer.

Now it was no matter. Otter had asked to call him by his childhood name, and he would have let her call him anything she wanted. After all, they had known each other for their entire lives as Otter and Wolf Pup. It would always be so.

He did not know whether his grandfather was even aware that he had used the childhood name. That, too, no longer mattered. It was plain that today Singing Wolf regarded him as a man. With pride, he too would regard himself so. At least, most of the time. There would be times, he knew, when he would wish that he could return to the status of childhood, when he had fewer problems.

Why is it that a child cannot wait to become an adult, thinking that many restrictions are to be removed? There is no way to tell one in advance that the restrictions are to be replaced by responsibilities. There comes a time when it would be desirable to exchange those responsibilities again for the restrictions of childhood, but that is not to be. So, a child longs for adulthood, and an adult longs to be a child again. It is the way of things.

But when one becomes truly adult, he realizes this. And this was so with the grandson of Singing Wolf. He was pleased and honored to be Pipe Bearer now. But there was a part of him that would always be Wolf Pup, son of Dark Antelope and Gray Mouse.

And it was good.

There was yet another shocking surprise before the People left the trail of Big Whirlwind. The wolves who had ridden some distance along the tattered path made by the monster returned, pale and shaken. They had found an area where there were strewn the battered carcasses of some twenty buffalo.

They were not lying in the Whirlwind's path, but some distance to one side, scattered across the prairie. Some were as far apart as two or three bow shots. The young men who made the discovery were badly shaken.

"There were no tracks," one told the People as he glanced nervously around him. "They had been *dropped* there from the sky!"

27
》》》

There was never such a Sun Dance in the memory of the People. It would be remembered in the legends and stories and yes, in the Story Skins. This was the year that Big Whirlwind struck the Southern band.

It might have been worse, everyone realized. The horse herd, representing the wealth of the band, was intact. What if, for instance, Big Whirlwind had swallowed the horse herd as he had the buffalo, spitting out the mangled bodies across the prairie somewhere else?

The families of the dead painted their faces in mourning as they approached the Sun Dance encampment, but they were few. Yellow Moccasin, the young chieftain of the Southern band, called a council on the last night before their arrival.

"The People know from our messengers what has happened to us," he reminded, "but we must show that we are still strong. We still have our pride."

There were those who had doubted that Yellow Moccasin would be a capable leader, because of his youth. At the loss of old Broken

Lance, the Southern band had been faced with the election of a new leader. They had not been forced to make such a choice for generations, it seemed. Old Broken Lance had seen more than ninety winters before he died in his sleep last season in the Moon of Falling Leaves. Others had been considered, but each had carried some disadvantage. This one was too old, another came from one of the other bands and was with the Southern band because of his wife's family. Dark Antelope had been a candidate in the minds of many, but he, like Black Fox, did not aspire to political office.

Yellow Moccasin had been a compromise candidate, and no one had really expected him to do very much. But the responsibility seemed to stimulate him, and as sometimes happens to a potential leader, he grew in the office. Old women nodded their heads sagely, and told each other that they had known all along.

It did appear that this would be the finest showing of the new young chieftain, as the Southern band approached the encampment.

"Let us dress in the finest that we have left," he said in closing his speech that memorable evening. "The Southern band cannot be destroyed, even by Big Whirlwind. He has broken big trees, oaks and cottonwoods, torn them away. But the willows still stand. Why? Because they bend but do not break. They bend with the wind and are soon upright again. It is so with us. Let the Southern band go in straight and tall, with heads high and our hearts proud!"

The council broke up with a feeling of excitement. No longer was this a band of ragtag survivors, but a determined, solidified unit of individuals who felt a pride and confidence.

It was a good speech, thought Pipe Bearer. Never mind that there *were* willows which had been torn away too. Grasses, even, had been plucked down to the very surface of the soil. But in general, Moccasin's simile was accurate. That which is flexible bends, but does not break, and survives. And the tone of the speech . . . *aiee*, it made one eager for morning, so that he could begin to demonstrate the pride of the Southern band.

It was customary for the young men of the bands already assembled to mount a mock charge on the new arrivals as they approached. Usually, it happened within sight of the camp. Granted, the smoke of such a large encampment could sometimes be seen from the distance of a day's travel. But that was too far, too inconvenient for those bent on fun and frolic. So the assault was normally within an easy lope of the encampment, requiring no planning, no responsibility, nothing serious that would spoil the fun.

It was startling, then, when about midday the wolves signaled that a large party of horsemen was approaching. The leaders called a halt and drew the straggling column into a more defensible formation. Could it be some unexpected party of potential enemies? The warrior societies assembled for a show of strength if needed.

It was a time of tension, of uneasy glances and sweating palms. Horses danced nervously, knowing by the attitudes of the riders that a major effort would soon be demanded. Old women clucked their tongues in disapproval, as they always did in unexpected situations. Tension continued to mount.

Just as suddenly as it began, the crisis was over. One of the wolves came loping back. It could be seen that his posture on the horse appeared relaxed, even before they could see that he was smiling. He drew his horse to a stop and explained.

"It is a party from the Sun Dance," he told the leaders of the Southern band. "An honor party, to show sympathy for losses."

"Who is with them?" asked Yellow Moccasin.

"I do not know them all," admitted the scout. "I am told there are subchiefs of all bands. The Eastern band, even!"

"But not the Real-Chief of the People?"

"I am made to think not."

"*Aiee*," mused Yellow Moccasin, a youthful grin flickering around his mouth. "It does not seem right that we should be pitied by the Eastern band!"

There was general laughter.

"Maybe," went on the young chief, "*we* should show *them* a charge!"

There was so much pent-up pride and excitement flowing in the veins of the young men that something had needed to happen, and this appeared to be the thing. Yellow Moccasin wheeled his horse and struck heels to its ribs. He was instantly followed by a score of young riders, yelling and brandishing weapons.

The blood of Pipe Bearer was racing. He glanced over at Singing Wolf, with whom he had been riding.

"There is a wise leader," said the old holy man. "He will be a great chief if he lives."

Pipe Bearer's horse was fidgeting, fighting the rein, wanting to join the others as they ran. Pipe Bearer himself felt much the same. He would have loved to race with the wind in the mock charge, to allow himself to escape the pressure of his position for a little while. But it would be beneath the dignity of his position. He looked at his grandfather again, and found the old man watching him. Just then Otter Woman rode up beside him, and paused uncertainly as she saw his solemn face. She looked from her lover to the holy man, trying to decide what to say, or whether to say anything. Unexpectedly, Singing Wolf spoke.

"Go ahead!" he urged. "Show our pride!"

The two young people kicked their horses into a run, sprinting after the others.

Rain looked at her husband in astonishment, a puzzled smile on her face.

"They are young," Singing Wolf explained gruffly, "and this is a special event."

"Ah, you have mellowed, Wolf," his wife chided. "You would like to ride with them!"

Singing Wolf snorted in derision, but he knew that it was true. He had changed a lot during the time that Wolf Pup had been with them. It had been good for him, to see his grandson mature and develop judgment and responsibility. And in seeing the world again through the young man's eyes, his own perspective had changed.

"I might have gone with them," he told his wife solemnly, yet with his eyes twinkling. "But I think my horse is too old."

. . . .

The young couple was able to overtake the main party of young riders before the charge began in earnest. The solemn delegation of sympathy was just over the next ridge, the wolves said. Yellow Moccasin held up a hand and signaled for silence. It would be more startling if the charge proved a complete surprise. He signaled for the party to spread out along the ridge and to advance slowly at a walk, as they would in a buffalo hunt.

The first rider to see the approaching honor party would signal and . . . *Ah!* a warrior near the left end of the line, perhaps a pace ahead of the others, suddenly raised his bow high over his head. Almost simultaneously he voiced the full-throated war cry of the People, struck heels to his horse, and charged over the ridge at a full gallop. The rest of the party followed, also bellowing the war cry.

The approaching delegation, accompanied by the messengers of the Southern band, was about two bow shots away. They were caught completely off guard. A few actually turned to flee before the mock attackers were identified. The first recognition, of course, was by the messenger scouts, who saw their friends and relatives among the attackers. One pulled his horse out of the column to meet the charge . . . Then another . . . They loped forward, answering the war cry. Then, swerving aside, they joined their brothers in the wild exuberance of the celebration, circling the column.

There were dour faces among the delegation from the camp, especially among the older citizens. Such foolishness was not appropriate, especially when the mischief seemed to be led by the band chieftain himself. *That is what comes,* it was said many times in the ensuing days, *from the election of a boy to do a man's job.*

"I was told that this was the Southern band, not the Eastern!" grumbled one old warrior whose head showed the snows of many winters.

Yet there were those, even that day, who saw this as a good thing. The Southern band had been nearly destroyed. Many were impoverished, and their hearts were heavy. Was it not good, then, that they had been blessed with a dynamic young chief whose enthusiasm could infect the rest of the band? An aging leader, no matter how wise, might have found it physically difficult to lead his people to recovery. Maybe this young chief was the man who had been needed at this point in the life of the Southern band. And are there, after all, really any coincidences?

There were also those who had opposed the election of young Yellow Moccasin who now approved. This tragedy, and the ensuing recovery of the band, furnished the *reason* for his election.

At the Big Council, when Yellow Moccasin made his speech, he summed it up, and quite possibly it was that very speech that started him on the path to greatness.

"We have mourned for our dead," he said in closing, "but that is only part of life. And life is for the living, so let us live it well."

Even some of the doubters among the elders had been impressed, and the Southern band had rallied behind their young leader.

And their possessions were few, but their hearts were good.

28
>> >> >>

Of course, Pipe Bearer and Otter Woman had been preoccupied with their upcoming marriage. That was much more important to them than the shift of political influence. Still, the political scene could not be ignored. It was perhaps more apparent to those who had actually ridden with Yellow Moccasin and the other young warriors in the mock charge. That escapade had been told and retold throughout the course of the Sun Dance. It had been an occurrence that was, depending on the teller, a joke, a scandal, a desecration, or an embarrassment. One thing was certain. It had brought attention to the Southern band in a way that nothing else could have.

There had been those, no doubt, who would have preferred to see the Southern band crawl. In their destruction by the storm, they could be expected to appear poor, downtrodden, and beaten. There had been none of that. It was with pride that the southerners immediately began to trade. Horses, for the necessities that they had lost. Not their best horses, of course. The best must always be saved for breeding and for the hunt. Those who would trade with the Southern band were keenly aware of this.

They were also aware that any trade must be *now*. After the Fall Hunt, the Southern band would be restored to its former glory, unless the hunt proved a complete disaster. There would be skins for lodge covers, and robes for winter. Not the huge lodges of thirty or more skins, perhaps. That would come gradually. But the time of deprivation would be over, along with the need to trade horses for necessities.

Even with all of this, the People were generous. Individuals of the other bands did not drive the hard bargains that they would in normal times. It was to their benefit, too, to have the Southern band recover quickly and remain strong.

There was pleasure among the young people. They had noted the manner in which Yellow Moccasin had handled the meeting with the delegation from the camp. His enthusiasm was contagious. Many considered that it had gone better than it might have under the leadership of an older chief. Broken Lance had been a great leader and his memory was honored, but *aiee*, even Lance could not have done for the Southern band what young Moccasin had just done. They were far from beaten, and had just achieved a new vitality, attracting prestige and respect.

Pipe Bearer was keenly aware of this, and looked to the band chief with admiration. From his earliest memories, when he was Wolf Pup, a small child in the Rabbit Society, he remembered Yellow Moccasin. One of the older boys . . . One to be admired and imitated. Possibly that was because this older boy was always kind to the younger ones. He had noticed them, talked to them, and helped them, and such things are remembered.

Why is it that some people are able to enter a crowd and seem to notice everyone as individuals? Each person is made to feel that *he came especially to see me!* Such is the charisma of the true leader, and it was so with Yellow Moccasin.

There had been a few seasons when Pipe Bearer had not noticed the activities of Moccasin. The older boy had reached puberty, become a member of a warrior society, courted, and married. Such activities remove a man from association with younger persons.

He had come to the attention of Pipe Bearer again with exploits in the hunt, and then with the election to replace the band chief at the death of Broken Lance. But the holy man's apprentice had been preoccupied with his own duties and his own courtship, and paid little attention. Like others in his family, Pipe Bearer had not aspired to politics. He knew that Singing Wolf had often acted in an advisory capacity to old Broken Lance. The two were not quite contemporaries, the chief being older. But they were friends, and had held each other in great respect.

Now Pipe Bearer was made to think on the remarkable cleverness of young Yellow Moccasin. Prior to this, Moccasin had seemed only a capable, friendly person, liked by all. In fact, Pipe Bearer had heard disgruntled whispers that the election had been only a popularity contest. How could a young man like Moccasin have the wisdom needed to *lead?*

These thoughts had been echoed after the mock charge, led by the band chieftain himself. It was beneath the dignity of a leader, some said, to engage in such childish foolishness.

Pipe Bearer, however, had begun to see that the event may not have been a childish whim, but instead well planned. The Southern band had been dejected, self-pitying. Something had been needed to put the band in motion toward self-respect, a better outlook. A distraction, maybe, to reorient the People to the world. A young, inexperienced leader with few serious thoughts? *No,* Pipe Bearer thought now. *Rather, a clever leader who leads without seeming to do so.*

He had been thinking along those lines one morning as he went to empty his bladder on rising. He encountered other sleepy individuals on the same mission in the area used by the men for that purpose. A figure approached, keeping a respectable distance as he adjusted his loincloth. He recognized Yellow Moccasin.

"*Ah-koh,*" said the other. "Wolf Pup? No, Pipe Bearer, is it not?"

"That is true."

"Ah, yes. You rode with us in the charge," Moccasin chuckled. "But I have not congratulated you on your name. You bring honor to the Southern band!"

"It was nothing," Pipe Bearer protested. "I was there . . ."

"Yes, yes, I know. But you handled it well. Your grandfather was wise to give the name. But I am told you will marry soon? Otter Woman, I am told?"

Aiee, he knows everything about me, Pipe Bearer thought. It was quite flattering. "That is true," he said. "After the Sun Dance, Singing Wolf says."

"It is good. I wish you the best, a good marriage."

"Thank you."

"I have had little cause to ask for the help of your grandfather," the young chief went on, "but I know him to be a powerful holy man. Broken Lance consulted him freely, no?"

"Yes, that is true. They worked well together, understood each other."

"Yes, so I understood. Well, may it be so with us. You and I."

"What?"

"You and I . . ." Moccasin answered. "Do you not see? I will call on Singing Wolf's medicine for now, but think on it. We are both young, and we will lead the Southern band for many seasons."

Pipe Bearer was dumbfounded. He had not even thought of such a future. He could not answer.

"No matter, for now," said Yellow Moccasin as he readjusted his breechclout. "You are busy with your marriage plans and your learning. We will talk of these things later."

Pipe Bearer stood, astonished. He was honored to be noticed by the band chieftain. It had not even occurred to him that this would be the logical progression of things, but of course! And a wise leader would see . . .

A little later, he told Otter of the conversation. She smiled, pleased.

"Of course," she said. "You will be the band's holy man. Not too soon, I hope. But Moccasin is already the band's chief. He is letting you know that he realizes it."

"But I had not thought, Otter . . . *Aiee*, I have been too buried in my learning, maybe."

"Maybe. But maybe I can distract your mind some."

"I am made to think so," he laughed. "But Otter, Moccasin knew of our coming marriage."

"Does not everyone?"

"Of course. But he gives things his attention. He will be a great leader, Otter."

"As you will be a great holy man, my husband-to-be!"

And his mind was distracted some.

The marriage took place on the last day of the Sun Dance. A simple ceremony, symbolic of their union. The two fathers, Dark Antelope and Black Fox, took the corners of a soft buffalo robe, and spread it from behind around the shoulders of the seated couple. Thus they were enfolded, and symbolically the two became one.

It would be perhaps three days before the encampment was entirely abandoned. They would camp during that time in a private, selected area a little distance away. Then they would follow the Southern band, easily traced by the lines scratched in the prairie by dragging lodge poles and *travois*.

Both had the feeling, as they lighted their symbolic first fire that evening, with its offering of tobacco, that their entire lives had been pointed toward this time. They were finally together.

A coyote called on a distant ridge, and its mate answered from another direction. It was fitting, and it was good.

"Thank you, Grandfather," Pipe Bearer whispered to his spirit-guide.

The final result, after all of the events of the Sun Dance were over, was an increase in the political prestige of the Southern band and its young leader. They had entered the encampment with pride. They had nothing, but had the means and the will to recover. They still had their horse herd. There were many vows and offerings to sacrifice next year in return for spiritual help in the recovery.

And when the Southern band made its way out of the Sun Dance encampment, instead of a loss of families, they had actually gained five lodges.

Sometimes these were the misfits and political discontents, changing loyalties and bands every season or two with the shifting of prestige. A prosperous band had a tendency to grow. One in difficulty would lose a few lodges. In this case, one or two lodges had abandoned the Southern band, but more had joined it, because of the charismatic leader. It seemed that these young families were the finest among the People. They sensed an opportunity to assist in the recovery and growth of the band to its former position of prestige and respect. A very unusual phenomenon, but it gave a good feeling.

29
>> >> >>

Pipe Bearer had some difficulty at first. He would waken in a panic, certain that he was neglecting his duties. Or, sitting with Otter and looking across the hills at the wide sky, he would become restless. Surely, he should be doing something constructive. It had been many moons since he had experienced anything like leisure with no responsibilities.

Fortunately, he had the distraction of a new and vital relationship. Otter had always been his friend, since the time they were small together in the Rabbit Society. Now she was his wife as well. He felt that he could hardly bear the happiness with which they woke to greet each morning and sought the sleeping robes at night.

During the day they wandered hand in hand along the sparkling stream. They watched the flash of silvery minnows in the sunlight, and felt the musical shift of the white pebbles under their moccasins as they waded across the ford.

Not since he was a boy had he found an opportunity to do something as simple as watching ants go in and out of their lodges, carrying burdens greater than their own weight. Otter, too, was fascinated by their complex work of butchering and carrying away for use the flesh of a grasshopper.

They watched a dung beetle, rolling a ball many times her own size. The pace or two traversed by the insect must have seemed like a broad plain. She tucked her prize in the crevice that would become the lodge for her young, still in the egg inside the ball. The two young people marveled at her strength and ability.

"*Aiee*, I am glad that our lodge will be easier to build!" laughed Otter.

"True. But we will be in the lodge of my grandparents for a while."

"I know. Pup, we will have to help with that. The Fall Hunt must be a good one, because the People need many lodge skins before winter comes."

"That, too, is true. But we need not think of that now."

They smiled in amusement at the plight of a crow, caught in the very act of robbing the nest of a smaller bird. They were alerted to the action by the raucous cries of a pair of bluejays. Jays are not entirely innocent of such depredation themselves, but now screamed angrily in righteous indignation, diving and striking at the dark marauder. Their attack was so fierce that the crow actually took refuge on the ground to avoid the jays' swooping dives.

Now a robin and a brown thrasher joined the fray, striking as they stooped at the crow. A mockingbird approached from a nearby thicket and the crow appeared to have had enough. He rose ponderously, hindered for the first few wing beats by the battering of the attackers.

Once airborne, he retreated as quickly as possible, trying to ignore the blows to his head and back administered by the tormentors. Nearly a bow shot's distance they chased him before turning back.

"Look!" laughed Otter. "The birds of different kinds all joined to drive the crow away!"

It is not unusual, of course, for a small bird to harass a crow or a hawk. It is their way, in an effort to protect their young. The crow in turn detests *Kookooskoos* the owl, who snatches young crows from their roosting places in the dark of night. It is the way of things.

But here, jays and robins joining together to fight a danger? Pipe Bearer was puzzled. The robin and the mockingbird were probably far more likely to find their nests in danger from the jays than from a passing crow.

"It is strange," he agreed.

Could this be an omen of some sort?"

"We will ask Singing Wolf later," he suggested. "For now, it is over, no?"

From time to time he thought about the scene, and wondered. Was this merely a glimpse into the daily world of these creatures, or did it have more significance? But the pleasurable distractions of the new marriage kept it from his mind most of the time.

It was by far the most pleasant time of his entire life, except for the occasional pang of guilt that he should be permitted such ecstasy. But Otter did much to assuage such guilt. In fact, it seemed that she could probably soothe any hurt that might befall him in this lifetime.

Best of all, his happiness was shared. It was apparent in the adoring gaze that the girl turned toward him constantly. Her large dark eyes in the moonlight showed so much love and affection as they embraced that he felt he could hardly bear it. Their lovemaking . . . *aiee! If everyone had such a marriage,* he thought, *no one would have time for any disagreement. Or for hunting or any other daily tasks, either.*

Sometimes it seemed that their appetite was insatiable. But after a few days it became apparent that merely being together was in itself a great reward. The joy in talk, in the sharing of thoughts and ideas, of things of the spirit, was equally pleasurable in an entirely different way. In this way they gradually came to understand that their hearts and their spirits had begun to meld together and become as one.

There seemed to be a clarity of vision, an exciting enjoyment of all things, that rivaled the experience of the vision quest. The stars were brighter and closer, the moonlight more silvery, the sunsets more beautiful. Even the glowing coals of the fire held mysteries more thrilling. When they rose and sang the Morning Song to the dawn each day, it was with a special feeling of thanksgiving for the world and all that is in it, and for each other.

All good things must come to an end, and this was true also of the idyllic few days of privacy together. It was time to rejoin the band.

There was little packing to do, for they had few possessions. The robes that they had used for their bed . . . Weapons for defense and for the hunt . . . Saddles for the two horses that they had hobbled by the stream.

They had kept with them one dependable old mare to use as a pack horse. Though there was little to pack, the mare could be easily caught in an emergency, in case the other animals broke loose and tried to follow the herds of the People. It is well to be prepared.

Their fire had died during the night, and this morning they did not rebuild it. Otter took one last look around as her husband led the horses into their private little camp and placed the saddles on their backs. It would always be a special place for them. The People would probably hold the Sun Dance at the same site again in a few years. Maybe she and Pup could steal away to this private place . . .

"Ready?" he called.

"What? Oh, yes. I was thinking."

He left the saddled horses for a moment and came to her.

"What is it, Otter?" he asked gently.

She was certain that he knew. "This place," she whispered. "It has been . . . *ours,* Pup. I hate to leave it."

He nodded and placed an arm around her waist, drawing her to him. *He does know,* she thought.

They looked across the rolling prairie, the colors different in the slanting yellow rays of the rising sun. The big cottonwood behind them quivered in the cool of the morning breeze, whispering softly the song which would be a part of their memories. A little green heron sounded his hollow cry from a thicket by the stream below. They had watched that pair of birds with great interest as they nested in a shrubby tree.

The stream itself spoke with its tinkling melody as it wandered over the white gravel of the riffle. The little world that they had shared for these few days as man and wife must be left behind now, and the parting was sad. Even for those whose lives are nomadic, and moving on a part of living, there are special places. Otter felt this keenly.

"My heart is heavy to leave this, our place," she told her husband.

"And mine," Pipe Bearer agreed, "but we can come here again."

"Yes. But when? It will never be the same."

He smiled and held her closer. "Maybe it will be even better," he teased. "And think: we will be together anywhere from now on."

Otter nodded, smiling now. "I know." A mischievous twinkle appeared in her eye, and she casually pressed her knee against his leg. "Pup," she whispered, "could we not stay a little while? Days are long now . . ." She snuggled against his chest.

For some reason, Otter had not yet bundled the sleeping robes. The horses were grazing contentedly nearby, and there seemed no urgency about the day's travel.

"Maybe a little while," he agreed.

Pipe Bearer, honored apprentice to the holy man, was, after all, only human.

The quivering leaves of the cottonwood and the murmuring water continued their conversation as if they noticed nothing.

It was several days later that the young couple overtook the Southern band. They had not expected to do so yet.

The first hint that something was wrong came as they rode casually one afternoon. The day was warming, and there was only a light breeze. They noticed a pair of vultures, then another, and more, circling over an area half a day ahead. They paused to study the situation, with a certain degree of concern.

Pipe Bearer dismounted and lay on his belly to steady himself. He then closed a fist lightly to peer through the tube made by his palm and fingers. With the extra light from the sides excluded, he could see distant objects more clearly. The vultures appeared to be circling an area still out of sight behind a ridge in the distance. At times there were so many that the appearance was that of a column of smoke rising straight upward in the heated air currents, twisting slowly as it did so.

He could not see the object of their interest, and a dreadful fear crept into his thoughts. He hated to even acknowledge the fear, and did not do so aloud. To do so might *attract* tragedy. He could see the concern in Otter's face, though she too said nothing.

"We must go and see," Pipe Bearer said as he rose.

"You can see nothing?" Otter asked.

"More vultures. Nothing else."

He was thinking that the carcass of a buffalo or a horse would attract the carrion birds, but probably not this many. They started on at a faster pace, but watching the surrounding country carefully. They were not close enough to see the area by nightfall, so they made a fireless camp and stayed awake and on watch most of the night.

They were moving at dawn, planning their route of approach carefully. By midmorning they were able to hide the horses in a patch of sumac, tying a thong around the nose of each to prevent its crying out. Then they crept quietly to peer over the summit of the ridge into the valley below.

"*Aiee!*" exclaimed Otter. "It is the People!"

Very quickly, the suspense and dread departed. They stood to survey the scene for a little while, and then hurried to retrieve the horses and ride on in.

The People had erected brush shelters along the stream, the horse herd was gathered and herded by young men in the upper end of the valley. All seemed in order, and people were butchering buffalo and dressing skins.

"Ho, Pipe Bearer! Otter!" called one of the wolves as they started down the slope. "Welcome back!"

The man quickly explained as they rode toward the camp. There had been a fortunate encounter. A moderately large herd of buffalo had been sighted by the wolves, and it had been decided to camp for a few days to hunt. They were several days short of the area selected for summer camp, but plans change. Especially when skins are needed for lodge covers.

30
»»»

The scene at the temporary camp was much like that following the Fall Hunts, although on a smaller scale. Since the People obtained horses a few generations ago, hunting was much easier. It had been almost forgotten that the People once hunted buffalo on foot. True, there were tales in the oral legends of the People . . . Stories of great holy men who could work among the herd, pretending to be one of them, and maneuvering the animals into the desired position, near the cliff's edge.

White Buffalo, a holy man of long ago, figured prominently in some of the stories about the coming of the horse. It was he, it was said, who first pointed out that the powerful medicine of the new creature would work well with his own, that of the great bison. More than one man bore the White Buffalo name, it seemed. Father and son, down through several lifetimes. The keeper of the sacred white cape had inherited the name with that priestly responsibility.

The cape had been lost at one time, according to the Story Skins. The cape now in use had been obtained on a quest only a few generations ago by Red Horse, a young holy man, who was a distant relative.

The change in hunting methods had led to what seemed a lessening of the importance of the white cape and its holy man in recent generations. It was easy to organize and plan a hunt, because the hunters were all well mounted and well armed. It was no longer quite so critical, the planning and timing, because the hunt would be good, anyway. There was a more comfortable margin of food supply during the Moon of Hunger. Singing Wolf recalled that in his own childhood there had been elders who had referred to that moon as the "Moon of Starvation." It had not been that critical for many seasons. There were probably children today who wondered why it was the Moon of Hunger. There were even jokes that it needed a new name.

Oh, yes, sometimes the Fall Hunt was less than successful. They had only to move to a different area, hunt elk or deer a bit more intensively into late autumn. It had been of no great concern.

Until now . . .

Singing Wolf was greatly troubled that the people of the Southern band did not seem to realize the seriousness of their situation. With the few lodges now in the band, an early freeze or a less than perfect Fall Hunt could be disastrous. The summer, even the early autumn, were no problem. Many of the People used brush arbors and lean-to structures during the heat of the summer anyway. But then must come a time when shelter was essential, and that must come from the buffalo. He had calculated that with some sixty or seventy families, even small lodges for winter would require more than a thousand buffalo kills. He thought of approaching Yellow Moccasin about the matter, but hesitated. He did not know the young chieftain well, and preferred not to seem to interfere. He would be glad when his grandson rejoined the band. Pipe Bearer was nearer the chief's age, and Wolf had seen them in conversation. That was good. His apprentice was progressing rapidly, and this relationship was as it should be.

Singing Wolf was pleased when Moccasin called a temporary camp and organized a hunt. It showed great wisdom. At least, he hoped so. It could mean only that a hunt seemed a pleasant diversion for the young men . . . No, surely this young leader had deeper insight . . .

There had been many changes in the lifestyle of the People in recent generations. Easy trade with the French, the coming of firearms, blankets . . . *aiee*, Singing Wolf recalled, most of it had happened during his own lifetime. Cooking pots . . . Fewer and fewer women were now skilled in the art of cooking with stones in a rawhide cooking pit. Glass beads for ornamentation. Were the spirits *really* as receptive to ceremonies where the designs and symbols were created in glass beads, rather than quills and paints? Sometimes he was not sure. It was too easy, and many of the People did not realize the things that are of real importance.

Well, a hundred, maybe a few more kills . . . It was a start. A great many more would be needed, a really big Fall Hunt.

There were problems with this hunt at the end of the Moon of Roses. The heat was oppressive, and there was more loss from spoilage. This led to waste of good meat, which was unfortunate. But Singing Wolf realized that the important gain from the hunt was in skins, not meat. Some of the older women, who had seen hard times, seemed to realize this too. They would not allow their families to go wrong.

A summer hunt led to other problems too. A stench of rotting offal hung over the valley and was carried on the breeze. Vultures and coyotes grew fat and their young prospered, even as the People prepared to move on to more pleasant surroundings.

The holy man had other concerns too. The Moon of Thunder was at hand, the moon when the great booming storms cross the prairie. Rain Maker sounds his drums and stalks through again and again, throwing big spears of real-fire at random targets. The People could survive, but it would not be pleasant. He was afraid that many did not realize this, and would make little effort to plan for their shelter.

Life was too easy. It had not been so during *his* younger days!

. . . .

It was decided at a very informal council that the Southern band should move into the heart of the Sacred Hills. That, after all, was the source of much of their spiritual strength. This was quite pleasing to the holy man. Even though Yellow Moccasin seemed shallow and irreverent at times, he seemed to grow wiser with each public utterance. The speech that the young chief made at the council was impressive.

There had been a suggestion that the band make a visit to the French trading post before going into summer camp. They could replace some of the items lost in the Big Whirlwind.

"They have a cloth from which they make lodges, too," a man pointed out. "We have seen their tents. It is like a blanket, but without the fur."

"And it will never shed water," an old woman insisted.

"It does for them," the man retorted.

Yellow Moccasin held up a hand for silence. "This is worth some thought," he agreed. "I would like to trade for some things I lost too. And we will surely need lodges. But *aiee,* I have nothing to trade. I traded all my furs *before* the Big Whirlwind!"

There was a silence. It had been easy to talk of trading, but it was apparent that no one had enough of material value to make the journey to the traders worth the trip.

"I am made to think," Moccasin went on, "that we should go back to the Sacred Hills, the Tallgrass. It has always been our source. The grasses have been nourished by the blood and bones of the buffalo *and of the People.* We are one, and when we are there, we are close to the source of our strength. The sun brings the grass, which feeds the buffalo, which feed us. Then all things feed the grass again, no? Let us go back closer to our beginnings."

Singing Wolf's heart leaped for joy. *He does understand,* he thought. *This young leader thinks like one of our elders! His body is young, but his is an old spirit!*

During the journey to the Sacred Hills, a thought occurred to Pipe Bearer. He sought out his grandfather to initiate the idea.

"Grandfather," he began, "tell me more of the white buffalo."

"Tell you what?" Singing Wolf asked. "You know the story. You have seen the Story Skins."

"That is true," the young man agreed, "but what of now? Is the medicine of the white bull not so important now?"

Singing Wolf pondered for a moment. "I had not thought of that," he said finally. "It would seem not, but maybe . . . You have raised a big question, Pup."

With the increasingly efficient use of the horse, maybe the ritual and the power of the white buffalo cape had lost some of its meaning. The old man who was keeper of the cape no longer held the prestige that had accompanied the name White Buffalo.

Singing Wolf was surprised as he thought about it now. When had it happened? In his youth, the White Buffalo medicine had been as critical as any ceremony of the People. Now it was not a thing of great significance. The old man, White Buffalo, carried out his ritual before the hunt. But it no longer carried the solemn importance that it once had. There were many hunters who performed the traditional apology to their first kill, *We are sorry to kill you, my brother* . . . Yet there were many who did not. White Buffalo probably did so in behalf of the entire band. Singing Wolf was embarrassed to think that he was not even certain.

"Pipe Bearer," he said seriously, "I am made to think that you have come upon something very important. Why did I not see it?"

The young man said nothing, but he noticed that his grandfather had called him Pipe Bearer, not Pup, as he usually did. He had bestowed the name and the honor that went with it. Even so, there were times when Singing Wolf seemed to take perverse delight in calling his grandson Pup. It was a way, perhaps, to remind him of his place.

Now, however, the holy man seemed to regard his apprentice more seriously.

"I wonder," Singing Wolf said slowly, "if our troubles are because we have forgotten . . ."

"The medicine of the buffalo?"

"Yes . . . Was the Big Whirlwind meant to show us? Have we left the old ways?"

"Are you made to think that, Grandfather?"

"I do not know," the old man pondered. "But it deserves some thought. Let us both pray about it and talk again."

Pipe Bearer was so surprised at being accepted almost as an equal that he had little to say.

"It is good . . ."

"One more thing," Singing Wolf said. "There is a thing we must do."

"What is that, Uncle?"

"We will go, you and I, to talk to White Buffalo."

"Now?" asked the young man.

"No. After we have prayed and slept on this matter. We must think, too . . . Shall we speak of this to Yellow Moccasin?"

"Are you made to think so, Uncle?"

"Well, not yet. After we have asked for guidance, and after we talk to White Buffalo. Let us talk of this tomorrow, Pup."

31
»»»

Singing Wolf and Pipe Bearer made their way among the few
lodges and the brush shelters that marked the camps of the families. Ah, there . . . On a pole near one of the fires hung a shield
with a pictograph of a white buffalo. This must be the place.

An old woman puttered around her cooking fire and a man of
similar age leaned against his backrest, eyeing them suspiciously.

"Ah-koh, Uncle," Singing Wolf began respectfully. "We would
speak with you."

"Why?" the old man asked bluntly. He took a puff on his pipe
and blew a cloud of bluish smoke.

"May we sit?" inquired the other. "I am Singing Wolf, and this,
my assistant, Pipe Bearer."

The old man nodded. "I know who you are," he said gruffly.
"Why do you come to me?"

"We wish to learn from your wisdom, Uncle," the holy man
answered.

There was a contemptuous snort from the other, but he did not
answer.

"You *are* White Buffalo, keeper of the cape?" inquired the holy man.

"And what is that to you?"

"*Aiee*, Uncle, that may be *everything* to us," Singing Wolf answered.

"How is that?"

There was suspicion in the old man's tone.

"I . . . well, yours is the medicine of the buffalo, no?" Wolf answered.

"Huh! I thought everyone had forgotten."

"No, no, Uncle! But first, let me say, I am sorry for the loss of your lodge. And for many."

The old man nodded, softening just a little.

"I would ask," Wolf continued, "of the cape . . . Was it spared?"

Indignation flared in the face of White Buffalo.

"That has only now occurred to you?" he asked irritably.

"*Aiee*, there have been many things, Uncle," Wolf said wearily. "*You* know. You have seen our People lose everything."

This did not seem to be going well at all. The old man was bitter, defiant, angry that he had not been consulted before. A bit confused, even. Wolf was somewhat embarrassed that he had not been aware of this. He should have known, but in the past few moons, the teaching of his assistant, the Big Whirlwind . . . *aiee!*

He also wondered why there was no evidence of any apprentice who would assume the name and the office of White Buffalo. A thought crossed his mind. Was the strike by the Big Whirlwind a reminder, to catch the attention of the People? To remind them of their utter dependence on the buffalo?

Somehow, he must break through the defiance of this old man. They must begin to communicate.

"The cape, Uncle? Was it saved? I am made to think that this is important to the People."

There was a long silence while the old man took a leisurely puff on his pipe again. Finally he knocked the dottle into his palm and tossed it into the fire.

"Yes," he said. "My woman saved it. Now, who are you, again? Who is this?" He gestured toward Pipe Bearer.

Singing Wolf's heart sank. Could this man be of any help at all? He was hardly aware of what was going on. Wolf looked at the old woman and saw the sorrow and misery in her eyes. She knew, but was helpless.

"I am Singing Wolf, Uncle. This is my grandson, who is also my assistant. He is called Pipe Bearer."

White Buffalo nodded. "I had an assistant once. He died."

"My heart is heavy for you, Uncle."

The old man shrugged. "It was long ago. No one remembers now, or cares."

This was going nowhere.

"We came to ask of you, Uncle. Your buffalo medicine . . ."

Even as he spoke, Singing Wolf realized the futility of this visit. Even if the old man could remember, did he have the strength to carry out any of the rituals? As Wolf recalled, even the Dance of the White Buffalo was a vigorous thing, and this man seemed so feeble. He rose.

"Thank you, Uncle. May we come again? We would learn from you."

The old man seemed pleased. "Of course!"

As they turned away, the woman at the fire came near enough to whisper quietly.

"I would speak with you, Uncle," she said to Singing Wolf. "By the river, there, in a little while?"

He nodded and they turned away.

They waited by the water only a short time until the woman approached, carrying a waterskin.

"*Ah-koh,*" she said hurriedly, and took a deep breath. "Ah, my heart is heavy, Uncle. You see how it is?"

She was a somewhat younger woman than they had thought, younger than her husband. Tears came to her eyes as she continued.

"I know why you came. The People need the medicine of the

buffalo. But my husband cannot . . ." She paused, unable to continue.

"It is true about the cape?" Wolf asked.

"Yes. But he is like this . . . Growing worse the past two seasons . . ."

"Ah, my heart is heavy for you," Wolf said. "We had no idea . . ."

The woman nodded. "I know. His medicine is no longer so important. That hurts him."

"But it may be important now," Singing Wolf answered. "That is why we came . . ."

"I know, *I know!* I have been with White Buffalo a long time, Uncle. I can see how it is, how many skins the People will need. But he cannot help."

Wolf realized that this was a highly intelligent woman, who understood the problems facing the band.

"It is true?" he asked. "He has had no assistant?"

"As he said. His only son, who died."

"I am sorry, Mother," Pipe Bearer said.

"It was long ago," the woman said sadly. "Now he cannot teach anyone."

"You have helped him in his work?" inquired Singing Wolf.

"Yes, of course."

"You know the steps?"

"Yes, Uncle. The ceremonies. *He* knows the ceremonies, but his body, his legs will not let him do them. Still, what you need is someone who knows how to work in the herd!"

"In the herd? Buffalo herd?"

Wolf now remembered. He had never seen it done, but had heard of this special skill. It had been part of the buffalo medicine. A young holy man, dressed in a calf skin, would enter the edge of a herd. By his antics, he could maneuver a number of animals into a vulnerable position. They could then be hunted or driven over a cliff . . .

The hunt on horseback had eliminated the need for this highly specialized and highly dangerous work.

"Your husband knows how to do that?" Wolf asked in amazement.

"Of course. He learned it as a young man. It is part of the buffalo medicine. It is no longer used, though."

"Yes, I know."

"You had not thought to use it now, this season?"

"No, I had not. We only sought his advice. As you have said, we need many skins before winter."

"That is true. But I only wanted to tell you how it is, Uncle. As you see, he cannot help."

Wolf nodded. "You have no family, Mother?"

"That is true. I only look after White Buffalo. A little longer . . ."

"Who hunts for your lodge?"

She chuckled. "*Aiee,* we *have* no lodge. But there are those who remember, who share their kills. My husband was once a greatly respected man!"

Again, Singing Wolf was embarrassed and ashamed. He had not realized the plight of this proud woman and her failing husband. He must find a way to help them, without offending their pride.

The two men walked in silence for some time, and finally Pipe Bearer spoke.

"The woman understands the need."

"Yes. But that is no help, Pup. I am made to think that she is right, though. One of the old hunts, a drive over the cliff, like the one at Medicine Rock. Yet White Buffalo . . . *aiee,* his body and his spirit are both very weak."

"Uncle, I have seen that when one begins to lose his spirit in this way, it is mostly for things not long ago."

"That is true, Pup. But . . ."

"Wait! Hear me. His memory of the buffalo medicine may still be as good as ever."

"True. But he cannot do it. His body is feeble."

"But he can *teach,* Uncle!"

"There is no one to . . . *aiee! You?*"

"Why not?"

"No, no, Pipe Bearer. You are a holy man. You have learned well. It is not good to risk that knowledge."

"What good is it if the People die when Cold Maker comes?"

"But you have a new wife!"

"That is true. A wife who will understand what I must do."

"No, I cannot let you. And we do not even know if White Buffalo remembers."

"Yes, but what he forgets, his wife will know. She has helped him. She knows the cadences, the songs. And she is wise."

"But does she know how to work the buffalo herd?"

"Ah, does anyone? If there is one who can tell us, it is this woman."

Grass Woman was dubious.

"I am made to think not," she said. "I remember the training of our son. It was two seasons, and he was not ready yet at the time of his death."

"But look, Mother," Pipe Bearer pleaded. "I am not just beginning. I have studied the medicine of my grandfather. I would not have to begin over. All that is needed is to learn to work the herd."

"*All* that is needed!" snorted the woman. "There are only a few moons before we must have the hunt. There is not time."

"And no time to kill a thousand buffalo without this," retorted Pipe Bearer.

"But it is too dangerous!"

"As dangerous as freezing?"

"*Aiee!* It is not the same!"

They argued long and hard, and gradually they came to agreement. At least partially. Then it was necessary to convince old White Buffalo. Most of the convincing was left to his wife, Grass Woman.

They took Yellow Moccasin, the band chieftain, into their confidence early in the game.

"It is good," he agreed. "I had seen this as a hard winter. It still may be. Now, how can we help?"

"I can think of nothing for now," Singing Wolf told him. "Later, we will need the help of the wolves and the Elk-dog Society, maybe, to help position the herd."

"You are thinking of Medicine Rock for the place?" asked the chief.

"We had not talked of that. It has been used before."

"It is good. For now, as we travel, we will move in that direction."

"But not too close!" Singing Wolf warned.

"No, no. I understand. And meanwhile, the wolves will range wide. We must know where the buffalo are, which way they move."

"It is good," agreed Singing Wolf.

"Let us keep closely informed," said Moccasin. "Come to me at any time."

It seemed that at least the leadership of the Southern band was in good hands.

To the surprise of them all, the old man seemed eager to begin. Possibly the urgency of the present situation had broken through his resentment and bitterness. However, much of the credit must probably be given to Grass Woman. She had patiently and gently convinced the old keeper of the buffalo medicine. These people were here to help him, not to steal the power of his gift. Day by day she had repeated this logic. When the time came that she felt he was ready, she talked to Singing Wolf, Pipe Bearer, and Yellow Moccasin.

"It is time," she told them. "I hope he is ready."

And so he was. Even Grass Woman was startled at his clarity of thought and his understanding. Maybe this was the best thing that could have happened for him . . . To be needed.

32

»» »» »»

Sometimes old White Buffalo seemed young and eager and alert as he taught. At other times he was forgetful, and confused. There were days when he did not seem even to recognize his frustrated pupil. The old man would ramble nonsensically, calling Pipe Bearer by names of people from the past, young men long since grown old. Names which meant nothing to the listener.

"He is like that sometimes," the wife of the buffalo priest apologized. "Let me talk to him."

Sometimes that was helpful, sometimes not. The frustration was made worse for them all by the knowledge that there was not much time. The long hot days of the Red Moon were almost upon them.

"Maybe," suggested Yellow Moccasin, "we will have a good hunt anyway, without the buffalo medicine."

The young chief had been taken into their confidence early, and had been very helpful. It was he who had suggested that they not make public their plans. There was too much possibility of failure, though they carefully avoided mention of that. To voice such an idea would only tempt the spirits, no?

Singing Wolf constantly prayed, sang his ritual songs of supplication, and sought assistance. This plan would be critical to the survival of the Southern band as a power in the political influence among the People. Possibly, to their survival at all . . .

"Or maybe we could winter with the Eastern band," suggested Yellow Moccasin.

The others chuckled, glad to know that their leader could retain a sense of humor in such a time of crisis. It was apparent, of course, that he could not be serious. For the proud Southern band to take shelter with the foolish people of the Eastern band . . . *Aiee!* There *are* limits to what one may endure.

So they traveled toward Medicine Rock, deliberately casual, so as not to draw attention to the plan that would become critical to the band's survival. The wisdom of Singing Wolf, aided by his medicine, was carefully heeded by Yellow Moccasin. The young chief announced when to move and in what direction as casually as if it made no difference. Yet each step was carefully planned.

It would be necessary, as the critical time drew near, for Pipe Bearer to have access to small bands of buffalo. For that purpose, Singing Wolf was carefully observing the condition of the grass. Where would the great herds be likely to come? And *when?*

As bad as some days were for White Buffalo, there were good ones too. Sometimes, Pipe Bearer thought, the man seemed bright and alert and highly intelligent. The old eyes would sparkle with interest and in a short while Pipe Bearer would be able to gain an immense quantity of information about the buffalo and their ways. And that was good, because one fact was apparent to each of the handful of people who knew of the plan. Pipe Bearer must learn, in a space of two or three moons, the body of skills which would normally take that number of years.

Exceptionally helpful in all of this was the wife of White Buffalo. It did not require many days to see that here was an exceptionally capable woman. Grass Woman understood from the first what was needed, and why. Pipe Bearer realized that much of the effectiveness of the old man's buffalo medicine had been due to the skill of this woman. He pondered to what extent Grass Woman had taken over the spirit-gift of White Buffalo, and when.

The woman was very modest and unassuming about it, as was befitting. She seemed to wish no prestige or recognition, but only support for her husband. White Buffalo had had another wife, it seemed, one nearer his own age. They had had two children, a boy and a girl. The boy was killed in a hunting accident before he married. The girl was now grown and with her own lodge and children.

It took a little longer to learn that the first wife had been a sister of Grass Woman. When the terrible spotted sickness struck the Southern band many seasons ago, Grass Woman, then a young woman, had been orphaned. She had joined her sister's lodge as a second wife, a not uncommon custom among the People. Apparently there had been no children of that union.

Now Grass Woman seemed extremely devoted to her husband. She had a way of gently guiding him into what might be necessary for him to function in the effort at hand. On days when he seemed confused and forgetful, she quietly placed familiar objects near him or in his hands. This seemed to reorient him to reality.

At least sometimes. On some days nothing worked, and Grass Woman would sadly shake her head in despair. On those days, she would take over the instruction herself occasionally.

"The White Buffalo Dance is not too important for what you will need," she told him. "You have seen it, no? Almost like the Buffalo Dance of the Bowstring Society. They wear the capes of the buffalo, and mimic all of his motions. The slow steps, swaying of the head, stamp of feet . . . The main difference is the white cape. But I am made to think that you do not need that anyway."

"That is not the buffalo medicine?" he asked.

"Well, yes, but not the part you need. Look, you only need to move the herd, no? To where they can be driven over the cliff? Besides," she chuckled, "I do not think that my husband would let you use the white cape anyway. And it is not used to move the herd."

"Then how . . . ?"

"I will try to let him tell you," Grass Woman said. "I am made to think that he cannot *show* you. It requires much bending and stooping, and . . ." She paused, her eyes moistening. "His bones are stiff," she continued. "My heart is heavy to see him so. But it is something you must learn yourself anyway."

She wiped away a tear.

There came days, however, when the woman would meet him with a bright smile.

"My husband is good today. Let us do all we can."

On those days, Pipe Bearer could see how dynamic a man this had once been. Though the office of White Buffalo had diminished in importance, he had once been a major factor in the band. It was sad to see.

The old man was still somewhat confused as to just who Pipe Bearer might be and why he sought only a part of the expertise of the buffalo.

"There is no easy way!" he protested.

"I do not seek an easy way, Uncle," Pipe Bearer protested. "Only the right way."

"You are called Pipe Bearer?"

"Yes, Uncle."

Grass Woman interrupted for a moment. "You remember, my husband? We spoke of that. This is the grandson of the holy man, Singing Wolf. This one earned the name by saving the medicine pipe."

"Oh, yes! I remember now. Well, so be it. And you wish to learn."

"Yes, Uncle. We must have a big hunt to furnish lodge covers . . ."

"Yes, yes," White Buffalo interrupted, "I remember now. Yes . . . Now, you have had your vision quest?"

"Of course, Uncle."

"It is good!"

Sometimes it became so slow and painful that it was like starting over each day. *And this is one of the good days,* Pipe Bearer would think sarcastically.

But there was usually a little progress.

"You remember," the old man said, "how you could get inside the heads of other creatures? On your vision quest?"

"Yes . . . That was helped by fasting."

"And so it is here. You will need to fast for this. And you have to get inside their heads . . . The buffalo. You must become one of them."

"*Become* one?"

"Yes! Here, Grass, show him the cape."

"The *cape?*"

"Not the white cape," Grass Woman explained. "This. You will wear this."

She unrolled a soft yellowish calf skin. There were thongs attached to the legs and to the cape which would fit over a man's head and shoulders. It was made to be worn.

"You must be a calf," the old man said. "You must watch the actions of the calves, how they play, how the cows and yearlings act toward them. Then you use their actions to move them where you want."

Pipe Bearer's heart sank. There was little opportunity to watch calves now. There were some scattered bands of buffalo across the plains, but the People would be hunting them. The animals would be disturbed and wild. And so little time. How could he possibly learn the skills needed?

"But Uncle, I . . ."

Grass Woman raised a hand to silence him. "Never mind. I will help you. I have seen this many times."

Aiee! That might be, but how could he learn enough to accomplish what he must in so short a time? And the danger . . . How could he, a new husband, have become involved in such a situation? The whole thing looked hopeless.

•   •   •   •

"Yes," Singing Wolf told him. "I remember now. I have seen it done. You know how, when a calf cries out, all the cows rush to defend it? Not just its own mother. And it is that which you use."

"I must watch this some more," Pipe Bearer said. "Yes, I have seen the defense by the cows."

He tried to sound more confident than he really felt. The idea of walking into the herd and among the great animals gave him a very uneasy feeling. And to be bent over, almost on all fours, in a vulnerable position, unable to defend himself or to flee . . . He could not remove from his mind the nagging vision of a great broad forehead covered with dark wool and framed by shiny black horns. He broke into a nervous sweat at the thought. But as he had said, he would watch from a distance at first. He must be completely familiar with the actions of cows and calves in their undisturbed state.

It was several days, however, before the opportunity rose. The wolves reported a small herd, no more than forty or fifty animals, in a little valley near their line of travel. There was a flurry of activity, as hunters prepared to take a few kills. But Yellow Moccasin called a hasty council.

"This is as we wished to have it," he explained. "We need this herd to be undisturbed. Our brother, Pipe Bearer, will perform some of his medicine with this small herd to cause more to come to us. So, be it known: no one is to approach this band of buffalo. Maybe later, but this is important for now. No one is to hunt on his own in this herd. This is a rule of the council, and will be enforced by the Bowstring Society. I have spoken!"

And so it was.

33

»»»

Pipe Bearer sat in semi-concealment on the slope above the herd. He was alone. Otter Woman had offered to accompany him, but he had refused. He knew that he must concentrate his full attention on the matter at hand. Otter would have provided a distraction which he did not have the strength to resist.

"Just watch the calves," White Buffalo had told him. "You will understand."

He had arrived shortly after dawn, and found a place among the stems of sumac on the hillside. It was not necessary to be completely concealed. At this distance, two or three bow shots, the vision of the buffalo was not very acute. Their sense of smell was quite another matter. He had chosen his position very carefully, downwind from the grazing animals to avoid alarming them.

He watched a group of crows, some five or six birds, as they gracefully made their way across the valley toward a distant line of trees along a small watercourse. A doe and twin fawns, cautious and alert, grazed on the slope below him. In contrast to the relatively poor eyesight of the buffalo, the deer could see distant objects with the ability of the eagle. The doe spread her ears wide, adjusting them to the slightest sound.

Again Pipe Bearer pondered the differences. Both are grazing animals. The deer depends on sight and hearing, the buffalo on smell. It is their way. Smell, and numbers. The sheer numbers of the great herds would be protection. In time of danger they would run. A few of the slower and weaker would fall to a bear or a wolf pack. The stronger and more healthy would survive to run another day.

But just now he must be aware of the calves. He drew his attention back to the herd. A movement on the far hill distracted him for only a moment . . . a coyote, trotting lazily along the ridge. A morning hunt . . . Mentally, he wished the animal good hunting. It was a good sign for Pipe Bearer, his medicine animal. He breathed a brief prayer that his own effort might go well today.

Now he settled into a serious concentration on the little herd. the day was still pleasant, though it would be uncomfortably hot later. The herd, now . . .

There were two or three old cows that appeared to be the leaders of the herd. Twenty-some younger cows . . . Some of those were followed by yearling calves. Most of the females of breeding age seemed to have a calf of this season, easily identified not only by size but by their lighter yellowish color.

Two . . . no, three herd bulls. Two of magnificent size, one slightly smaller and younger. One of the old bulls seemed slow and thin, past his prime. This season or next, the younger bulls would probably drive him away. Pipe Bearer had once watched one of these old bulls, alone, no longer able to move fast enough to defend himself. A circling family of wolves had been harassing the venerable old monarch, nipping at his heels, stalking, watching, preventing him from taking food or water . . . It was only a matter of time.

Pipe Bearer turned his attention to the younger animals. He must observe their actions. The younger of the adult bulls was quite active, moving among the young cows and yearlings, sniffing . . . One or more of the cows must be in season, and the bull was searching . . . The other, larger bull rushed at the younger, diverting attention from the cows. The sheer size and massive strength of such an animal was impressive.

Still, he knew that when the time came for him to move within the herd, the danger was not so much from the bulls. Unless provoked, they were unlikely to be aggressive.

The cows were another matter. Their total activity revolved around the welfare of their young. And this was what Pipe Bearer must learn. He saw that as the herd grazed, most of the calves were bedded down in a group. In two groups actually, eight or ten calves in each. One cow . . . no, the larger group of calves had two cows watching over them. It was as if by agreement. A mother accepted the duty for a while, as the others wandered some distance away to feed. Then one would return, seek out her own calf, and relieve the sentry to go and graze in turn.

Then he saw a moving shadow. A young wolf, probably this year's litter, was creeping forward on its belly toward one of the calves. Pipe Bearer wondered why it should be alone. It would normally be running with the family pack. Maybe this individual had been separated somehow . . .

The calf which seemed to be the quarry of the young wolf was bedded down at the extreme edge of the herd. It was curled in the fetal position, head tucked in its left flank, apparently asleep.

The wolf crept closer, moving ever so slowly, and Pipe Bearer was entranced by the scene before him. He could see the yellow eyes, fixed unmoving on the helpless calf. Now, a sudden rush . . .

The calf scrambled to its feet, bawling in terror, the wolf pup's jaws fastened on a hind leg. Instantly the watching cow whirled and rushed at the intruder. And not only that cow. From every direction came the rush. Every mother recognizes the cry of an infant in distress, and it is not different with other species. In the space of a heartbeat the young wolf was facing a forbidding array of sharp black horns. He tried to retreat, attempting to slip between the angry buffalo. The tip of a horn caught his flank and he was tossed, to land with a yelp, running hard. Still one more time he was struck. An old cow came at him, rushing and pounding at the squirming form with stiffened forelegs. Even at this distance and amid the bawling and confusion, Pipe Bearer could hear the impact . . . thud . . . thud . . . thud. It must have been on the third or fourth pounding strike that one of the cow's hooves struck the pup. It was apparently a glancing blow, not a lethal one. Fur flew, the wolf yelped in pain and scrabbled away, limping on a hind leg. He was still limping but running hard as he crossed the ridge a hundred paces to Pipe Bearer's left. The cows pursued only a few steps. Then they turned back to seek their own calves and complete the mothering-up process that would reassure each that all was well after the emergency.

The scene had had a profound effect on Pipe Bearer. It was apparent that in a short while he, disguised in a calf skin, must be moving *within* such a herd. He would have no means of self-defense. If he were perceived as a threat, he would be subjected to exactly the treatment that the wolf had received. *Aiee!*

He took a deep breath, unsure whether he could manage. A wrong move, a moment of panic, and it would be over. How had he managed to become involved in this way? It was a useless question that he asked himself, because he already knew the answer. He would do this thing because he must, for the good . . . No, possibly for the *survival* of the Southern band of the People.

"But the cows will not see *you* as an enemy," Grass Woman explained. "You are the calf, to be protected!"

"*Aiee,* how do *they* know that?"

"Because you have *shown* them. You must think like a calf. Get inside their heads. *Move* as one of them. Then they will protect you from any danger. Once they do that, you can move them where you wish. You pretend to be a calf in trouble, and they will follow you."

Grass Woman had gone into much more detail than her husband. It was one of his bad days, and he seemed not to understand.

"You know these things," White Buffalo had insisted. "I taught you, many years ago."

It was no use to argue. The old man was confusing Pipe Bearer with someone else. Probably his lost son, his understudy so many years ago. Fortunately, Grass Woman was able to intervene. At least, to the extent that she could help Pipe Bearer to understand the principles involved. Once more, the young man was impressed by the wisdom of this woman.

"I am made to think," she told him, "that you want to go too fast. Wear the skin, move around the edges of the herd. Watch the other calves, do as they do."

The *other* calves? *Yes*, he finally realized, *I must think of it in that way.*

He went back to the meadow again, and tied his horse. He had brought the calf skin, and carried it with him to his place of concealment in the sumac thicket. He did not yet put it on. More observation was needed.

It was the cool of evening this time, and the calves were playful. They raced and bucked and played, butting heads and pushing each other around. Several times he saw calves attempt to nurse a dam not their own. This was corrected by a gentle kick or a nudge from the offended cow. The calf would jump quickly aside and retreat. He began to notice that the cow never made a move to pursue the errant calf. It was as if a calf might be mildly chastised for an honest mistake, but with no hard feelings.

Pipe Bearer began to see how this could be used. Now he was eager, interested, and impatient to begin.

He glanced at the lowering sun. Not long until dark. But there should be a moon. Yes, he would try it.

Pipe Bearer quickly donned the calf skin, tying the thongs to wrists and ankles. It was not easy on the wrist ties, but he managed, by holding one end of the thong with his teeth. Then he stooped and made his way down the slope.

It was not easy to walk in this manner, crouched almost double in an effort to look like a calf. He tried to make his gait look believable too. Amble slowly, pause to nose at the ground, jump around a little when he encountered another calf.

Once he almost panicked as a large bull calf playfully challenged him to a pushing match. He could not match the strength of the animal's push, but resisted for a little. Then he slid aside, allowing the calf to brush past him. He had seen the calves use this device to avoid pursuit. *When the weaker concedes, there is no further pursuit,* he noted.

It must be admitted that there by the light of the rising moon, Pipe Bearer began to enjoy his new understanding. Soon he was moving freely among the animals, even venturing to brush against the flank of an unsuspecting cow occasionally. A massive head would swing, but now he began to see . . . that was only a reprimand, as a mother might correct her child. It was not intended to do harm.

He wanted to stay longer, but knew that Otter Woman would be concerned. He worked his way out to the edge of the herd and slipped away.

His back was tired and stiff as he stripped away the calf skin and walked to where he had left his horse below the hill. But he felt a great satisfaction. He could hardly wait to tell Otter. And next time, he would try it in daylight.

34

》》》

"**B**ut my husband, there must be much danger in this!"
Otter protested.

She had taken great pleasure in calling him "my husband" since
their marriage. It was a personal thing between them, a delicious
private joke. At the same time, it was an announcement of her
pride in her new status, brought about by their union.

Neither of them could yet quite believe their good fortune. All
their lives they had been friends, looking forward to this time
when they would be together. Now it had happened. All of their
pretending as children had come to reality. Part of the beauty of it
was the sharing of the little personal jokes that were half teasing
and half love.

"My husband . . ." Otter Woman had waited for a lifetime to
call him that, to announce such status publicly.

Yet all was not as they had imagined it. The problems of the
Southern band had fallen on the new couple with a vengeance.
They had no lodge of their own, but that was not unusual. Most
couples started their lives together in the lodge of relatives. Usu-

ally, that of the bride's mother. In this case it was different. First, in that their marriage was to begin in the lodge of the holy man and his wife. That in itself was no problem except that now, they had no lodge. Neither did Otter's parents, nor the parents of Pipe Bearer, nor virtually anyone else.

There will always be problems, and just as surely, they will always be unexpected. Looking for troubles, trying to anticipate and avoid them, is useless. The ones about which we worry seldom come to pass. They are replaced by others, of which we never dreamed. It was almost amusing to Otter Woman sometimes, the way in which she had envisioned her marriage to her childhood sweetheart. Everything would be perfect. Their lodge, their love, their every moment together.

Instead, there was no lodge, not even a borrowed one or a bed in that of a relative. Their moments together were scarce, because of the urgency of Pipe Bearer's learning. There was the ever present worry of the danger to him.

One thing that they did have, of course, was their love. If one must be limited to a very few possessions in a new marriage, certainly a bed must rank high on the list of necessities. In this case, sleeping robes. Snuggled together for warmth in the cool of the prairie nights, whispering together in private intimacy . . . There was little that could threaten them then, for a little while.

It was out of that amusing contradiction, maybe, that Otter Woman had begun to call him "my husband." It was a public announcement of her satisfaction with life, of a defiant challenge to any problem that might arise. There was a touch of wry humor too. Otter realized that there would come a time when she would tell her grandchildren of their early marriage, and they would all laugh about it.

Just now, it was not easy to see the humor. There was too much danger in what Pipe Bearer was doing, and it was a matter of great concern to Otter. She had been ready and willing to accept the sacrifices that fall to the wife of a holy man. She understood, and had no problem with such a lifetime. But the risks that he must take with this buffalo medicine . . . *Aiee!* That had not been in the bargain!

"There is really not much danger," Pipe Bearer assured her. "Look . . . horses almost never injure their young. Buffalo do not either."

"That is fine," Otter said, with a little irritation, "if you are a young buffalo!"

"Yes, I know, Otter. But you know that this is what I must do."

She softened. "Yes, I know, my husband. But you will be careful? It bothers me that you are *enjoying* this danger."

"Ah! I had not thought of it that way. No, Otter. I am made to think it is not the danger that I enjoy. That would be . . . Well, disloyal to you. I would not . . ."

She held up a hand. "I know, Pup. Say no more. Only be careful."

He nodded. "I promise. But let me tell you. It is not the danger, but the *success*, that feels good. You do something that turns out right, and it is good. That is what I am feeling."

Otter seemed confused. "But you have not yet . . ."

"I know, I know. It will be some time yet. But Otter, I can walk among them, and they accept me! You should see!" He paused. "Yes, you *could!* I will show you."

"*Aiee*, is this wise, my husband?"

"Of course! You can watch from the hillside. Then you can see that there is little danger!"

They rode out the next day. It had been decided to stay in this camp for a few days to permit Pipe Bearer to work with the herd. Since it was going well, Yellow Moccasin suggested, let it continue. Hunters had made a few kills in other areas, and there was no urgency to move on.

Pipe Bearer and Otter hobbled their horses on the near side of the ridge, allowing them to graze.

"Will they not cry out, and alarm the buffalo?" asked Otter.

"I am made to think not. They are far away, and anyway, there are always a few wild horses. Buffalo do not fear horses, and these have not been hunted by men on horses."

He carefully placed Otter among the sumacs, donned the calf skin cape, and made his way down into the bowl-like valley. The herd was some distance away, several bow shots.

"You cannot see well from here," he had told her. "I will bring them."

"*Aiee! Bring* them?"

"It is what I am learning to do, Otter. This will see if I am *really* learning."

He approached the herd and initiated play with some of the calves. He could now recognize individuals among them. He chose a small but aggressive female calf that had played with him before. This one was a bit darker in color than most, a reddish hue. She appeared to be the daughter of one of the old lead cows. Maybe she, too, would be a leader someday, if she survived to maturity.

Come here, Red, he thought at the young heifer. *Let us play!*

For a little while he trotted around, pushing, butting, and behaving as calves do. Then he retreated away from the herd, enticing his playmate. The calf stood staring for a little while, and then loped after him.

A low mutter of warning from the old dam seemed to make it prudent to pause. A little more play . . . He was working his way toward a dense clump of brush in a low spot, where he might find concealment.

He slipped into that cover and watched his erstwhile playmate for a moment. The calf stood stiff-legged, staring in confusion at the brushy spot where her playmate had vanished.

Now . . . Pipe Bearer cupped his hands around his face and uttered a short, staccato bleat of fright. He had practiced this cry for help many times, well away from the herd and from any human observer. This was its first real trial.

Response was immediate and quite impressive. Several cows came pounding toward him and then paused, confused. They could see the red calf standing alone, but seemingly not threatened. But then the powerful protective instincts of the bovine mother began to come to the fore. There had been a cry for help. Here stood a calf, staring at something unseen in the thicket. It must be . . .

The old lead cow charged into the brush before Pipe Bearer realized the danger. It was perhaps fortunate that he did not have time to take any action. If he had jumped up or tried to run . . . *Aiee!*

He curled himself into a form as small as possible, drawing the cape over as much of his body as he could. The cow nearly stepped on him, jumped *over* him, and whirled, still looking for the unknown predator that had caused the cry for help. She thrust her face close to him and he could feel the hot breath of her angry snort. The cow's nose, wet and shiny, was within a hand's breadth of his face. She nudged him a time or two, shook her head threateningly, and stepped back, confused.

Pipe Bearer breathed a cautious sigh of relief. It was not over yet, but he did have time to think now. It had not occurred to him that the protective reaction must be directed toward an enemy. Here, there was none. A calf in trouble. A very strange calf, to be sure. One which was misshapen and which smelled very strange. But a calf is a calf and must be protected with all the instinctive aggression of the ages since Creation.

The confused cows were calming somewhat now. One ventured to take a nervous bite of grass, and they began to draw back. The lead cow stepped over to smell and nose the figure curled in the bushes once more. She gave a deep, sighing snort, and turned away.

It was some time before the animals drifted away. They were grazing, and grazing animals in good grass do not find it necessary to move around much. Time passed very slowly for Pipe Bearer. The red calf finally wandered off to follow its mother, but he was reluctant to move. He wondered what the old cow had thought as she nosed him. *A dead calf?* At least, not hers. A calf that no longer needed help.

He had learned a valuable lesson. It was the first time that he had used the distress cry, and its effect had been little short of astonishing. If it worked as well when its use was essential to the success of the great hunt, that too should go well.

One thing he should have realized, though. When he, acting as a calf in danger, gave that little bleat of terror, he should have planned better where he would go to avoid the rush of the defending cows. They had nearly trampled him in their eagerness to save him.

This would take some thought. And what would happen to him when the real hunt happened? How was he to avoid being pushed over the cliff with the herd?

He finally rose and moved toward where Otter Woman still waited on the hill. He stood to remove the cape and work the stiffness from his back. He had spent a long time in the cramped and unmoving position.

Otter came running to meet him.

"*Aiee*, Pup, I feared for you! I nearly came to see if you were hurt!"

"It is good that you did not," he laughed. "They would have thought that *you* were the danger to me."

Her eyes were sparkling with admiration now.

"You were wonderful, my husband. I can see now how it works. You can move them where you wish!"

"Ah, I hope so, Otter."

"But only a few cows came to you. How do the great numbers be killed?"

"The hunters drive the ones behind, and crowd those near the edge."

"Oh . . ."

She said little more, but he could tell what she was thinking. What happens to the man in the calf skin, who is nearer the edge than any when the stampede starts?

The next day when he went again to the little valley, the herd was nowhere to be seen. They had moved on. It had been intended that after his period of learning and instruction, this small herd could be hunted.

He considered for a moment trying to track the moving buffalo, but then abandoned the idea. He felt that he owed this particular band a great deal. He knew individual animals intimately, their likes and dislikes. This one steady and dependable, that one flighty and unpredictable. Had he not been inside their heads to know how they thought and felt? And the calves, his playmates . . .

He stood looking across the wide prairie toward the horizon, but could not see them. It was as if this little herd had never existed. Or maybe just for the short while, when he needed them. Whatever, they had served their purpose well.

"May it go well with you, my brothers," he said softly, as he turned back toward his horse.

35
» » »

$\mathbf{A}$s it happened, nothing could have been better than the disappearance of the little herd. Singing Wolf, long an expert in the swaying of public opinion, managed to suggest in a subtle way that there was involved something mystical and of the spirit.

He did not actually *say* so. There is a power in suggestion beyond any that may be seen. Fear of the dark is rooted in the unknown, the unseen terrors that *might* be lurking there. Mankind can adjust to almost any fear if we know what it is. Sunlight sends the terrors of the night fleeing, because even the worst of them may be avoided if they are identified. This is why some stories are at their best when told only at night. The circle of firelight is barely able to push back the shadows far enough for relative comfort. Who knows what might lie beyond?

The reverse side of this principle of human nature deals with that which may be good, though we do not understand it. Much of the task of a holy man is in interpretation of his gifts of the spirit to his followers. Not a complete explanation, but a hint here and there. A complete explanation of the ways of God would be impossible anyway, because of the finite nature of the mind of man. Even if the explanation were possible, man could not understand it. More marvelous things may be imagined than can be described, at best. A mere suggestion here and there is the expertise of a skilled holy man of any faith.

It was so with Singing Wolf and the Southern band. There was no major public announcement. There were those who were disappointed that there was to be no hunt of the herd where Pipe Bearer had been working his skills. When the question arose, there were hints that somehow the disappearance of that herd had been linked to the buffalo medicine. No one *said* so. It was only that the hunting of those animals had been forbidden. Then Pipe Bearer had spent a part of each day with them. Some special ritual . . . Then they had disappeared. It must be part of the medicine, no?

Some whispered that maybe it had not been a real buffalo herd at all, but a vision. A spirit-herd called temporarily from the Other Side, maybe. After all, who had even *seen* that herd? A couple of the wolves. Beyond that, only the holy men and once, it was said, Yellow Moccasin. Whatever the nature of that herd, its presence appeared to have been successful. The band's leaders and holy men all seemed pleased.

Rumors flew, of course. This small herd had been given instructions by means of the special medicine of Pipe Bearer. Maybe they would cross over and bring back many more. Maybe the herd had been sent on ahead, to reproduce and multiply en route to the Fall Hunt. A spirit-buffalo might not require nine moons to produce a calf, no?

On the other hand, some argued, can the skins of spirit-animals be used for lodge covers? Who knows?

Yellow Moccasin, well aware of the gossip and rumor, called a council for the purpose of deciding to move. He announced blandly and at the beginning that the special tasks required of Pipe Bearer had been accomplished. No one knew what those tasks might have been. But as they were unknown, they were now magnified in the imagination. The tasks took on more and more of a magical quality in the telling. Soon it was said that a successful Fall Hunt was virtually assured. It was due to this that a move was advisable. Why tempt the spirits? A move would provide a distraction, and possibly even quiet some of the speculation.

A move under the present circumstances required much less effort than usual. The personal effects and baggage of the People were at a minimum because of their losses. The heavy part of the work involved in a move was the handling of the lodges. Heavy poles, heavy lodge skins . . . Where there are no lodges, such chores are nonexistent, though this is not a good trade-off. Nonetheless, the Southern band was ready to travel soon after sunrise the morning after the decision by the council.

Probably no council would have been required. Yellow Moccasin could simply have announced the move. But for a young leader, Moccasin was showing a remarkable amount of diplomatic skill. Why not allow the subchiefs to participate in the decision? Having had a part in it, they would be more supportive in any problems that might arise.

Besides, a vote in the council allowed them a certain prestige and recognition. This would not be forgotten. Their loyalty to Yellow Moccasin would be strengthened, and the band would become stronger.

It was on the second day of travel that the weather changed. The air had been heavy and hot. Only at night did the prairie cool enough for real comfort. During the day people and animals appeared greasy with sweat that would not dry. Occasionally the breeze stirred for a little while, cooling the moist skin, and that was good. Dark patches on sweat-stained buckskins became white-ringed spots as the drying perspiration left a thin crust of salt behind.

The prairie streams slowed, and although water had not yet become a problem, it was apparent that it *could* be so. There were still deep pools, even along the smaller watercourses which had ceased to flow entirely until they could be replenished. The wolves ranged a little wider, to make certain that each night's camp would have access to water for people and horses. A herd of perhaps a thousand horses required a great amount of water.

These precautions were really not considered with any degree of urgency. It is only common sense when one travels in late summer. Besides, the area where they were going in the Sacred Hills was known for its large springs and streams. Medicine Rock itself towered over the river, which had always had a dependable flow. Once called the Sycamore by the People, its name had now become the Medicine River after the powerful events that had occurred there. They would strike the river several days' travel downstream from the Rock, and then there would be water in plentiful supply.

So no one was really concerned yet. It was only for creature comfort that they began to long for a rain. The damp and sweaty atmosphere made each day's travel seem longer and more exhausting by the time for the evening camp.

On the day before the storm it had been noted that there was some change in the making. During the afternoon the high thin clouds had been replaced by sky of brightest blue. But in the distance the People could see the rapid growth of towering white columns.

"Rain Maker taunts us," an old woman said. "There is no rain in those!"

"That is true," said another. "But they tell of change! It will come!"

"Look how the swallows fly low," said another as they made evening camp.

And yet a little later, when twilight had fallen and the coyotes began to sing, it was noted that their song sounded clear and close.

"Did you see Sun Boy's dogs?" Singing Wolf asked his assistant. "It will rain within three days."

Pipe Bearer had noticed the bright spots of light just before sunset, one on each side of the sun as it sank. He had mixed feelings about the unmistakable signs of coming change. It would be more comfortable, of course, to have a cooler weather pattern.

But he doubted that some of the People realized what they were hoping. Cooling rain might sound pleasant to one who is hot and sticky in sweat-soaked buckskins. But even a cooling rain is wet, and the People had virtually no shelter. There were only a few lodges in the whole band. That, of course, was the entire purpose of the special hunt which would ready the Southern band for winter. It is easy to forget, in warm weather when the rain has stopped, how uncomfortable it is to be wet and cold.

The first warning of the coming storm came from the wolves. One of them rode back to meet the column and explain the situation to Yellow Moccasin. They had seen a low, gray-blue cloud bank from the ridge ahead. It lay to the northwest, stretching for a considerable distance across the horizon.

"How far away?" asked the young chief.

"Maybe a day's travel. Maybe farther. But we are made to think that it is traveling fast."

Yellow Moccasin glanced at the sun. It was only a little past midday.

"It will be here today?" he asked.

"Oh, yes! Well before dark. There is a place where we might camp, over there." He pointed.

"Let us look, then!" Yellow Moccasin reined his horse aside and urged it ahead. "Keep moving," he called back to the travelers.

He was soon back, passing the word along the column. They would alter their course slightly to take advantage of an area of shelter, and would camp early. A storm was approaching.

"*Aiee!* Big Whirlwind?" cried a little girl.

"No, no, child," her mother comforted. "Not this time."

The camp site chosen by the wolves was a good one. There was a good stream with timber in a thin strip along its banks. That would furnish some shelter. Yet it was low-lying, and would not attract the spears of real-fire which Rain Maker loved to throw.

Already, they could hear the distant mutter of Rain Maker's drum as they hurried to establish camp. Not too near the stream . . . It could easily flood. Some improvised shelter . . . But first, fires. If everything were soaked by the rain, it would be hard to start the campfires. But once they were started, even wet wood could be used.

In a very short while, smoke drifted through the timber and along the creek. The air was still, waiting. People began to construct brush shelters and to tie such robes and skins as they might have over pole frames.

They were none too soon. There was a restless stirring in the still air, and a sudden coolness descended. People hurried to complete their makeshift shelters as the breeze quickened. Sparks, fanned by the rising wind, danced along the ground and threatened piles of belongings. But not for long.

The first fat drops of rain spattered on the skins of improvised shelters almost without warning. A flash of light, followed by the boom of thunder only a few heartbeats later . . . *Aiee, Rain Maker moves fast . . . run for cover!* A closer spear of real-fire, then another. Then one at almost the same instant as the crash of the thunder . . . The *smell* of Rain Maker's real-fire.

Then the sheets of water descended and the whole world turned gray. It was impossible to see more than a few paces. The fires which had not had time to become well established were smothered and drowned, and the others struggled to stay alive.

Pipe Bearer and Otter Woman huddled together under a robe which they held over their heads.

"The People wanted a change," Pipe Bearer remarked.

"Yes," Otter answered. "And it *is* cooler."

36
» » »

Medicine Rock. Its spirit reached ahead of it as the People approached the area. It was always so. Sometimes they camped within sight of its gray cliffs. There were no taboos, no reason to avoid the place, but few went there. Its spirit was too powerful. A young person on his or her vision quest, perhaps, as Pipe Bearer had done. Occasionally, a bold young warrior demonstrating his manhood. But for most, there was a hesitation. Not fear, exactly. It was more a feeling of inappropriate actions. One does not tread on sacred ground without good reason.

In this particular season, the Southern band discussed the coming hunt in council. Strict rules were laid down. The coming hunt would be so important to their welfare in the coming winter that *no one* must go near the Rock, except for the holy men. This would be strictly enforced.

There was some minor grumbling, but no real objection. The need was apparent. The camp of the band was some distance downstream, well out of sight of the Rock.

"If you happen to see it, you are too close," Yellow Moccasin warned. "Back away quickly, with apology to the spirits."

The entire importance of this approach was that nothing should intrude between the massive herd-spirit of the migrating buffalo and the powerful medicine of the Rock. Singing Wolf and Pipe Bearer spent much time in discussion.

"But Grandfather," the young man asked, "is it not wrong to camp downstream from where we hope to make the hunt?"

"Yes, it would be, *after* the hunt," the holy man agreed. "The water downstream would be fouled. But for now, we must try to keep the spirits of the Rock undisturbed. Our horses and our people must not affect the area at all. It might keep the herds away. We can move the camp upstream after the hunt."

Of course. That was logical. The camp would be better if it were nearer after the hunt, anyway. It would be easier to transport the great number of skins and the quantities of meat that they hoped to acquire. The results were not discussed, only the procedure.

The wolves would range widely to the north, hoping to locate the large migrating herds. At that point, the holy men would take charge of events. The wolves might make themselves seen by the buffalo to encourage the animals in the right direction, but that was all.

This morning, Singing Wolf and Pipe Bearer had gone to look at the Rock, to learn what they could of the terrain. It would be important to know in advance. They had come partway on horses, but left the animals hobbled as they neared the cliff. Now they stood at its foot, looking upward.

"I am made to think," Singing Wolf pondered, "that here is the area that has been used. Did you not tell me there are bones in the crevice there?"

"Yes, Uncle. I thought it so."

"Good. We must look at the top, then. *That* is the important part."

It took some time to climb the face of the cliff.

"*Aiee*," exclaimed Singing Wolf, "my bones are not as limber as they once were."

He was also breathing hard, and they stopped to rest before climbing higher. Finally, though, they reached the flat rim and stood for a moment to catch their breath.

"Now," Singing Wolf pointed, "we can see . . . Look, the herds will come from the north, that way. The cliff faces south. That is how an ancestor of ours wintered here, you know. See, how the winter sun would warm his cave?"

Pipe Bearer nodded. He had heard that story many times, but to *see* where it happened, and how the angle of the winter sun could be used . . .

"But we have more to think of," Singing Wolf said. "Now, if the lead cows come through that notch in the ridge, there . . . the wolves can direct them this way, and then you use your buffalo medicine."

Pipe Bearer was looking downward. It was a long way, and he did not relish the idea of coaxing the herd *toward* him at the very rim. Again he wondered . . . *Where* does the man wearing the calf skin go? How does he escape? Or does he? A thought struck him like a blow to the groin: *Is the one who calls the buffalo expected to . . . Aiee! Is that part of it?* Surely he would have heard . . . Would there not be stories?

He was about to ask Singing Wolf, who might or might not know. If not, maybe old White Buffalo could tell him.

It was then, as he visualized the rush of the herd over the edge of the rim, that his eyes fell upon the rock. It was a block of stone, partly pulled away from the shelf at the rim. There was a narrow crevice there, just large enough for a person to crouch . . . Yes, that must have been useful.

He looked around to orient himself. Yes, if the herd came from the north, there, gently urged along by the wolves . . . On the east, the crevice up which they had climbed. And right at the point where the crevice met the rim, this small hiding place!

But what would keep the herd coming, to push the leaders over the edge? White Buffalo had said something about people waving blankets and yelling. That must have been along the west side, there, or the herd would simply turn west along the rim and be gone.

He took a few steps in that direction. There appeared to be a clump of sumac . . . Could a person hide there? It would be dangerous, because a buffalo might easily run directly over a mere human waving a blanket. But he stepped a little closer. A rock formation . . . No! This had been a pile of stones! It was a hiding place that had been *built* for the purpose, now partially tumbled and overgrown. And there beyond, another, and another.

In an instant, he began to see the whole plan. This was a line of ancient hiding places, possibly used by the People long before the First Horse. The buffalo could be encouraged by people on foot, walking at a distance behind. Once there were a number of animals inside the corridor between these rock piles and the crevice, those at the north end could rise up and shout and wave blankets. He walked over to the crevice itself and yes, there were several natural hiding places there too.

"Grandfather," he called. "Look at this . . ."

Quickly, he pointed out his discoveries, and his theory as to their use.

"It was useful once," he said eagerly. "It could be again!"

"I am made to think that you are right, Pup. I had forgotten. Yes, the old men used to tell of these things."

"A little repair . . . A few stones here and there . . . Grandfather, this may be even more useful now than when it was new. The growth of sumac helps to hide the places."

"That is true. Did White Buffalo tell of this?"

"No, Uncle. He mentioned yelling and waving blankets or robes. Not the hiding places. You know, his spirit wanders sometimes."

"Of course," said old White Buffalo. "It is as I told you. The hiding places. Wave a blanket . . ."

"Yes, Uncle," Pipe Bearer answered. "It is as you said. But I did not think to find them. You have seen them used?"

The old man became suspicious.

"Of course," he said confidentially, "many times."

Pipe Bearer nodded. He was not certain whether White Buffalo actually remembered, or had merely talked to someone who remembered. Or did the old man *know*, anymore? He decided that it did not really matter much. It was obvious, the use of the stone hiding places.

They explained the situation to the chief, and the necessity to have a number of people for this dangerous part of the hunt.

"The Blood Society!" Yellow Moccasin said instantly. "They usually hunt or fight on horseback, but this will appeal to them. The Bloods are a little crazy anyway!"

"It is good!" said Singing Wolf. "Let us take one of them to show what is needed. Then he can tell the others. Who is their leader?"

"Lone Antelope, is it not?" the young chief asked.

He knows quite well, thought Pipe Bearer. *That is his way, not to appear haughty.*

"I will talk to him," Yellow Moccasin went on. "I will tell him to talk with you, Uncle. Then you can decide how and when you will show him."

"Do you wish to come with us?" asked Singing Wolf.

"No, no, Uncle. I am made to think that the fewer people who go to the Rock before the day of the hunt, the better it will be. I would like to see, yes. But it is more important that the spirits be left undisturbed. This is yours to say, not mine."

Singing Wolf smiled, pleased. "It is good," he said.

They watched the retreating young chief, the old holy man nodding his approval. "There," he said softly, "is a man wise beyond his years. He will be a great leader, Pup. He understands the things of the spirit."

Pipe Bearer took Lone Antelope to the rock the next day and showed him the hiding places.

"The wolves will follow the herd in from the north, there, very carefully," he explained.

The Blood warrior nodded. "And these rocks . . . ?"

"Yes, a man behind each pile. Maybe some along the crevice to the east, there. Then when the leaders are inside, here, the Bloods jump up and yell, wave blankets."

"I have heard of this. How do you get the herd to come this far?"

"That is my part. I call them to me."

"And where are you?"

"There. At the rim."

The eyes of Antelope widened. "*Aiee*," he said softly.

What was left unsaid was a great compliment to the young holy man. For the leader of the Blood Society, with their reputation for fearless courage, to recognize the situation and the danger faced by Pipe Bearer, and for him to be so impressed . . . It would be just as well not to mention the hiding place clear out on the rim. At least, for now.

"You think this is made to be?" asked Pipe Bearer.

"Of course. *Aiee*, it is a good plan! And who pushes the herd on from behind?"

"The wolves. They will push in closer as they come near."

"You will need more horsemen, Pipe Bearer. Look, no more than fifteen or twenty are needed here behind the rocks. The rest of the Bloods can ride in with the wolves."

"It is good. Thank you, my brother."

They had thought to have the horsemen of the Elk-dog Society for this part of the scheme.

"You have maybe twenty more Bloods?" he asked Antelope. "Maybe some Elk-dog warriors, too? And we should have some *below* the cliff, no?"

"It is good," answered the Blood leader. "Wherever we can be of help, Pipe Bearer."

On the way back to the camp, Antelope spoke again.

"Tell me, holy man, do you not study your grandfather's gifts?"

"That is true."

"But also this, the medicine of the buffalo?"

"Yes. White Buffalo has no apprentice, and his skill is needed, but he is too old."

"I see. Yes, it is true that the medicine of the buffalo has not been needed in recent seasons. The hunt has been good."

"Yes. But this time it was needed badly, no? I have wondered if this season, the Big Whirlwind may have been a warning. The buffalo medicine was nearly lost."

"So now you study *both?*"

"That is true."

"*Aiee!*"

That was Antelope's only comment, but it carried a great deal of respect.

37
»»»

Now there was nothing to do except wait for the buffalo to come. That was perhaps the hardest of all. All plans were made. Yellow Moccasin had talked to the Blood Society, whose tasks would be critical to the success of the effort.

Pipe Bearer had gone over his part in his mind a thousand times. He dreamed about it at night, and slept poorly. For a while he tried to interpret the significance of his visions, but that was futile. He was always, in his dream, wearing the calf skin cape, and the buffalo were rushing toward him. Then he would waken, sweating and terrified.

He went to his grandfather for help with the problem. Singing Wolf listened, nodded thoughtfully, and asked a few questions.

"Are you gored in this dream?"

"No, I . . ."

"Are you falling?"

"No."

"Are you afraid?"

"Yes, Uncle, that is it!"

"Good. It would be foolish not to be. Now, *what* do you fear? In the dream, I mean."

Pipe Bearer paused, uncertain. In his waking days, he feared many things. The charging buffalo, the height of the cliff, whether the plan would work . . . What if it did *not*, and the People had no shelter for the winter? But in the dream, it was all one. He could not say, could not identify that vague, free-floating fear which always brought him up short and jerked him out of his sleep to lie sweating in his robes.

"I . . . I cannot say, Uncle. There are many things that can go wrong."

Singing Wolf nodded, thoughtfully. "But I did not ask that. In your dream, what do you fear?"

"I . . . All of it, maybe!"

His grandfather nodded and puffed his pipe for a moment.

"When the time is nearer, I will cast the bones," he said. "For now, I am made to think that this is not a bad thing. There are many kinds of dreams, Pup. Some have great meaning. Some are just dreams. It would be strange if you were *not* having something like this, no?"

That helped some, but there were other concerns. Pipe Bearer visualized this hunt, the herds migrating from the north, arriving at the Rock to be pushed over the cliff. Something was wrong with the plan, and it took him some time to identify just what it was. The *wind*. Prevailing winds on the prairie are from the south. Even their neighbors, the Growers with whom the People often traded, called themselves "Kenzas," which in their own tongue means "South Wind People."

If the buffalo were moving south toward the cliff, they would be moving into the wind. They would easily catch the scent of the hidden Blood warriors behind the piles of stone. Yet there was no other way. The People had placed the camp far downstream to prevent the scent of humans from pervading the area. But was that precaution all for nothing? The Bloods must be in position when the leading buffalo approached. The breeze would be blowing the human scent directly into sensitive black noses. *Aiee!*

He hurried to Singing Wolf again, to tell him of this concern. The old man's eyes twinkled.

"You thought of that!" he said, smiling. "Good!"

"But what . . . ?"

"When the time comes, we will make a ceremony. With the smoke of some of the plants, we will purify the Bloods who are to be there. Yourself too."

"But I have the cape."

"Yes. Have you wondered why the buffalo do not seem to catch your scent? The cape has already been purified. White Buffalo told me of these things."

Pipe Bearer now recalled that the calf skin did have a distinctive smell. The smoky odor of well-tanned buckskin, yes, but another too. It was a pungent, not unpleasant herbal smell . . .

"Of course, we will try to change the wind too," Singing Wolf was saying.

The holy man seemed serious, but there was a mischievous twinkle in his eye. Pipe Bearer decided to let the matter drop. And the two elder holy men *had* discussed it between them.

Pipe Bearer and Otter Woman were snuggled together, wrapped warmly in the sleeping robes against the prairie night's chill. He was nearly asleep.

"Pup?" she whispered.

"Yes? What is it?"

"I have been thinking."

"Ah! I too!" He drew her to him.

"No, no, not about that. About the buffalo. How to get them to come."

"What do you mean, Otter?"

"I am made to think . . . Would White Buffalo know a way?"

Pipe Bearer thought about it for a moment. In the past, was that not an important part of the office of White Buffalo? To know the ways of the herds, to be able to call them to a desired area? That function had been lost, or taken over by other holy men, as hunting became easier.

"But he is forgetful, Otter. Would he even remember?"

"I do not know. But I am made to think of something . . . You remember, soon after our marriage . . ."

"Ah, yes!"

"No, listen to me, Pup! We saw birds of different kinds, who worked together to chase the crow. Was that a sign?"

"I do not understand."

"Nor do I. But that day, the medicines of Robin and Jay and Red Bird joined to a useful purpose. Maybe it is the same. Your medicine, that of Singing Wolf, and of White Buffalo . . ."

He began to see. Was it the sensitive spirit of Otter that allowed her to understand that sign when he had missed it?

"I am made to think," he said slowly, "that you are right, Otter. I will go and tell Singing Wolf of this!"

He threw back the robe and sat up.

"*Aiee*, not now," Otter whispered. "They are asleep. Tell him in the morning!"

She lifted the robe invitingly, and such persuasion was hard to resist.

"That is true," he admitted as he lay back down and Otter drew the robe over them.

Still the buffalo did not come. A few scattered bands, a few kills, but these would not supply the hundreds of skins needed for lodge covers.

The weather continued warm and pleasant, which may have been a part of the problem, Pipe Bearer reasoned. There must be some cold weather to the north to drive the great herds south for the winter. And that had not yet come, apparently. The warm late summer and early autumn had become a mixed blessing. It was good, because the People had little shelter. At the same time, they needed buffalo to provide lodge skins for that shelter. And the buffalo would not begin to migrate south until cold weather forced it. *Aiee!*

So the People waited. The days passed, through the Moon of Ripening and into the Moon of Falling Leaves. There were probably those who did not realize that time was growing short, but most people did. Already it was apparent that there would not be time to move southward into winter camp. They would winter here, because they must. Even if the buffalo came tomorrow, there would not be time both to prepare the lodge skins and to move. One or the other, but not both.

And what if the herds did *not* come? No one had the courage to voice such a question aloud. There had been seasons when the buffalo took a different path in their migration, farther west. If it happened this year, it would be a disaster. This knowledge made the waiting even worse, because there was nothing that could be done.

Pipe Bearer did not tolerate this knowledge well. With the impatience of youth, he craved action. Yet the wolves reported nothing to the north. They ranged two and even three days' travel in that direction, and found nothing. Only the twos and threes, and small bands left behind when the herds had moved north in the spring. The hunters continued to harvest some of these, but it could be plainly seen that it would never be enough. All the skins that had been removed and tanned since the Southern band arrived at the Rock would make scarcely two or three lodges.

It crossed the mind of Pipe Bearer that maybe the buffalo had taken the western route because of Big Whirlwind. He approached Singing Wolf with that idea.

"I am made to think not, Pup. They must choose their path for the food and water, not for something that happened many moons ago."

"But many were killed."

"A few hundred, maybe. Not enough to notice."

"Would the *spirit* of the Big Whirlwind linger, Grandfather?" Pipe Bearer suggested. "Would the herd avoid that?"

"Ah, that I do not know. But it should be considered, Pup. White Buffalo should know. Let us go and ask him!"

It was such a simple thing, yet neither of them had thought of it before. They approached the campfire where Grass Woman was preparing stew.

"*Ah-koh,* Sister," Singing Wolf began. "We would speak with your husband."

The woman straightened and glanced around the area.

"Ah, I do not know where he is, Uncle! This is a good day for him. He knows people, and is visiting. Do you want to leave your message?"

"No, no. We only wanted to ask him something."

"Maybe I can help. Is it about buffalo?"

"Yes. We were wondering, Sister, if the herds avoid the place where Big Whirlwind has passed?"

"Ah! I am made to think not. My husband has never spoken of it. Shall I ask him for you?"

"No, we can ask him later. Do not trouble yourself, Sister."

They turned away.

"Wait!" she called after them. "You are wondering why the herds do not come?"

They turned back to her fire. Once again, Pipe Bearer was reminded what a very intelligent woman this must be.

"Yes, that is it," he said simply. "Has White Buffalo said anything about it?"

"No, no." Grass Woman shook her head sadly. "Most of the time, you know, he hardly knows who he is."

"But you have said . . ."

"I know. That this is a good day."

"Well, yes . . ."

"And that is true. But his thoughts do not . . . how shall I say it? He does not realize, Pipe Bearer, that the herds are late."

The two men started to turn away again, and then Singing Wolf paused.

"Sister," he said thoughtfully, "I seem to remember a ceremony . . . One to bring the buffalo?"

The woman smiled. "Yes," she said, "there was one, long ago. It has not been used for many seasons. It was not needed. The wolves range widely, the young men ride like the wind . . . Ah, yes, one of my favorite ceremonies! One of his too."

"White Buffalo knows the dance, the songs?"

"Of course. The white cape is used. It is a beautiful thing."

"Could he do this?" asked Singing Wolf.

"I suppose so, Uncle. One does not easily forget things learned long ago, no?"

"That is true. May we wait for him here?"

"Of course, Uncle. He should not be long."

They waited impatiently, but shadows were long when he returned.

"These guests would speak with you," Grass Woman told him. "Singing Wolf and Pipe Bearer. You remember, you taught him of the calf skin?"

"Yes, but I thought . . ." His look of confusion told the tale. In his troubled mind he was confusing this young man with another, long dead.

"I have come to tell you, Uncle. That part goes well. But we have heard of a ceremony to bring the buffalo to us. You know of this?"

"Of course. I have done it many times. But you cannot learn it. It requires the white cape."

"Ah, Uncle, I could not presume to learn it. I only wondered if you would perform it."

"For what purpose?" White Buffalo asked suspiciously. "It is not something to be done for amusement."

"No, no," interrupted Singing Wolf. "I know that, Uncle. We would not ask you to misuse your powers."

"Then *what?*" White Buffalo snapped.

"We want you to call the buffalo," Singing Wolf said simply.

A broad smile broke across the face of the buffalo man.

"It is good," he said. "When?"

"Soon," Singing Wolf promised. "We will talk of this again."

Grass Woman followed them a little way.

"I am not sure now," she admitted. "He knows the songs, but can his knees let him do the dance?"

38
» » »

A site for the ceremony was discussed at length. It would be best, of course, for White Buffalo to dance at the place where the actual event was to happen. That seemed impractical. Pipe Bearer wondered whether the old man could ride a horse that far. Even then, there was the cliff. The holy man, the chief, and the Blood Society leader had all climbed to the rim by means of the crevice in the cliff's face. It was doubtful whether the old buffalo priest would be physically able to do so.

Maybe the ceremony could be carried out at some chosen neutral spot nearer the camp. After all, it was intended to bring the great herds of thousands of animals. It should make no great difference, because the breadth of their frontal advance might reach as far as the eye could see. Probably farther.

It was Grass Woman who made a better suggestion. "Could we take White Buffalo there on a *travois?* Cross the river here?"

Singing Wolf and Pipe Bearer exchanged looks of surprise. Not up the crevice, of course, but to approach the cliff from the other

side, from the north. It would be a long way around, but it might
be undertaken in a half day.

"It is good!" agreed Singing Wolf. "Have you told him?"

"Not about the *travois*. But he knows that his help is needed.
Aiee, Buffalo is pleased, Uncle."

"What will he need, Sister?" asked the holy man.

"The *travois*. I will help him, as I have done before. The white
cape, the paint . . . the drum for his dance. I will prepare everything."

"Good. Tomorrow?"

"Yes. When it is light enough to travel."

"We will bring the *travois*."

It was a strange procession, the four people who crossed the
river at the gravel bar that morning. Pipe Bearer led the way on
horseback, followed by Grass Woman, riding the horse that pulled
the pole-drag. She had insisted that it be so. White Buffalo sat on
the platform of the *travois,* dignified as he could be while the
contraption rattled and bumped over the gravel.

Singing Wolf brought up the rear, riding closely behind the
drag to watch after the old buffalo priest. There had been a nervous moment when it appeared that White Buffalo would refuse
to ride the *travois.*

"Am I a child or a cripple," he demanded, "to be assigned to
such an indignity?"

Grass Woman was able to calm him, and to assure him that this
was a sort of ceremonial honor.

"Do not disappoint them," she pleaded in a whisper. "The People need you."

Still grumbling, he took his place on the platform. "They have
forgotten that!" he muttered.

"No, no. That is why we go this morning."

White Buffalo nodded. "Where is it that we go?"

"To Medicine Rock, to the buffalo leap."

"Oh, yes. Are the buffalo here?"

"No. You are to bring them."

"Ah! Of course. I remember."

All of this was rather disconcerting to Pipe Bearer. Could this old man, confused and disoriented, possibly be of any help? His wife was telling him everything that he should do or say or think. It was an uncomfortable situation, yet Grass Woman seemed confident.

There would be no one else at the ceremony, and Pipe Bearer was thinking that this was good. If the People could see how desperate their plight must be, to depend on an almost forgotten ceremony, performed by a feeble old man . . . *aiee!* The People knew, of course, that the ceremony was to be held, but not the entire circumstances. They would stay away from the Rock because of the edict of the council. They saw one of the wolves at a distance as he rode northward to relieve one of the others. The man waved a greeting.

As it happened, they need not have worried about the ability of White Buffalo to handle this, his priestly function. When Grass Woman drew out the white cape, he became a changed man. He appeared dignified, confident, and capable, as well as years younger. Once again he was White Buffalo, keeper of the white cape. She adjusted the cape around him and carefully painted his face.

When the first tentative beats of the small dance drum began, an even greater change took place. His stiff old limbs seemed to take on a rejuvenated life, and soon he was stepping proudly to the rhythms of the dance.

It was simple, but long. Grass Woman had kindled a tiny fire, and burned a pinch of tobacco to initiate the sequence. The south breeze carried the slender wisp of smoke aloft and northerly. Pipe Bearer prayed that the ritual smoke and the spirit of the dance ceremony would reach the desired goals.

It was a strange transformation that took place as they watched. The old man in the ancient cape seemed able to mimic every swaying move of the buffalo. His steps, the casual toss of the horned headdress recalled exactly the motion of a grazing bull.

Pipe Bearer failed to understand the words of the song, sung by the old priest and his wife. Such ritual songs are often so. But is it really the word or the spirit that communicates what is in the heart of the worshiper?

Four times the caped figure withdrew from the scene and danced back in again, honoring the four directions. Each time there were repetitions, and each time Pipe Bearer was impressed that here was a man who truly understood the way of the buffalo.

When at last it was over, Grass Woman helped him remove the cape, and led him over to sit on the *travois* platform. White Buffalo was sweating, exhausted, and trembling. It seemed impossible that a few moments before he could have been engaging in the intricate steps and motions of the Buffalo Dance.

"He will be all right," Grass Woman assured them. "He can rest on the way back to camp."

They departed quickly, because the day was growing late. Pipe Bearer stayed behind to remove all traces of the fire and of their presence. It must be as before.

He overtook the rest of the party without difficulty. They were moving slowly for the comfort of the exhausted White Buffalo, who seemed to be sleeping.

He woke briefly when they arrived at the camp a little while before sunset. The others helped him to his bed and he thanked them briefly as he sank onto the soft robes.

"It is good!" he said.

Pipe Bearer devoutly hoped so.

The camp was wakened at dawn by a plaintive wail that rose and fell, quavering as it echoed across the valley. Pipe Bearer recognized the Song of Mourning.

"What happened?" Otter asked sleepily. "Someone is *dead?*"

People were rising, moving around the camp, questioning. Pipe Bearer had a feeling that he knew. The first person that he encountered was Singing Wolf.

"Grandfather . . ." he began.

"I am made to think so," the holy man answered.

They hurried toward the sound.

Grass Woman stood over the still form in the robes. She had gashed her forearms in mourning and tossed ashes over her head.

"Sister," Singing Wolf greeted her. "My heart is heavy for you."

A young woman rushed forward, glanced quickly at the body and at the mourning Grass Woman. Then she too raised her voice to join the Mourning Song. The daughter . . .

White Buffalo lay on his back, arms folded over his chest. Pipe Bearer wondered if Grass Woman had arranged him so for burial, or if the buffalo priest had assumed this position himself when he lay down.

"He knew?" Pipe Bearer asked.

Grass Woman paused in her wailing song for a few moments, while the other woman continued.

"Yes," she said. "I am made to think so. My husband's heart was heavy when he saw that his head was not working right. This was his last gift to the People, and he was proud. His heart was good for the Buffalo Dance. I thank you for him. I am made to think that this is as he wished it."

"My heart is heavy for you, Mother," Pipe Bearer said sincerely.

Grass Woman had already joined the other woman in the song, and the two men turned away.

"He was a good man," Singing Wolf said.

And unappreciated, thought Pipe Bearer. In his lifetime, White Buffalo had seen his responsibilities as buffalo priest become less important. The increasing use of the French muskets had made the procuring of meat and skins so much easier. A man could go out and find food for his family almost without effort now.

There was a certain feeling of guilt now on the part of Pipe Bearer. They had exploited the old man's skills, used his medicine, sucked the life from him to obtain what they needed. It had resulted in his death. And it was not even certain whether the ceremony had been successful.

At least, that question was answered the following day. It was late afternoon and shadows grew long when one of the wolves pounded into camp and slid from his sweating horse.

"They come!" he shouted. "The great herds! More buffalo than we have ever seen!"

There was great rejoicing in the camp, even as White Buffalo's family continued their ceremonial mourning. His funeral-wrapped body had been carried with great honor and placed on a tree scaffold a few bow shots downstream. The singing would continue there for two more days.

Meanwhile, life is for the living, and there were excited preparations for the big hunt. It was time now for another council, for specific plans to begin.

"Let us say again," Yellow Moccasin reminded, "no one hunts on his own. Our lives depend on it!"

There were solemn nods of understanding.

"Now!" The chief turned to the wolves who had brought the news. "Tell us of the herds. More than you can count?"

Clever, thought Pipe Bearer. *He is using their story to rouse the excitement.*

"More than stars in the sky, my chief!" one of the scouts insisted. "More than the grains of sand by the river!"

"How fast are they moving?" asked Yellow Moccasin. "When will they be here?"

These were things that could have been asked in private, but young Moccasin was using the occasion for all it was worth.

"They move slowly," explained the wolf. "Maybe three days."

"You are pushing them?" someone asked.

The scouts laughed. "*Aiee!* They *come*. We stay out of the way!"

"It is good," Yellow Moccasin said. "Now, here is the plan."

He outlined in some detail the plan that was already known in general. The Bloods would arrive at the Rock during the night to take up their positions. Pipe Bearer would go at the same time, to use the medicine learned from White Buffalo. The Elk-dog Society would try to separate a section of the herd to push gently toward the Rock, beginning at dawn of the appointed day. Others would wait below to finish any injured animals that might survive the fall from the cliff.

Pipe Bearer was becoming so excited inside that he doubted whether he could sleep until after the hunt. But there was still a nagging doubt. The breeze continued to blow steadily from the south. What effect would the heavy human scent from the hidden Blood warriors have on the advancing herds?

39
»»»

Despite the excitement and anxiety, the intervening days passed quickly. The People were so curious about the approach of the herds that the council was forced to announce another edict: no one was to go to *look* at the advancing animals. To do so might alarm them. A stampede away from the desired area would be a disaster. Now the People's winter survival depended entirely on the success of this one plan.

Singing Wolf cast the bones, and seemed pleased, though he was not specific. He suggested that Pipe Bearer *not* cast the bones this time.

"Yours is a different role, a different medicine in this," he explained. "I am made to think that we should not let them mix too closely. This time is too important. Maybe later, when we know it better."

It was a strange statement. Pipe Bearer had been thinking in terms of a very temporary use of the teaching of White Buffalo. This one time only . . . He wondered why his grandfather had cast the bones in private, and why his grandfather had been so vague. He worried about it for some time and finally asked bluntly.

"What did the bones show?"

"*Aiee,* you know how that reading goes, Pup. It is a matter of suggestion and interpretation. There is a sign of danger, but any hunt shows that, does it not?"

"There must be more. What?" Pipe Bearer insisted.

"I am made to think," Singing Wolf said soberly, "that they showed the death of White Buffalo."

Ah, the young man thought, *so that is it. But wait!*

If the toss of the bones indicated danger and death, what if it was *not* related to that of White Buffalo? *Who* then? He could see now, the reluctance on the part of his grandfather. There was one who would be in the most dangerous position of all during the buffalo leap . . . *Pipe Bearer.* This, then, must be why the holy man did not want him to cast the bones. It was a thoughtful kindness. But now he could say nothing. To speak of such a thing would surely tempt it to happen. He must say nothing to anyone.

Singing Wolf now withdrew from the camp, accompanied by his wife, and began ceremonies of his own. They could hear the distant beat of his drum and scraps of song. Pipe Bearer was unsure what his grandfather might be doing. Certainly it would be connected to the coming hunt, but how? What more could be hoped for? The buffalo were coming, and the plan was in place.

The only element in doubt was the direction of the wind. *Ah! The wind.* He smiled to himself. *Of course!* Singing Wolf was aware of the potential problem with the herd moving upwind. In fact, now he recognized snatches of song. A prayer for a change in the weather would surely be appropriate.

It was late in the afternoon when it happened. The wind had died, but in the distance could be seen towering white clouds growing as they rose. Everything was still and heavy, and even the birds and the insects of a summer day were silent. Pipe Bearer felt a sense of something about to happen.

The first hint was, oddly, a feeling of coolness in the air. Even before it began to stir, it was apparent that something had changed. Could this be Cold Maker's first thrust of the season? Now some scraps of clouds went scurrying high overhead. For the brief time that the sun was obscured, there was a definite chill in the air, warming again as the shadow passed.

Then a subtle stirring of air, a mischievous puff in this direction or that. A surprising spatter of fat raindrops from what appeared to be a clear sky . . .

Finally the pattern became clear. The breeze sprang up again, this time from the northwest, and it was good. And before dark, the wolf who rode in with his report told of another change. The herd was becoming restless, and had begun to move more rapidly.

"They will be at the Rock by daylight!" he announced.

The calf skin felt warm, and Pipe Bearer pulled it around him as a protection against the chill of the north breeze. He was sitting, waiting for dawn. He could not see, but could smell and *feel* the presence of the thousands of grazing buffalo out there in the darkness. The Bloods were in place. Only daylight was needed now, and already the eastern sky was turning from black to yellow-gray. He had a vague sense of shifting shapes near at hand, and now could hear the low muttering of the animals as they spoke to each other or to their young. He gave a contented little bleat, to let them know his location. It would not be long now, for better or worse.

He could begin to make out the forms of individual animals now. A great black bull . . . lighter-colored cows. The easiest ones to see were the yellowish calves, cavorting in the pleasant stimulation of a cool morning. A calf came near and paused to stare at the figure on the ground. Pipe Bearer "spoke" softly and the calf came closer. It was growing lighter now, and quite rapidly.

He engaged in a pushing match to establish his presence, and began to frolic with the others. The cows seemed to take no notice. He moved among them, again feeling the rush of excitement at his ability to do so. He touched a cow's flank as if he were the calf of another cow, trying to steal a meal. Then he retreated from the expected disciplinary kick and moved on.

The time was growing near now. It was light enough to see. Even though he had expected it, the sight of buffalo blackening the whole prairie came as a shock. He must draw the nearest animals as close to the edge as possible now, before the Elk-dog warriors tried to stampede them. What if someone made a mistake and started *now?* There would be no way that he could avoid the crush of the panicky animals.

He tried not to think about that as he saw the riders in the distance begin to split off a section of the herd. They rode quietly at a walk (*aiee,* that is good!), separating the close-packed buffalo and maintaining an open lane which widened as they passed back and forth. Their position, too, was one of danger. What if the whole herd began to run in the same direction? Pipe Bearer tried to estimate how many buffalo there might be in the portion that had been detached from the main herd. Thousands, maybe.

But now he must not look. He must keep his head down and concentrate. And hope, of course, that no one alarmed the herd before he was ready. The thought crossed his mind that the Bloods, who would give the signal, were notoriously unpredictable. What if one of them became overeager, and fired his musket early . . . He must not think of such things.

He now engaged in play with a calf, and a third joined in. Farther and farther he led them into the corridor that led to the rim of the cliff. One of the cows raised her head and gave a low rumble of warning. Her calf looked at her for a moment, and Pipe Bearer butted it playfully to distract it. The cow seemed to sense something wrong and began to trot toward him.

It was now no more than twenty paces to his hiding place and to the rim. But the approaching cow was no farther away than that either. He could wait no longer. He voiced the frantic bleat of terror that he had practiced for so long, and raced for the split stone. He was still bending over to look like a calf, so he could not see well. He could hear the pounding hooves of a few animals, and another bleat of terror from one of the confused calves.

A musket boomed from the flank, and there was a volley of shots and shouts from the line of horsemen along the north. Then yells and the waving of blankets, more shots . . .

As Pipe Bearer scrambled into his little crevice, he caught a glimpse of the split widening where the riders were. The main herd was moving away from the portion that had been separated. The horsemen were pushing those, and the rumble of their hooves was like distant thunder. Except, of course, that thunder does not shake the earth like this. He wondered if the shaking might cause the stone block that formed his hiding place to fall away to drop with the buffalo. It was too late to worry about it.

He scrambled into the crevice and looked up. An angry cow, her horns only a hand's span above his face, peered down at him with her bloodshot little eyes. Her horns swung, and clashed against the protecting rock of the crevice. He thought of a cow's next move, the stiff-legged stamping that he had seen used on a young wolf. The knife-edged hoof would easily reach his unprotected body.

But now the cow was pushed from behind. She turned, scrambling for footing. A hind leg slipped into the crevice, striking his lower leg. At the same time the bulk of the animal rolled across his shelter, darkening the world for a moment. He heard or felt bones snap, and was unsure whether they were his leg bones or those of the buffalo. He screamed, but the sound was lost in thunder.

Then the dark form fell away and over the edge, and for a moment he saw sky. Then the body of a shaggy beast, and another and another, an endless procession. They pushed, shoved, fought, and leaped into space to escape the crush behind them. He could hear and feel the thud of massive bodies on the rocky face of the cliff. There were shots from below. His crevice was filled with thick choking dust, and mud and dung spattered down on him.

Then things quieted. The rumbling of the earth became more distant. The sounds that he heard now were distant shots, shouts of triumph, and an occasional deep-throated war cry from the Bloods. Cautiously, he raised his head and looked into the face of a grinning warrior.

"Ah! Pipe Bearer," the man said. "Are you hurt?"

"I . . . I am not sure," he replied honestly. "My leg . . ."

"Let me help you."

Strong hands lifted him out of the crevice and he stood on his good leg, gingerly placing his other foot on the ground. It was very tender, and blood from his calf darkened the buckskin legging. But he could bear weight. Maybe the little bone . . .

"Did it go well?" he asked.

"*Aiee,* Pipe Bearer, it was perfect! Look below!"

He peered over the edge. There appeared to be hundreds of carcasses, by ones and twos and in piles. A few animals had struggled across the stream before dying or being shot or lanced by the hunters. The prairie to the north was covered by a pall of dust. The main herd would find a way around and continue the migration.

"Can we help you?" asked the man who still stood beside him. "Can you walk?"

Pipe Bearer took a step or two, gritting his teeth against the pain. But there was no grinding of bone.

"I am made to think so. Could someone tell my family? My wife, my grandfather, parents?"

"It is done!" agreed the other. "You want a horse?"

"Maybe. I will sit here a little while."

He was feeling a little faint, and he moved away from the edge of the cliff. His body ached from a hundred bruises. Maybe he could sit for a little while and then make his way down to the river. Cool water would feel good on his injuries.

He took a deep breath, and winced only a little from his sore ribs. *At least,* he thought, *now the People can winter well.*

Even with all the hard work that must be accomplished quickly, it was a time of joy. After the forced inactivity it seemed good to return to familiar things. The camp was quickly moved to a spot on the south side of the river, and a few bow shots upstream. That should avoid the fouling of the water by the butchering and by the dung of the myriads of buffalo.

It was a time of joy and feasting and celebration, and the prestige of Pipe Bearer was greatly enhanced. The Bloods and the Elk-dog men told in great detail how the young holy man had virtually *changed* into a buffalo calf and enticed the animals over the edge.

"We thought he was dead too!" laughed one warrior as he retold the tale for the hundredth time.

"There was a little while," Pipe Bearer admitted, "when *I* thought so!"

Otter was very proud, and was constantly looking after his injuries. When, of course, she was not working to dress the skins that would become their lodge.

It was after the heaviest of the work was behind them that Grass Woman approached the camp of Singing Wolf and asked for Pipe Bearer. She was carrying a bundle.

"I have heard it told," she began, "how you became a calf and moved the herd to the cliff."

"It was nothing, Mother . . ."

She held up a hand to silence him. "My husband would have been proud," she went on, "to know that one he taught . . ." Her eyes filled with tears and she paused.

"Without his teaching, I could not have done that," Pipe Bearer said. "He taught me well. And did he not call the herd? *Aiee*, Mother, the People owe much to White Buffalo."

She nodded. "And I to you, for helping bring back his pride. Here, my husband would want you to have this."

She opened the bundle and shook out the white buffalo cape.

"*Aiee*, I could not take this," he protested. "It is *his* medicine, that of the buffalo."

"But think about it," Grass Woman said. "You have part of it already, or you could not have done what you did. There is no one else."

"But I do not know the medicine of the white cape!"

"Ah, but *I do*," she smiled. "I can teach you. It has already been shown that it works well with yours, no? You will have both medicines, and will be the greatest of holy men!"

Pipe Bearer's modesty would not let him aspire to such an honor, but what is one to do?

"It is good, Mother," he smiled.

So that is how the old men told it later.

Grass Woman moved into the lodge of her daughter, and gave instruction in the medicine of the white buffalo to young Pipe Bearer.

There had been a time, it was said, when the bearer of the white cape was the principal holy man of the band. The two offices had grown apart. At one time, the white cape had been lost, and then returned to the People.

Now, under the best of circumstances, it had come again to be of major importance. Its medicine had been returned to its proper place of respect in the band, and was joined now to that of the holy men. The white cape was once again one of the most important objects in the band, along with the sacred pipe and the Spanish bit that helped the People control the elk-dog, the First Horse.

These things were painted on the Story Skins, and it was good.

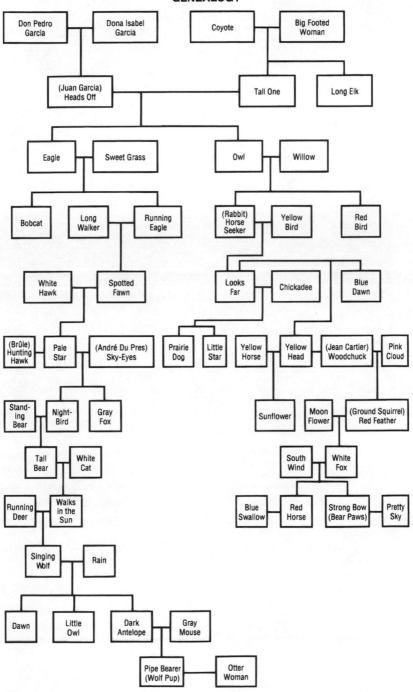

Don Coldsmith was born in Iola, Kansas, in 1926. He served as a World War II combat medic in the South Pacific and returned to his native state, where he graduated from Baker University in 1949 and received his M.D. from the University of Kansas in 1958. He worked at several jobs before entering medical school: he was a YMCA Youth Director, a gunsmith, a taxidermist, and for a short time a Congregational preacher. In addition to his private medical practice, Dr. Coldsmith has been a staff physician at the Health Center of Emporia State University, where he also teaches in the English Department. He discontinued medical pursuits in 1990 to devote more time to his writing. He and his wife of thirty-four years, Edna, operate a small cattle ranch. They have raised five daughters.

Dr. Coldsmith produced the first ten novels in the Spanish Bit Saga in a five-year period; he writes and revises the stories first in his head, then in longhand. From this manuscript the final version is skillfully created by his longtime assistant, Ann Bowman.

Of his decision to create, or re-create, the world of the Plains Indian in the early centuries of European contact, the author says: "There has been very little written about this time period. I wanted also to portray these Native Americans as human beings, rather than as stereotyped 'Indians.' As I have researched the time and place, the indigenous cultures, it's been a truly inspiring experience for me. I am not attempting to tell anyone else's story. My only goal is to tell *a* story and tell it fairly."